Holy Smoke

Books by Frederick Ramsay

The Jerusalem Mysteries
Judas
The Eighth Veil
Holy Smoke

The Ike Schwartz Mysteries
Artscape
Secrets
Buffalo Mountain
Stranger Room
Choker
The Eye of the Virgin
Rogue
Scone Island

The Botswana Mysteries
Predators
Reapers

Other Novels
Impulse

Holy Smoke

A Jerusalem Mystery

Frederick Ramsay

Poisoned Pen Press

Library of Congress Catalog Card Number: 2012910490

ISBN: 9781464200908   Hardcover
        9781464200922   Trade Paperback

Poisoned Pen Press
6962 E. First Ave., Ste. 103
Scottsdale, AZ 85251
www.poisonedpenpress.com
info@poisonedpenpress.com

Printed in the United States of America

Acknowledgments

As always, a shout-out to the folks at Poisoned Pen Press. I won't list them by name. I attempted to do that in the past and invariably left someone off the list. It's enough to say, modesty aside, that they consistently publish the finest mysteries here and abroad. They do that because of their abundant enthusiasm, and professionalism, and because they really love what they do. Those of us who have the privilege to write for the Press can never thank them enough. So, to the gang over on Goldwater Boulevard and also to Loretta Warner, many thanks.

Holy Smoke is the second in a trilogy set in first-century Jerusalem. The action in the first in the series, *The Eighth Veil,* took place in Herod's palace. *Holy Smoke* is set in the Temple. I have appended a few notes at the end of the book which I hope will help readers make their way through the vagaries of that time and place and connect them with a few of its major players. Some of the words used in the text are transliterated Hebrew, Greek, or Latin. Most particularly *Ha Shem,* The Name; *kohen, kohanim,* priest, priests; *Elohim,* The Lord. I have italicized them even though many have made it into the English lexicon. I have done so to emphasize them and the place they held in the thought processes of the time. For the same reason I capitalized Law, when it refers to Torah, and Temple, the heart of the city and its peoples' faith.

Enjoy.

Whoever did not see Jerusalem in its days of glory,
never saw a beautiful city in their life.
—Talmud: Succah 51b

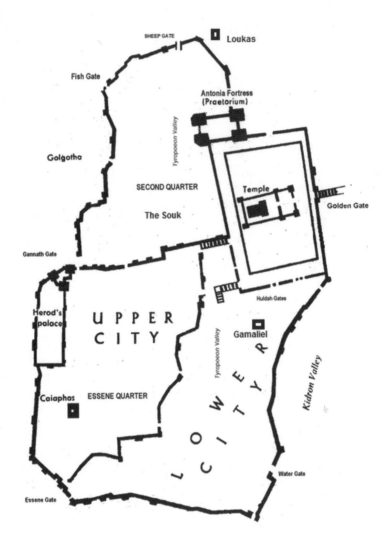

Gamaliel's World

ASSYRIA: A Semitic kingdom on the Upper Tigris; today, northern Iraq

BITHNYIA: Bithnyia/Pontus, a Roman province lying along the south coast of the Black Sea; today, Turkey

CAPPADOCIA: a Roman province in Central Anatolia, capital Caesarea; today, Turkey (Kayseri)

EGYPT: still Egypt

KHORASAN: a country that straddled the trade routes into India and present-day China; today, Afghanistan

MACEDONIA: a kingdom on the northeast of the Greek Peninsula that rose to great power under Philip II and Alexander; today, the Republic of Macedonia

JUDEA: a Roman province; today, Israel

PARTHIA: a political power in Persia; today, northeast Iran. Note: Gamaliel has trouble distinguishing between Assyria and Parthia

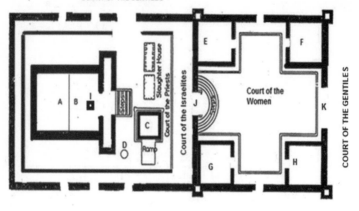

Jerusalem, 29 C.E.

A = Holy of Holies	E = Lepers	I = Incense Altar
B = The Holy Place	F = Wood	J = Nicanor Gate
C = Altar of Sacrifice	G = Oil	K = Beautiful Gate
D = Laver (water basin)	H = Nazarenes	

Herod's Temple

This diagram represents what scholars suppose the Temple might have looked like in the early first century. It is offered here to help the reader visualize the relative locations of the places mentioned in the narrative. The thin vertical line between A and B is the Veil, a curtain the thickness of which has been the subject of debate. Some affirm it had to be thick and heavy, other insist it was a single layer of fabric. No one knows for sure. The four rooms at the right, frequently called the Treasury, were designated for their use, either to store material or deal with a particular issue common to the time.

The Temple was destroyed in 70 CE, and nothing was built on the site until the seventh century, when Muslim Umayyad Caliph Abd al-Malik restored the city's walls and the mount, and built the structure commonly known as The Dome of the Rock.

Chapter I

Because his cadre of *kohanim* had drawn this particular week to perform the priestly functions, Josef ben Josef would be the one to discover the body. Had he remained by the Altar of Sacrifice where he'd been assigned, had his curiosity not willed his feet across the porch and into the Holy Place, had he not paused and looked at the Great Veil, he might not have been the one to raise the alarm and cause the high priest's face to turn as red as Moses. Also, he would not have lost his place on the roster of *kohanim* and ended his days in Bethlehem herding goats and sheep instead of remaining a priest in the service of *Ha Shem*. He had one glorious moment as a priest in the city of David, in the Temple, and then—finished.

There could be no doubt about the body, although it had yet to be brought into view. A heavy cord of elaborate construction snaked out from under the Veil and, indeed, provided the only evidence of its existence, but what else could be attached to its other end? Josef's cries of alarm at the edges of the Holy of Holies brought his colleagues scurrying into the most sacred area of Herod's Temple. The steps of Nicanor Gate, which lead from the Court of the Priests into the Holy Place, the antechamber to the Holy of Holies, seemed to be as far as they dared go. There they gathered, wailed, and seemed incapable of moving one way or the other. Instead, they stood like the pillars of salt one sees down by the Great Salt Sea, like Lot's wife. Even after being joined by the high priest, Caiaphas himself, they remained inert, in a state of fearful confusion. That is until the rabban of the Sanhedrin arrived. His presence seemed to restore a small measure of order and calm. He paused, seeming to measure the mood of the moment, studied Josef, the other five priests, the high priest, and then asked for an explanation. Josef stammered his story as best he could.

"Has anyone determined with certainty that there is, in fact, a body attached to the end of this cord? Pulled on it, perhaps?" the Rabban asked. The men glanced at one another and shuffled their feet, embarrassed. "No? Then doesn't it seem reasonable to do so?"

The *kohanim* turned to the high priest for confirmation. Holy Writ did not prescribe the lashing of a cord to the ankle of anyone entering the Holy of Holies, although there had been talk about it for years and many assumed it was part of Temple protocol. In any case, there could be no accompanying instructions as what one was to do if the worst actually happened, that is if some unclean person did, in fact, dare to enter the Holy of Holies, approach the Name-That-May-Not-Be-Spoken, and been struck down for his impiety.

The high priest put his fists against his ears, clenched his teeth, and growled something in Aramaic that Josef did not catch. The rabban, on the other hand, had a half smile on his face that he did not attempt to hide. Did this most honorable man find this awful situation amusing? Perhaps his enjoyment derived from the high priest's discomfort. Josef had heard talk. He had not paid it any mind at the time, but now he wished he had.

"High Priest," the Rabban said, "you will have to bring this dead person to light sooner or later. Let's have it done now."

The high priest nodded. There were no precedents for this. How could there be?

"And let us hope that it is, indeed, a man at the end of that rope and not one of your sacrificial animals gone astray."

An animal from the pens that held the bulls and rams: was that even possible? Again, it seemed to Josef that the rabban took some perverse pleasure in the high priest's discomfort.

"Or perhaps this is some pagan's idea of sacrilege and he turned swine loose in there."

The image of a dead pig lying behind the Veil with the other end of the cord tied to its leg caused Josef's stomach to turn over. He swallowed the vomit that formed in his throat. It would not do to add to the desecration by being sick, not now. He took a deep breath and forced the blasphemous image from his mind. The rabban, he saw, stood with his head cocked to one side, apparently waiting on the high priest. Time ground to a halt. Whatever lurked behind the Veil was too appalling for any of them to contemplate. But contemplate it they must.

"Impossible, Rabban. What a thought!" Finally, it seemed, the high priest had found his voice. Turning to the priests he added, "All of you will go to the Laver and wash. Sacrifice an unspotted ram and dip your hands in its blood and sprinkle it on your tunic. You must pray the prayer of consecration as you do so. When you have done all these things assemble in the Holy Place and await my direction. You, Nathan, you climb into the observation room. It is early, but there may be enough light for you to see what lies at the end of this cord."

The priests hurried off to do as they had been directed. Surely Caiaphas would know what needed to be done. Had he not served as high priest longer than anyone in memory—recent memory at least? He had. Josef refused to listen to the talk in the streets of his corruption and political maneuvering. Caiaphas stood last in the line of Aaron, the one man closest to the Lord. Even Gamaliel, the rabban, did not sit so close as that.

Josef rushed to catch up with his co-workers and begin the rite of purification the high priest decreed.

Chapter II

Gamaliel served the Sanhedrin as its rabban, the rabbi's rabbi, so to speak, the final arbiter of what was, and what was not, an acceptable interpretation of the Law. In addition, and more to his liking, he trained young men in the art of disputation and reading the same Law. Because of those two undertakings, he found himself frequently in the company of the high priest. The two of them did not always agree on the nature and enforcement of the Law and were frequently at odds both publicly and, more often, privately. Even so, he would never have anticipated that he would spend the next several days dealing with the consequences of a corpse in the Temple.

On awakening that morning at his usual early hour, he felt wearier than when he'd retired. He blamed Caiaphas for that. They had passed the previous night in disputation. Would the high priest never let the issue of the marginally heretical rabbis go? It seemed obvious to Gamaliel that proper instruction in the righteous interpretation of the Word by those capable of doing so should be sufficient to counter any of the eccentric interpretations being offered by the Nation's wandering band of self-proclaimed rabbis, prophets, and would be messiahs.

Gamaliel told the high priest that when he found the time, he made a practice of drifting along the edges of the crowds gathered around these well intentioned, but ignorant, teachers and almost without exception believed there could be no dangerous outcome stemming from any of their teaching. That is, with the possible exception of the tall one from Nazareth. Yeshua, he was called. That one had a very different view of the Nation, the Lord, and the Law.

"That man seems to prefer teaching by telling stories or asking questions," he'd said to Caiaphas.

"He's Greek? He's studied Aesop or Socrates?"

"I rather doubt it."

He did not add that after listening to him, Gamaliel had decided that with some formal training and a firm hand to guide him, this Yeshua might someday make a good teacher of the Law. At the same time he wondered whether the Galilean might have spent some time with the teachers from Persia or Parthia, which if true, could slow that process down. Gamaliel didn't know a great deal about the tenets held by the worshipers of Mazda, the Zoroastrians, and had only heard of the *Avesta*. His most immediate experience had come at the hands of a bullying Roman Tribune who'd hawked Mithras as the one true way, not Gamaliel's "angry god." Gamaliel harbored some doubts about the connection between the Mithras the Roman worshipped, who seemed pretty punishing himself, and the Mithras the Parthians held to. What little he did know of their odd monotheistic sect persuaded him that on the whole it was not a bad thing to discuss so long as the declaiming rabbi eventually turned his listeners back to see Judaism as the final and perfected Way. If this Yeshua harbored any notions in that direction, he would doubtless understand that important distinction.

In any event, Gamaliel had needed every bit of his reserve of patience. Someday, he thought, he would end up in a shouting match with the high priest—the sort that when it involved younger men, often led to blows. Gamaliel would never resort to violence, of course. He was reputed to be the calmest of men. Still, there were times when disputing with Caiaphas pushed him close to the brink.

So, on rising after his restless night and still agitated by the high priest's argumentative nature, he'd dismissed his students as they'd arrived and headed for the Temple. Merely standing near the Presence had a calming effect on him. And thus it was that on this soon to be historic morning, he strode through the crooked streets of the Lower City alternately assaulted by the chattering voices of men and women sharing the day's ration of gossip, and the pungent aroma of spices, roasting meat, and excited humanity. It was only when he had mounted the steps to the Temple Mount that he stopped short, perplexed. Something was missing. He paused to stare upwards at the Temple walls. No smoke rose from burning sacrifices, no Shofars sounded to mark their procession to the altar. What could this mean?

As he attempted to reconcile these anomalies, a frantic young man dashed up to him and began to babble. Gamaliel had to ask him to repeat the message twice before he could make any sense of it.

"The Holy of Holies…defiled," he gasped. "A man, unclean… dead."

From this, he assumed that death had somehow visited the Temple. He picked up his pace and hurried across the Temple Mount, through the Beautiful Gate, across the Court of the Women, then through the Nicanor Gate to the Court of the Priests. There, the rostered *kohanim* and their leader, all in a state of high excitement, chattered and gestured, glancing furtively at the Veil that screened the Holy of Holies from them. He listened as the youngest of them, Josef Somebody-or-Other, blurted out his story. With some trepidation, Gamaliel ventured into the Holy Place but only far enough to confirm the presence of the cord which disappeared under the Veil.

The situation presented a certain irony and in spite of the obvious seriousness of the situation, he had to smile. The practice of attaching a rope to the ankle of the high priest when he entered the Holy of Holies had not been his idea. The possibility of having to retrieve a body thence, the result of the Lord's anger at an unworthy entrant, had circulated in the vestry and palace for years. If he remembered correctly, it was first suggested during the time of the Maccabees as that complicated revolution wound its way through history and ended in the ascent of Herod, the builder of this gaudy Temple. Then, as now, the perceived distance between the appointed high priest and the line of Aaron had been called into question by some of the Nation's more conservative leadership. Gamaliel did not know if their scruples made any difference in the first place—who could say after a lapse of four millennia how closely related to Moses' brother-in-law, Aaron, anyone could claim to be, or whether the practice of attaching the rope had ever been instituted.

The previous year when he suggested that it might be something to consider, his colleagues had shouted him down. There is no mention, they'd insisted, in any of Torah that could support such a thing. He'd replied that he knew that and suggested that if one thought about it, there wouldn't be—that even admitting the possibility of an unprepared, unrepentant priest meant that the builders of Zerubbabel's Temple and the drafters of Torah as they knew it had doubts about the Truth and the Way. No, they would not have written anything of the sort into the documents. But he asked them to consider their current situation.

"Pause for a moment and ponder this," Gamaliel had said. "We worship in a Temple built for us by a king who practiced the faith only when and as it suited him. His successor son shares that marginal faith. The Temple is far removed from the simple Tabernacle the Lord decreed as to size, construction, and more importantly, spirit. King Herod built this one as a memorial to himself more than to glorify the Lord. And as much as it pains me to say it, our leader is an unreconstructed Sadducee appointed not by our elders but by our Roman overlord who has no interest in nor respect for our ways. What do you suppose are the chances Caiaphas, or indeed, any high priest who owes his selection and allegiance to a pagan, could survive a confrontation with an out-of-patience *Elohim* in a place designed and built by a king who was for all practical purposes also a pagan? If, as you claim, you cherish him as your leader, you must consider the possibility. If I am wrong, will any harm be done? If I am correct, how will we proceed if the worst happens?"

It had been a delicate conversation, as some of those in the disputation were close supporters of the high priest and any question of his position and legitimacy would be awkward.

"But he has been in and out of the Holy of Holies every *Yom Kippur* for years and the Lord has not been offended yet."

"Operative word, friends—yet."

They had reluctantly agreed with his argument, but had insisted it not be made public knowledge.

"What will people think if they were to know we have doubts about our high priest?"

They decided that on next celebration of *Yom Kippur* they would urge Caiaphas to adopt the cautionary cord.

Now, it seemed that the worst had happened. True, it was not the high priest who lay inert behind the Veil, but someone else, and he or she—one had to acknowledge that remote possibility—most certainly had to be removed lest the Lord's anger increase.

It did take a push to put the high priest into motion, but soon whoever lay within would be brought to light. Then a determination could be made as to what must happen next. As an afterthought Gamaliel sent a messenger to fetch the healer, Loukas.

"Exit through the north gate and go out from the city through the Sheep Gate," he said to a still agitated Josef. "You will find the man in the house that backs up to the hillside. Tell him The Rabban of the Sanhedrin requires his presence. Tell him it is urgent. No, tell him it is a puzzle. That will bring him when *urgen*t might not. Hurry."

Chapter III

By the time Loukas the Healer arrived, neither the high priest nor any of the *kohanim* had made any progress toward removing the body, which by this time had been confirmed by Nathan, who'd climbed into the observation chamber built high on the wall that allowed visual access to the Holy of Holies. He had called down that, though little light penetrated the place, he could see what he was certain must be a body lying on the floor.

Gamaliel managed to bring the priests together and calm them down enough to take direction. Unfortunately, no help came from the high priest, who stood immobile like one of the ubiquitous statues of the current Caesar that seemed to grace all the city corners where the Romans gathered. Caiaphas' face by this time had turned as white as the marble used in those same busts and the alabaster slabs that lined this Holy Place. He had given his initial instructions about the need for purification and appeared to have run out of ideas as to what to do next.

Gamaliel met Loukas at the steps and briefly described the situation to him and the lack of progress in retrieving the dead man.

"What is the hold-up?" the healer asked.

"Two things. Our priestly class seem reluctant to admit that a body exists behind the Veil in the first place, even though it has been confirmed, and then there are the mechanics of pulling it free from its folds. I am told it is very thick and heavy, which would make an extraction nearly impossible and might defile the fabric in some way."

"You've been told? You don't know?"

"I'm not sure anyone does. Well, the high priest might. He has to make his way through it once a year."

"How long have those sheets of material been hanging there?"

"It is hard to say. As long as the temple has existed, presumably."

"From Solomon's time? Surely not."

"No, not that temple. This one is Herod the king's attempt to rival Thebes, Athens, and Rome for grandeur."

"My, my, Rabban, do I detect a small hint of Greek cynicism in your tone?"

"To be a Cynic is only to accept a certain view of things. It is not the exclusive property of your Greeks."

"Not my Greeks, please, but I take your point. And so this temple…?"

"Has been here forty years or more. It depends on when you start counting. It replaced Zerubbabel's, built in an attempt to replace Solomon's. That one Nebuchadnezzar burned to the ground centuries ago. Yet, the tradition holds that except for the annual entrance to the interior on *Yom Kippur* by the high priest, the space is as it has always been."

"We will discuss the illogic of that presumption later. In the meantime, tell me about these layers of cloth. How many and how thick?"

"As I said, I have no idea. Caiaphas tells me it is composed of many layers of cloth, as many as twenty, and together they measure perhaps a cubit in thickness."

"Yet he manages to come and go—at least once a year."

"Yes, but…"

"It begs the question, does it not? How do you suppose the body came to lie in the space in the first place? Surely the means of its insertion will be the same needed to retrieve it."

"Insertion? No, I believe the person walked in and died for his impiety. I do not know why. It is a very foolish thing for someone to do."

"Because he would stand in the Presence and to do so is proscribed by Torah, he was struck down. Do you believe that?"

"How else, then?"

"I have no idea, but consider the possibilities. There is first this notion that he walked in and was stuck down by an offended deity, as you say. Alternatively, whoever is in there was shoved in under the Veil after being dispatched elsewhere. Or, could it be he—I'm insisting it is a *he* in there until proven wrong—was forced by someone to enter, perhaps to steal the Ark."

"There is no Ark. Not for six hundred years."

"No? I must brush up on my reading. I suppose this is what I get for being a skeptic about the Lord and his works."

"Be careful with your tongue, Loukas, and remember where you are."

"Sorry. So, no Ark. What then?"

"There is a slab of stone set on uprights like a bench with the marks designating the laws given to Moses engraved on it. It is where the high priest pours the blood sacrifice each year."

"I see. Consider me corrected for the time being. However, we have a problem to solve irrespective of the circumstances that created it. For the moment, let us assume he was placed in the space. It may not have been so, as you prefer to believe, but for now, suppose it so. That being the case, if you wanted to do such a blasphemous thing, how would you do it?"

"How? I have no idea. It is not possible I would say. The weight and thickness of the veil alone—"

"You are not with me, Rabban. I asked you to devise a method in spite of your belief that it can't be done. It is not important that you believe it, only that you assume it for the moment. It is the pathway one takes to uncover new wisdom. One assumes the unlikely and then sees where it leads."

"You make my head ache, Greek, but let me think a minute." While the priests stood in confused disarray, Gamaliel paced the length of the Veil, pausing briefly at the point where the cord exited from its folds. "Can you find a sturdy pole," he said to the priest nearest him, "about twice the length of a guard's spear—six or seven cubits in length? Two such poles would be better. Find me two, if you can."

The *kohanim* exchanged glances and when the high priest nodded, one darted off to search.

"When he returns, we will slide them under the Veil on either side of the point where this rope comes through. Then while two of you lever the Veil up and away, the rest will haul on the rope and drag our infidel out."

"Very nice coming from a man who does not think the deed can be done."

"Loukas, you have my permission to have both sets of your teeth in close approximation for the time being."

"I should shut my mouth?"

"Isn't that what I just said?"

During this exchange, an apparently upset Caiaphas had been eying Loukas.

"Ah, High Priest," Gamaliel said, "You are wondering about our Greek friend here and his presence in the Holy Place. Be at ease. In spite of his outward appearance and demeanor, he is one of us and properly entitled to be here."

Designating Loukas as a Levite might have been a stretch, but Gamaliel reckoned that with the passage of time and the effects of the Exile, the purity of the lines from Aaron and the tribe of Levi had been blurred, the present high priest being a case in point. Another justification for the safety cord. Anyway, he felt it important to anoint Loukas with Levitical status. He hoped an understanding Creator would forgive the breach if in fact he'd overreached.

Caiaphas nodded, but did not seem reassured.

The priest returned quickly wrestling two long poles wrapped in sacking—too quickly, Gamaliel thought.

"That did not take much time. You were only gone for a moment."

"I found all these things just outside lying up against the wall near the Beautiful Gate, where the grain sacrifices are received."

"A convenient coincidence, Rabban, would you agree?" Loukas said.

"Too convenient a coincidence. Very well, let us see what we have on the other side of the veil."

Chapter IV

Gamaliel's double lever worked well enough to raise the Veil a cubit or two and allow the priests to drag the corpse from the Holy of Holies. Their location on the end of the cord blocked their view of the body at first. Just as well. Loukas exhaled through pursed lips and Gamaliel gritted his teeth. What now lay at his feet had to be a man, but beyond that little else could be said. From forehead to knees the man had been burned to near nonrecognition. The priests turned from their hauling and seeing the body, either fell to their knees or raced from the room.

"There, you see, Loukas? This man has stood in the Presence and paid for his offense. The fire of judgment has scorched him past identification."

"So it would seem, Rabban. And yet—"

"Please don't say any more. Not here, not now." Gamaliel eyes narrowed and flicked in the direction of the high priest.

"Ah!"

The high priest, in his turn, wheeled on the *kohanim* and began barking orders, most of them contradictory. The priests still in the area rose from their knees and scurried off in different directions attempting to follow Caiaphas' direction.

"We must remove this…this…"

"Body?" Loukas asked.

"Thing," Caiaphas said. "But how? There is no one here who dares touch it."

"I can," the healer said. "Please hand me the sacking found with the poles."

One of the priests handed the cloth to him and stepped back, unwilling it seemed to stand too close to the abomination on the floor. Loukas spread the cloth out. It appeared to be a long sack which at one time must have held grain, perhaps an omer or more—enough barley to provide sacrifices for a dozen people. Also, it had been opened at both ends. Loukas arranged the two poles and slid the sack over the ends and into the center.

"There, you see, Rabban?"

"See? What is it I am to see?"

"The means by which this poor man was carried into this place."

Loukas placed the poles with the sack next to the body. He spread the poles apart and with some difficulty shifted the man's remains onto the sack.

"Now, if I can borrow two of your priests, honorable sir," he said to Caiaphas, "I can remove this offense from your presence. They will not have to touch it, only the poles which, as you can see, now make a stretcher which we can use to bear him away.

"Away? Away where? My priests cannot be expected to carry this obscenity all the way to Gehinnom."

"No, of course not. Only as far as the Court of the Gentiles. There I will hire men to take him the rest of the way. I should think it would be in your best interest to have this man out of this place and out of your sight as quickly as possible."

"Yes, yes, of course. You," he pointed to two of the younger and presumably stronger priests, "take an end of this stretcher and remove this…this thing from my presence."

Loukas threw his cloak over the body. "You should come, too, Rabban. There is work for us to do."

"Us? Work? How is that to be?"

"You are the solver of great mysteries, are you not? Here is another to test your skill."

"I solved one mystery and vowed never to attempt another. What makes you think I will be drawn into this one? As far as

I am concerned this man, for reasons that defy common sense, walked into the Holy of Holies and was struck down for his foolishness."

"Then how will you explain these poles and sack? Is it not obvious that they were the means by which he was brought here?"

Gamaliel closed his eyes and sighed. What had happened here? And, more importantly, did he want to know? He did. It is the nature of the sort of mind Gamaliel had that required answers to important questions irrespective of their origin. Sometimes he felt this trait a curse bestowed on him by a deity who enjoyed taunting him.

"Why must it be me, healer? You can solve this thing as well as I and moreover you are the only one interested in the solution."

"You do not really believe that. This will nag at you forever if you do not get to the bottom of it. Come along, we will tackle it as we have done before. Granted it is not as exciting as a murder in the king's palace and it is unlikely you will have a chance to accost royalty as you have done in the past, but you must admit it is a fascinating puzzle."

"Take him away. I will follow later when I have had a chance to consult with the high priest."

Two nervous priests followed Loukas, the dead man in the makeshift sling. They made an ungainly procession as they exited. The remaining priests were set to scrubbing the floor outside the Veil where he had lain. Gamaliel found Josef ben Josef and had him repeat his story. This time he asked him to try remembering what else, besides the cord, he had noticed.

"Were there any indications, for example, that those poles might have been used before as we used them just now? Perhaps there were marks on the floor, scrapes…anything?"

Josef frowned and shook his head. "I cannot say, Rabban. I don't think so, no."

"A smear on the tiles? A footprint? Anything?"

Josef again shook his head. Gamaliel guessed that the young priest was in such a state that not much would be forthcoming. Too bad. The priest who'd discovered the poles could not add anything more to what he'd said earlier. Next he asked each member of the *kohanim* what they knew about the practice of attaching a cord to the ankle of those entering the Holy of Holies and if so, how did they come by the knowledge.

They all claimed to know and assumed it was an ongoing practice, although none had ever seen it done, as they had not served at the Temple during the Day of Atonement.

"Then why do you think it is customary?"

"It is spoken of in the vesting rooms. When we arrived for our tour of duty, the priests who were leaving spoke of it. Everyone knows."

"But it has never been done, has it?"

The men shrugged. They would not know, of course, because as they said, they had never been assigned to the Temple on *Yom Kippur*. If these men knew, could he assume the other *kohanim*, who also had not served on *Yom Kippur*, also knew? Was the presumed practice general knowledge among all the priests? If so, who else besides them would know and believe this practice served as part of the Temple routine? The answer to that question could be important.

Satisfied he'd heard all that the priests were likely to tell him and unwilling to tackle Caiaphas just then, he excused himself and headed to Loukas' house. There, he knew, he could think in peace. He would consider what had occurred in the past few hours and maybe enjoy one of the healer's wines— the one from Cappadocia that tasted of honey and soft summer days.

Chapter V

Gamaliel did not go immediately to Loukas' house. First, he dropped by the vesting rooms where the *kohanim* donned the various tunics designating the station assigned them, or the leather aprons if their assignment was at the Altar of Sacrifice which, for some, entailed the slaughter of animals. The vesting room also served as a place where older, no longer serving priests would gather to sit in the sun, reminisce, or offer gratuitous advice to their younger counterparts. He particularly wanted to speak with Jacob. Jacob ben Aschi had served the Temple for as long as Gamaliel could remember. Only the clouded vision caused by his advancing years had curtailed his active role in the workings of the Temple.

Gamaliel greeted the old man. "*Ha Shem*, Jacob ben Aschi,"

"Is that you, Rabban? Greetings in the Name to you, too. You are here about the scandal, yes?"

Gamaliel noticed the old man's empty cup. He retrieved a flask from a table covered with vessels of various sizes and shapes and filled it. He took Jacobs' hand and guided it to the cup. Jacob smiled his thanks. Gamaliel sat opposite the old man and cleared his throat so that he could be located and the old man could fix his milky eyes in his general direction.

"You speak of the dead man in the Holy of Holies, Jacob, that scandal? Well, yes and no. Yes, if you have something to tell me that will shed light on who the wretch was or why he did what he did."

"I am sorry, but I only know what I hear. I hope our high priest will puzzle out the mystery. So what else brings you here?"

"Besides wishing to see my old friend? I have a question for you. I am told that all the *kohanim* believe that we now attach a cord to the ankle of the high priest whenever he enters the Presence. Is that so?"

"Ah, these rumors. You are responsible for them, you know. It is your fault. All that talk last year about the risk we take with *Elohim* because of the possible corruption in Aaron's line or in the high priest's mind. It is your doing. You sit with the Sanhedrin and discuss this possibility and make a decision to suggest—suggest, mind you—that Caiaphas should adopt the practice, and by the time that debate found its way outside the Sanhedrin's walls, it became a policy in place."

"So, all, or nearly all, of the active priests believe it is the practice. Is that correct?"

"I think so. It can do no harm, you know, but oy, such a babbling. You and the remainder of the Sanhedrin should learn to be more discreet."

A gust of wind wafted a tendril of smoke at them. The aroma of burning flesh assaulted their noses.

"Ah, they have finally begun. If I am not mistaken, it is bulls, now," Jacob nodded his approval.

"So it seems. You would know."

"It is holy smoke, Rabban. It comes from the sacrifices."

"Yes, of course. And you can tell just from the aroma?" Jacob grinned and nodded. "So, Jacob, as to the Sanhedrin's membership, most of us are, as you say, discreet, but one or two cannot stop their gossiping. For some people, to be important means to be in possession of special knowledge. But, unless others know you possess it, they will never know how important you are. The temptation to let slip bits and pieces of information, no matter how trivial, is irresistible to some of my colleagues. They drop a hint here, a scrap there. Listeners are suitably impressed and the status of our important person is secured in their eyes—or ears to be precise."

Jacob shook his head. "It has always been thus. Well, you have your answer, and now so does everyone who might have wished to know about the practice. The fact that it has not been implemented and probably never will be makes no difference. It has found its way in the culture, you could say, and will surface in one form or another for as long as people speak of the Temple."

"So, the conclusion we can draw is that anyone or everyone might know about the practice?"

"I am telling you only what I surmise, Rabban. I am at an age when I can confess that I don't know anything for a certainty. So, will our high priest find out the who and the why?"

"I suspect not, Jacob. He is content with the notion that a madman dashed into the room and was struck down for his foolhardiness. It will serve as an object lesson for the Nation. And unless I miss my guess, now he will never allow the cord to be attached to his ankle, so that when he emerges unscathed from the Presence on the Day of Atonement, his position and standing with the Lord will be confirmed in everyone's eyes."

"You are not suggesting he arranged this to happen with that in mind?"

"Jacob, you know our Caiaphas better than anyone serving in the Temple. Do you think he would or could do such a thing?"

"Do not tempt me, Gamaliel. What he would or could do is not a sufficient reason to prompt an accusation. You can answer that question as easily as I."

"I believe he is capable, but not bold enough to do it. Furthermore, if I know anything about Caiaphas, it is that he sincerely believes he is the direct descendent of Aaron and has a duty to maintain and, if necessary, to cleanse any heresy, blasphemy, or breach of the Law that crops up during his time in office. He is comfortable with his relative purity before the Lord and would never dare to desecrate the Temple."

"There is your answer then. That is, it is your answer so long as you believe those bold words. What your answer will be if you come to doubt them later is another thing."

"There is one other thing about the high priest that disturbs."

"Just one? I hear the two of you are at odds over many things."

"In the case of the dead man in the Temple, then. Our high priest is not angry. He should be outraged at the very thought of a desecration of such magnitude—frothing at the mouth."

"But he is not?"

"He is in shock, I think. Perhaps in a day or two he will react to the enormity of the defilement and actually do something, but as yet, nothing."

"It is not a subject I am qualified to discuss, although I feel as you do, surely, Rabban."

"Yes, well, here is another question for you and then I must go. How is the Temple guarded at night? Would it even be possible for someone to enter the Holy Place without being seen and do such a thing? Remember, he had a cord tied to his ankle and that presupposes—"

"He wasn't alone. Yes, of course. Could someone or several people enter the place unseen and unnoticed and do this thing? I do not know how. At night, the guards are not as closely placed as they are during the day. They may not even be permanently placed at the Beautiful Gate, but move about. No one in their right mind would dream of assaulting the place, day or night. It would mean certain death."

"But a madman?"

"Ah yes, possibly a crazy person, as the high priest prefers, could do it, but I don't think so without being seen. He might make a dash for the entrance and penetrate the Holy of Holies before a guard could stop him, but then we would all know immediately, wouldn't we? The deed would have been reported last night, not this morning."

"Carrying in an already dead man?"

"Couldn't happen."

"Not possible?"

Jacob scratched his beard and considered. "Only if a guard— no, make that several guards— were bribed to look the other way."

"Do you think they would dare?"

"They would if two conditions were met. The bribe must be large enough to tide the guard over in the event he was found out and dismissed. And then, assuming he went along with the plan, even the most disreputable guard must not know the true purpose of the thing."

"Pardon?"

"However corrupt a man might be, he will not willingly give up his life just for money. But if he were led to believe only a prank was in play, he might turn a blind eye and a deaf ear. He would have to be both bribed and deceived."

"And a little stupid."

"That, too, yes."

"As I expected, Jacob ben Aschi, you may no longer see the things on earth, but you see into the mind of man with great clarity. Thank you. I must go."

Chapter VI

Before they were deployed, the Temple's guard assembled near the Pinnacle at the Mount's southwest corner. A room to one side provided space for the captain of the guards. Gamaliel had to backtrack to call on the captain, but he felt he had needed to hear what Jacob had to say before he tackled the men tasked to secure the Temple, the mount on which it stood, and the people who served in it. The day shift had been in place for several hours by the time Gamaliel arrived. He knew the captain only as Yehudah. Normally he would have known his patronymic as well, but it had been some time since he'd been required to look into security at the Temple. He believed that job fell more appropriately in someone else's area, or at least to someone with an interest in such things.

"Greetings, Yehudah. You are well?"

"It is the rabban, is it not? I am very well, Excellency. Is there something I can do for you?"

"You know of this business in the Temple, of course. Everyone does by now. I am curious how such a thing could have happened without one of your guards witnessing some part of it." The captain shuffled his feet and studied the rough paving stones beneath them, but said nothing. "Captain, can you help me here?"

"The person who should answer that question is Zach. Zach ben Azar'el commands the night company. He would know. All I can tell you is he said nothing to me when the guard changed at the first hour. I believe if he had seen or heard anything, he would have reported it."

"Yes, no doubt he would." Gamaliel paused and studied the Pinnacle for some moments while he thought how best to ask his next question.

"You are wondering how to ask me if any of my men might have been bribed last night, yes?"

"I hate to ask it, but I must. Is this a thing that could happen? It is important, you know. The Holy of Holies…"

Yehudah let his eyes drop to the pavement once more. "A bribe, like anything else, is always a possibility. We live in an uncertain world, Excellency. Money is scarce." He glanced in the direction of the Temple. The late morning sun's rays glinted off the gold finials and fretwork that adorned its top, and the alabaster panels set on the walls reflected the light like beacons. "Not so much for our priests. They can finish this," he waved his arm toward the Temple, "in gold and alabaster. No expense spared for that, but for the poor—"

"I think you have said enough, Captain." Gamaliel feared the guard's frustration would get the better of him and he would say something that would not be permitted, something that could cost him his position.

"It's just that…I am sorry, Rabban. It is for *Ha Shem*, I know."

"Captain, I understand how you feel, but remember we are on this earth for the blink of an eye. *Ha Shem* is forever. When we are gone, He remains. It is for Him we build this temple, not for ourselves."

"Sir, do you truly believe King Herod—"

"Enough, Yehudah, enough." The captain's jaw snapped shut with an audible click. "When will Zach and the night cohort report?"

"They will start straggling in from the eleventh hour until sunset. You will be able to speak to them then."

"Thank you, Captain. I will bid you good day. And Captain…it is for *Ha Shem*."

Gamaliel turned on his heel and made for the gate at the north end of the mount. It would be a long walk. Herod had made sure the mount that would lift this temple up so that it could be seen for miles around was larger than any other like it in the known world. Gamaliel did not have a ready answer to those who saw the Temple's opulence as a travesty when paired to those who daily struggled to put bread on their tables. He'd given Yehudah the stock answer, one he felt he could justify, but he believed it had fallen on deaf ears, and there were days when the plight of the poor caused him to question the Temple party's insistence that the construction continue. These last adornments added nothing to the building's utility. Would the Sanhedrin do anything to rein in the Temple Party's extravagance? Would they? Could they? He doubted he'd ever know.

The sun stood near its zenith, not quite the sixth hour. It had taken Gamaliel nearly two hours to seek out Jacob, question him, traipse across to the Pinnacle to speak with Yehudah, and then reach the Sheep Gate at the city's northern extreme. It would be exactly at the sixth hour when he arrived at Loukas' gate.

Since he had first made the healer's acquaintance, he made it a practice to visit him through the side gate that opened onto the back court. At first he did so because of his mistaken notion that Loukas was not of the Faith, and he preferred not to enter an infidel's house. Later, when Loukas had disabused him of that notion, the habit was too firmly entrenched to change, and so it was still to be through the gate, not door, he would enter Loukas' premises.

Loukas met him as he entered. Another man stood to one side. His dress suggested he might have traveled from the north and east.

"Greetings, Rabban. I expected you hours ago. You were detained? Not by the high priest, I hope."

"I was delayed, but not by his eminence. I felt the need to visit the captain of the guard and also Jacob ben Aschi."

"I do not know Jacob ben Aschi. Is he someone who has connections that can shed some light on our mysterious death?"

"Connections? No. He is a former *kohen* and blind, but he hears things and has the gift of the aged."

"And that is?"

"Perspective." Gamaliel turned to the stranger. "Forgive me if I sound rude, sir, but my position constrains me. To whom do I speak?"

The man bowed slightly and smiled. "I fully understand. You are the Rabban of the Sanhedrin, Loukas tells me, and consorting with those not of your faith can cause some discomfort if certain proprieties are not kept. It is the same with me and mine. So, you see we have the same conundrum with which to wrestle."

"Your…?" It had never occurred to Gamaliel that practitioners of other faiths might see him as the infidel and have scruples about being in his presence. It was a novel thought and one he would have to mull over at his leisure, if that time ever came. "I see. Well, you know me, but I do not know you."

"Then you must be told. Loukas, your manners are appalling. I am Ali bin Selah. Loukas and I share a mutual interest in the healing arts. Whenever I visit your handsome city, we come together and discuss the things we know or have discovered since our last meeting. Now I must be off. I am joining a caravan travelling down to Jericho and thence up the Jordan and beyond. It has been a great pleasure to make your acquaintance, Rabban Gamaliel."

With that, the man slipped through the gate with a swirl of silk and sun-bleached linen and was gone.

"Loukas, you must tell me what that was all about."

"It is simple enough. It is as he said. Assyrians possess skills we don't. I know Asclepius, Hippocrates, and their teachings, which he does not. He has knowledge of a vast pharmacopeia and mathematics, which I do not, and so on."

"Assyrian, Loukas? That empire expired years ago. You mean Parthian, don't you?"

"Some of the people who trace their lineage back to that time refuse to accept any other designation. They are Assyrian no matter where they live, you see."

"Really?"

"Consider the following. Suppose the city were destroyed and the Nation scattered—"

"That can never happen. As difficult as it is to live under Roman rule, no one but a madman would challenge them and even if they were that foolish, the ruckus would be over in days, a handful of survivors punished, and life would go on. It is not in the Lord's plan to destroy his city."

"It has happened before."

"Because we earned the Lord's wrath. That is no longer possible. We have the written Law now."

"For your sake I hope you are right, but you miss my point. Again I ask you to assume the impossible and see where it takes you. Were that to happen and you found yourself exiled to Memphis or Alexandria, would you call yourself an Egyptian or an Israelite?"

"I see—Israelite. What my descendents might call themselves I do not know, but I believe that if that were to happen and we were all scattered again, it would be only a matter of time before we returned and reestablished the Nation. It would be the wish of *Ha Shem* that we live in the land he gave us." Gamaliel frowned, "Sorry, you were saying?"

"Only that Ali and I share professional secrets. Also, he teaches me about his culture. I tell him what I know of ours. It is very broadening, Rabban, you should try it."

"Indeed? Why?"

"Never mind. You are an unreconstructed rabbi from Jerusalem. The effort would be wasted on you. Come sit in the shade, drink some wine, and tell me of your interviews with the man Jacob and the guard and I will tell you what I have discovered about our corpse."

"Good. Stick with the problem at hand. I must say, however, that your friend intrigues me."

"How so?"

"I can't say exactly but…Some wine and to work."

Chapter VII

Gamaliel sat on the bench which Loukas had previously moved into the shade. "I did not see your servant, Draco. Is he not well?"

"You know the story of poor Draco, how I pulled him from the gutter and of his terrible disease. He has had a turn for the worse. I'm afraid he will not live to see Passover. My hope is that he does not suffer much. The disease has ravaged all of his body. His pain, in spite of the medications I gave him, is terrible."

"Medications you gave. You no longer offer him relief?"

"No, I still do. I am trying a new one that Ali, my visitor, brought to me. It seems to have worked a small miracle. At least Draco is sleeping quietly for a change—something he has not done for days."

"And what is this new potion you have from your Assyrian friend—or is he Parthian?"

"I cannot say. He tells me it is the extract made from the sap of poppy flowers. But I have tried that before with only limited success, so this must be something new."

"Well, as long as it works."

"Indeed. It is a palliative only, Rabban, but it works. In the end it will only make his passing easier. And for him a quick death would be a blessing."

"A blessing certainly, but not to be wished for, Loukas. You are a healer. Doesn't your code call for you to do all in your power to preserve life?"

"It also states 'First, do no harm.' What good can come from prolonging a man's suffering? In Draco's case there is nothing to hope for and only pain to keep him company. I can ease that, and I may not deny him treatment. I will not stint in doing everything I can to ease his way, but a speedy death? Yes, I will pray for it."

Gamaliel would not argue the point. He had seen Draco on his previous visits and knew that death would be welcome. The ethics of advancing or delaying a death were far too complex to wrestle with today. Besides he wanted to know what Loukas had discovered.

"Well, to the business at hand. Tell me the dead man's secrets, then."

"His secrets? I cannot tell you much of them. I think, rather, it is his murderer's secrets we should be digging out."

"You insist the man is a murder victim and his death is not the result of stupidity. Loukas, the poles and sacking notwithstanding, doesn't the evidence point to a crazed or foolish man tempting the Lord? He enters, perhaps on a dare, perhaps as a test of his own faith, or perhaps out of lunacy. In the Presence he is consumed, or nearly so, by *Ha Shem's* wrath."

"It would be the high priest's desired story. I know that faith in the Temple, its traditions, its history, and Torah would be strengthened if that were the case. But that body lying in my storage area will not cooperate. I am sorry, Rabban, but something else happened to that man first."

Gamaliel sighed. Would nothing end simply? "And you say that because of what you found on inspecting it?"

"What I discovered and had confirmed by Ali bin Selah."

"You had the pagan look at him. Was that wise?"

"Why not? The man is dead. What harm can come to him now if a pagan or a dozen pagans look at him? He will be no less dead, and a worse state is not possible."

"But…" Gamaliel started to object to the thought of a pagan, an Assyrian at that, inspecting the body of one of the Faith, maimed and unrecognizable as it might be. But he knew Loukas and his acquired Greek ways and let it slide. "So, then what did you and your colleague find?"

"You remember the general condition of the body? He had been badly burned from just below his knees to his forehead."

"Yes I remember, and…?"

"Assuming for the moment that your notion of a wrathful deity scorched him, why not from the feet to the top of his head?"

"No one knows how holy fire might be applied."

"No, of course not, but one would think it would be mighty and all consuming. Yet this man is merely seared on the front. In fact, his clothing, what is left of it, on his back is hardly soiled, much less burned. Doesn't that suggest something less than the wrath of the Lord?"

"It suggests one of two things, each of which must be considered. On the one hand the Lord does not utilize fiery punishment in the magnitude we assumed or, on the other, the burns were administered by some other entity."

"Good. We are agreed. Now the next thing I discovered was the presence in the burns of ash and bits of burnt wood."

"Wood? Then you suppose he must have fallen into a fire pit or the like and died."

"Except there is evidence he had been bound for some time and was still bound when he died."

"You can tell that?"

"It is the matter of where and how the blood settles in wounds and so on. There is no mistaking it. This man had been bound before he received those burns."

"Then you are saying he did not fall into a fire. He was pushed?"

"I believe he was thrown in, Rabban. He had been tied up, I don't know exactly how. I am still working on that. Then carried to and dropped into the flames."

Gamaliel shuddered at the thought. "It would be a terrible way to die, face down in a pile of red hot coals."

"If that is the way he died."

"Pardon? If? What are you suggesting? That he didn't die in the fire? How then?"

"I think the man died before the burns occurred, although I would not put my seal on it."

"You have doubts?"

"I could state for certain that the worst of the wounds were post mortem, but not all. I do not think it significant, but suggest we keep it in mind when we make our inquiries."

"Our inquiries? You are not supposing that you and I…that we are setting out to unmask a murder?"

"It would not be the first time."

"I made a solemn promise to myself after the Feast of Tabernacles that I would never allow myself to be drawn into another investigation. Finding murderers and evil doers is the function of the guards, of those tasked to enforce the Law, not I, never again."

"But you are the rabban of the Sanhedrin. The Sanhedrin is the keeper of the Law."

"Only as long as the Caesar in Rome allows it to be so."

"True enough, but Rome does allow it, and as the rabbi's rabbi and the chief officer in the Sanhedrin, you are ultimately responsible for the keeping the Law. *Ergo,* the discovery of this man's killer ultimately falls on you."

"Nonsense. I am the chief interpreter of Moses' Law, of Torah, but breaches of the peace and the lawbreaking of thieves and murderers is for others."

"The circumstances of his death, if the high priest has his way, make it Torah. And if you do not pursue it, this man's killer or killers will go free. You know that in your heart. You know that if the generally accepted notion that the Lord struck this man down like Uzza is upheld, a murderer goes free. You cannot let that happen, Rabban. It is your duty to see that it doesn't."

"Uzza died because he reached for the Ark as it fell from a cart. He did not invade the Temple."

"It is a difference without a distinction and, as you so recently educated me to the fact, there is no Ark in the Temple."

Gamaliel shook his head and set his cup down on the table with a bang. "Of course you're right. That is, if your notion of murder is correct. I must withhold judgment as to that for now. You know, Loukas, there are days when I wish I had never met you. Please refill this cup and help me decide what I must do next."

Chapter VIII

The Shofars sounded the eighth hour as Gamaliel stepped through the doorway of his home. He felt dizzy and his stomach growled. Loukas' wine, he thought, must have gone to his head. Three draughts from the sixth hour on was neither usual nor prudent, especially since he had missed breaking his fast. The murder at the Temple had severely disrupted his routine and Gamaliel, if nothing else, was a creature wedded to routine. His servant scowled disapprovingly at him and laid the remains of his afternoon meal on the table, supplemented with a bowl of lentils Gamaliel supposed was meant to make up for a missed breakfast.

The burning question was, if Loukas had it right, what sort of person would stage such a grotesque murder? That assumed it was murder. He held out the hope that, in spite of the evidence pointing to this conclusion, Loukas had it wrong. But for now he had to accept that Loukas had the correct line on the circumstances surrounding the death, that it had been a murder committed elsewhere. He wished it were not, wished the more conventional solution would prevail. If the dead man were only a lunatic or fool who'd barged into the Temple, everyone would be happy and the case quickly forgotten. But in his heart Gamaliel knew that conventional thinking would not serve. Whether he or the Temple Party liked it or not, what occurred the previous night in the Holy of Holies probably constituted murder, pure and simple.

But who had been killed, and by whom, how, and why?

"Benyamin," he said to the servant who hovered at his side, "assume you are a murderer."

The servant held a ewer of goat's milk in one hand and a cloth in the other. "Master...I am what? I don't follow you."

"This is a hypothetical —"

"A what?"

"You remember being young. Didn't you and your playmates sometime pretend to be warriors, or great men?"

"Of course."

"Well then, suppose in this game you are a desperate murderer. How would you go about the deed?"

"I cannot imagine. A murderer, you say, Rabban. Surely you are not suggesting I am capable of such a thing?"

"I believe, Benyamin, as the prophet says, people are capable of all sorts of evil under the sun. You are, I am, and everyone is, if pressed hard enough, capable of doing nearly anything. It is why we are so determined to keep the Law, why Moses carried it to us exactly as delivered to him by *Ha Shem*."

"You wish me to commit a murder?"

"Not a real one, Benyamin, a pretend one. Just tell me your thinking if you were to contemplate such a thing."

The servant put the jug of milk on the table and sniffed. The scent of cooking still lingered in the room. He twisted a cloth in his hands. Gamaliel thought he looked miserable.

"I had hoped that would never come to light," Benyamin said.

"You hoped what would never come to light? Benyamin, now I am as confused as you look."

"I assure to you, Rabban, as the Lord is my witness, it was an accident. Yes, I carried a great deal of anger at the time, and, yes, I brought the club to the meeting intending to harm the man who had dishonored my sister, but I did not mean to kill him."

"Benyamin, I have no idea what you are talking about. What man dishonored your...you have a sister?"

"Sir, I...I thought you knew."

"We have gotten off on the wrong foot, I think. Perhaps you had better tell me your story now and then I will ask my question again."

Benyamin wiped his eyes and haltingly poured out his tale—of a younger sister dishonored by a neighbor. He did not explain how she'd lost her honor and Gamaliel did not ask. Benyamin, then the hot-tempered brother and filled with righteous anger, confronted the miscreant and words led to blows and blows to a clubbing and the neighbor then slipped and fell against a boulder. The wound inflicted by the stone had caused the death and Benyamin had been cleared of any wrongdoing, but it had preyed on his mind all these years.

"I see. Well, Benyamin, you were found not to be responsible for the man's death then. So be it. You must put it aside and trust the Lord to be forgiving and understanding."

"Yes, Rabban. So, is that what you wished to have me confess?"

"No, it is not. What I hoped you would do is consider in a pretend fashion...pretend, you understand...how you would plan a murder if you wanted to commit one. But I can see that exercise would be useless at this point."

"I could try."

"Yes? Well, go ahead."

Benyamin screwed up his face in concentration. If there was a machine between his ears Gamaliel thought he surely would hear the wheels clacking away.

"It is no use, sir. I am not capable of such a thing, despite my sordid past. Only..."

"Only what?"

"Well, I would say that if I were contemplating such a terrible thing, I would make sure that I masked the reason why I did it so as not to lead the authorities back to me."

"You would separate the deed from the motive. Well, thank you for that, Benyamin. I think I will sit in the sun for a while. If anyone stops to talk, I am not available. That is especially true of the high priest and any of the Temple officials."

"You are not at home. I understand. Ah…when do you plan on being at home?"

Gamaliel scratched his head, measured his fatigue which by now, and after a meal, nearly overwhelmed him. "I will be away for at least three hours."

"Yes, sir."

Gamaliel walked into the inner court and reclined on a bench which he'd earlier covered with mats. He would lie down and bask in the afternoon sun. He would consider the problem set before him. Perhaps if he turned over the facts of the case, as he had done in the past when called on to sort through something as grisly as this, he would begin to understand.

The sun hovered near the western horizon when he awoke. Benyamin stood over him with a damp cloth and a cup.

"Sir, I did not want to disturb you, but it is nearly evening and I know you always have your devotions before supper. Are you all right? You've been asleep for a long time."

"I am fine. What's in the cup?"

"A little wine thinned with water, sir. I believe you were dreaming and I thought you might…I thought it would freshen your mouth."

"Thank you." He sat up, took the cup of watered wine, sipped, swirled the liquid in his mouth, and swallowed. It did remove the sour taste.

Dreaming. Had he been? About what? He relaxed his mind and allowed his waking thoughts to return. A man with a mask, a very large mask that nearly covered the upper portion of his body bobbed, and danced before him, a cup in his hand. The whole area seemed filled with smoke which only made the place darker and more forbidding. The face, if that is what the mask depicted, changed, first sad, then happy, then fierce and danger-ous. Suddenly a body appeared at the mask bearer's feet. It was the burned man—only he wasn't burned. Then the masked figure waved his hand over the body and it thrashed about and the burns appeared. The mask smiled and that was when Benyamin woke him. What on earth did all that mean? Oh, to have the mighty Josef of Egypt here to interpret it.

His sleeping resulted in his missing the guard change at sunset. Tomorrow would be soon enough. Maybe by then Loukas would have discovered something new from his inspection of the body. It was time to sup and then read until sleep came again. He would think about his dream later.

Chapter IX

As it happened, reading did not occupy Gamaliel's evening as he'd planned. After eating his evening meal he'd retired to his reading room, the one room in his house which he insisted be exclusively his. Even when his wife lived and his children were young and underfoot, they rarely entered his personal version of the Holy of Holies. It was here that he kept his scrolls and books, his writing materials and blank sheets of papyrus in neat stacks on a table in one corner. There he would retreat to study, to find quiet and, since the death of his wife, peace and solitude. He lit his specially designed lamp with its multiple wicks. It alone could provide sufficient light for his failing eyesight to read the crabbed glyphs that marched across ancient panes. Because he had slept so soundly during the afternoon, he added a larger portion of oil to the lamp so that it would burn longer than usual. He would read, he thought, and let his mind find loftier things to occupy it than the sordid business in the Temple.

But it never happened. Even before the night's second hour had elapsed, his eyes strayed from the words on the sheet before him to be replaced by images from his dream—the man behind the grimacing mask, bobbing and weaving over the body. He could almost smell burned flesh. Did this uncomfortable apparition have anything to do with the desecration of the Holy of Holies? He shuddered.

As much as he wished it otherwise, he knew the mystery must be resolved and quickly. He pushed aside the document in front of him and replaced it with a fresh sheet of papyrus, part of a lot he'd purchased the previous week. The seller had assured him that, though the leaves had been used before to record some official transaction or other, each one had been carefully sanded and could be used without fear of introducing an error caused by an unintended *neqqudot*.

He smoothed the sheet and moved it closer to the light. How does one sort though the discontinuous strands of this murder? He dipped his stylus in new ink and made a tick mark on the edge of the page. He would list all the possibilities and their various bits of data, however tangential. So his first entry would be the simplest.

> *A man, either no longer in his right mind, under the influence of too much wine, or possessed by the notion he was entitled to do so, entered the holy place and was struck down by* Ha Shem *for his impertinence.*

But would that really have happened? If the man was insane, drunk, or otherwise innocently unaware of the consequences of his actions, would the Lord strike him down? The insane and those similarly afflicted were like babies, were they not? Is that how we are to understand His Justice—killing babies?

He made a double tick mark.

> *The man had a cord attached to his ankle which must mean one of two things: He was accompanied by others. He acted alone but considered the possibility he would be struck down and made provisions for it.*

But doing so presupposed premeditation and that, in turn, eliminated the insane and anyone possessed with the notion he could enter the place with impunity. That left a person with little common sense. Perhaps a young man filled with bravado and youthful cynicism and urged on by his peers to tempt fate or to prove the Faith to be empty.

> *However, if alone, would not the cord have followed him into the Holy of Holies, and then it would not have*

*been where it was found—so, not alone. There had to
be accomplices to the deed. Why else tie the cord?*

Why else, indeed? No, this will not do. To suppose that the
dead man entered under his own volition made no sense. Maybe
he had been pushed? With a cord tied to his ankle? It would
be a stretch.

He made a triple tick mark and wrote again.

*A man is murdered and brought to the Temple and
placed in the Holy of Holies.*

Why? Why dump the body there and not in any of the dozens
of places which the city's murderous element routinely used to
dispose of their victims? In Gehinnom or a wadi off the Jericho
road, for example. It made no sense. He put the writing materials
aside. He needed to think. What possible reason would anyone
have for depositing a body in such a manner?

He returned to contemplating his dream. Gamaliel was not a
great proponent of dream interpretation. He assumed the story
of Josef and the pharaoh to be accurate. It was in Holy Writ,
after all, and represented one of those instances when the Lord
interceded directly in the affairs of men, in this case, in the
sleep of a pharaoh. That fact made it important, if nothing else.
However, he felt certain that most dreams were merely the result
of a surfeit of drink, food, or conflict endured during the day
and a dream was the mind's way of disposing of the discomfort
such events caused in the same way as a daily visitation to the
toilet marked the elimination of the actual cause. Nevertheless,
he determined to take this last one seriously. He dare not presume, but perhaps *Ha Shem* had tried to tell him something by
visiting him with the images of the masked man and the corpse.
Certainly a possibility, but if so, what did he make of it?

He returned to his writing, adding four tick marks.

*A man is murdered and for reasons that as yet do not
make sense, his body is inserted into the holy place. This
is borne out by the poles and sacking that Loukas made*

into a stretcher. If so, there had to be no fewer than two persons complicit in the deed, plus the means of slipping their burden past a cohort of guards. And to be convincing, the body is scorched at some point.

Five ticks.

It follows then that some, perhaps several, guards must have been bribed to permit this travesty. What sorts of people have sufficient status to suborn Temple guards? Did the guards simply turn a blind eye? Did they vacate their posts for a prearranged time? Were they directly involved—could the dead man have been one of their own? Would any of them admit to having done so?

Probably not, so why ask?

He paused and read his notes. Had he forgotten anything? Yes, he'd omitted the knowledge of the cord. He must make a note.

Six ticks.

It is critical we determine who knew about the cord around the ankle. It would not be any of the Yom Kippur Kohanim *because they knew that the practice had not been implemented. It must, therefore, be any one of the other twenty-three groups, their families, or friends.*

How many might that be? He shook his head. The number could be legion.

One final entry, seven ticks.

The bribing of a guard or two does not confirm or deny any of the possible explanations. Whether a madman, a fool, or a corpse inserted into the Holy of Holies, guards must be bribed.

Gamaliel pushed the papyrus sheet aside and replaced the stylus in its holder. His eyes burned and fatigue had finally caught up with him. He would tackle this again in the morning. Better yet, he would take this scrap of papyrus with him and call on Loukas. Two minds would be superior to one, and Loukas had been trained in Greek logic. He, better than Gamaliel, knew the intricacies of deductive reasoning. Spending a lifetime training rabbis did not often entail the use of that skill and, as Gamaliel did spend his days teaching candidates, what little ability he had in that line had long since dried up.

He blew out his lamp and went to bed. He would call on the healer in the morning.

Chapter X

Gamaliel arose the next morning alert and refreshed. He'd slept without dreaming—at least not one he remembered. He found it difficult to accept that only twenty-four hours had elapsed since he'd been summoned to the Temple, since the man had been discovered dead in the holiest place on earth. He stepped into the street and found a boy loitering near his door. He gave him a coin and sent him to Loukas with the message to meet at the south end of the Temple Mount in an hour.

At the appointed time he found Loukas waiting for him at the Hulda Gates. "Greetings in the Name, Rabban. You have survived the night without incident. Did you speak to the night cohort of guards as you planned?"

"No. I fell asleep, and by the time I was myself again, I had missed the opportunity. I blame your wine for that, but am not complaining. It is extraordinarily fine wine. I did draw up some thoughts to consider." He handed the scrap of papyrus to Loukas who frowned and read his notes.

"Your Greek is terrible."

"Pardon? My Greek is terrible? Do you read Hebrew?"

"Some."

"Aramaic?"

"Not at all."

"Then my Greek will have to do. Why is it terrible?"

"It is illiterate, the Greek of the streets. Literary Greek is beautiful. It begs for the accompaniment of the lyre. You know Homer...Sappho?"

"By name. Listen, my friend, we can discuss the aesthetics of Greek rhetoric and my awkward Greek some other day. Tell me what you think of this first bit of analysis."

"It is a start, surely. It seems to me that you need to consider something else before you commit to this."

"And that is?"

"Like you, I have been thinking and it occurred to me that if I wanted to commit a perfect murder, I would first separate the victim from his killer. That is to say, I would place the act in such a way as to make the motive disappear or be invisible to a less inquisitive eye. Then, unless someone witnessed it, things like opportunity and means would have no utility."

"That is approximately what my man, Benyamin, said."

"I mean a complete separation, one that cannot be reversed, at least theoretically. The dead man was involved in something. Separating him from any hint as to what or who that might be leaves him isolated and leaves you with no place to start."

"And then what? If I cannot connect any of the key elements, what do I do?"

"As the Romans might say, *cui bono?*"

"Who benefits?"

"Yes. Did the dead man know something someone wished to keep quiet? Did he have something someone else wanted, and so on? Who is your dead man, Rabban? Find him out. Find his recent history, follow his days backward from yesterday, and you will find his killer. That is, of course, if you want to."

"That is the ultimate question, isn't it? I ask myself, why should I? Given the near impossibility of tracing this killer, assuming there is one, wouldn't it be simpler to accept the conventional wisdom and be done with it?"

"Of course it would, and if you had even a scintilla of moral flexibility you might do so. But, as that isn't the case, you are stuck with the need to press on. In my opinion, the evidence as we have it thus far denies the conventional option."

"Tell me again."

"Read your own analysis. Take, for example the fact that your dead man has been burned from head to knee."

"Yes, so? Those who would have the easy answer would say he entered the Holy of Holies and gazed on the face of the Lord. The burns are expected. Even Moses could not do that and not be affected. Though he averted his eyes, his face was permanently reddened."

"Forget all that for the moment, and look at the man. Pretend he was found in the street. So as you gaze upon this dead man lying in the road, what do your deductive powers tell you? Who is he? Why is he burned so badly?"

"He was brutally murdered."

"Exactly. It is only because he was found where he was that you entertain any other notions, you see? Look past the idea of an invader into the Holy of Holies and think of alternatives. He has a severe wound to the back of his head, I have discovered. He is burned across this face and front. Was the blow sufficient to kill him? I don't know, but combined with the terrible burns, probably."

"Very well, Healer, tell me what I am not seeing."

"Your high priest will not like it."

"Lately, that is his usual response to practically anything I suggest."

"Very well, what you have here is a clear-cut murder by person or persons unknown. Until you can identify the victim, you will be stuck. However, it seems to me you might make some progress by nibbling at the edges of this piece of cheese."

"Cheese? Loukas, I hardly think..."

"Hear me out. Your mystery is like a large lump of cheese that has a coin embedded in it. You've been to affairs where prizes are inserted into food, cakes usually. Assume the cheese is too hard to cut or you do not have a knife, but you know the coin is in there somewhere. So you nibble here, and you nibble there. Finally, when you have consumed enough—"

"You get ill from overeating moldy cheese and die."

"Nonsense. Start with the guards. Nibble there for a while and see what turns up."

"Very good. I will sample the cheese. You can do me a favor for your part."

"And that would be?"

"If the dead man was someone of substance, his people will be looking for him. You move about and hear things. Find out who's missing. Also, could you inspect the dead man again and see if there is any possibility of identifying him. A scar, a mark… his teeth or…I don't know…anything."

"I will try. Now, let us find a place where we can sit in the shade, drink some wine, and eat a little something. We will not speak of this problem while we refresh ourselves. We will let the inner workings of our minds mull over the facts for us."

They found a cool spot that served food and sat. The wine was good but could not compare to Loukas' Cappadocian.

"Tell me about your friend, Ali."

"There is not much I have not already told you. He visits once or twice a year and, as I said, we exchange information."

"This was one of his annual visits?"

"No, as a matter of fact he was to meet a colleague in Caesarea by the Sea, he said, but the man did not turn up. So he traveled to Jerusalem in hopes of finding him."

"Did he? Why did he assume he would be found in Jerusalem?"

"I don't know. Ali seemed less than eager to talk about him. I didn't think it polite to press. He left yesterday and did not seem upset, so whatever the two of them were about, it seems to have worked itself out."

"His friend was from Jerusalem?"

"So I believe. Business or…I don't know to be honest."

"No matter. Tell me something else. Where or from whom do you buy your wines? I would like some of the vintage you served me yesterday."

"Ah, well, that is courtesy of Ali as well. When he visits he brings me as much as he can, depending on the amount of his other baggage and the length of the trip. Wine, as you know, does not travel well."

"I had hoped to purchase some."

"I will tell Ali when I write to him. Maybe he can have some sent."

"Yes, I would appreciate…oh, do you recognize that man standing in the shop across the road?"

"What? What man?"

"Turn your head slowly to your right. There is a man with a great black beard and a striped headdress. He has been watching us since we sat down, and I am almost certain he was in the street where we met earlier."

Loukas did as he was directed, gazed absently at the shop fronts and the people in the general area of the man in question and then turned his attention back to Gamaliel.

"I may have seen him before, but I do not remember when. It will come to me eventually. But…well, very good, Rabban, you have become properly suspicious. This bodes well for your future as a solver of mysteries and a foe of criminals."

Gamaliel snorted.

Chapter XI

Gamaliel had been followed once before but in that instance he had set the act in motion. It had been a device he'd used to convince a killer of the need to act quickly. Then there had been no real danger, or he believed so at the time. Thinking back on it now, he wasn't too sure.

"Who do you think he is following?"

Loukas shrugged and sipped from his cup. "This wine is very good, isn't it? I mean for a local vintage."

"If you say so, Loukas. I am no expert. I know what I like and that is enough. The finer points of wine tasting are lost on me, all that sipping and sniffing. You haven't answered my question."

"No, I haven't. There is only one way to find out. One of us must leave and the other can see if our stalker follows. If he doesn't, then it must be the one who remains."

"Let's arrange to meet at the north end of the temple mount in an hour. We can weave our way through the streets. I judge him to be a stranger to the city. If I am correct, he will soon be lost in the crowds and when we meet, we can decide what to do next."

"You leave first. I will wait until you are out of sight and then move off in the other direction."

Gamaliel nodded, stood, and walked away. He headed into the busiest area of the Souk. Once in the crowded street, he risked a quick look behind him. If the man in the odd headdress were on his trail, he didn't see him. He meandered through the streets, pausing now and again to look at merchandise, haggle with a vendor, all the while keeping an eye on the sun. When it had made its transit toward the west and he deemed an hour had passed, he hurried to the Antonia Fortress and then to the mount's north gate. Loukas arrived moments later.

"I don't think I was followed. Was I?"

Loukas grinned and shook his head. "He did not budge when you left. I made a show of disputing the price of our food and drink and then left in the opposite direction as we planned. He hesitated and then followed me. In fact he is lurking behind that archway down the street."

"You didn't try to shake him off?"

"No. I thought I would rather have him in sight where I could keep an eye on him than lose him in the crowd and never know what he wanted."

"You still don't know what he wants."

"Not yet, but while I harangued the wine merchant, I also arranged for some men to follow our follower."

"Ah, and they will follow him to where he is staying later?"

"No, they are waiting for my signal to take him in hand."

"Won't that be dangerous?"

"I don't think so. If he were a danger, we would have known that long ago. I suspect he thinks I will lead him to someone else."

"Who?"

"No idea." Loukas tugged at his ear and in an instant a struggle ensued under the archway. Loud voices and then Gamaliel heard what he guessed was a series of punches. Two burly men approached supporting the bearded man between them. Swelling had already started under his left eye.

"Here's your man," one said. Their captive attempted to pull away but they only tightened their grip on his arms.

"Now, my good man," Loukas seemed quite amiable. "Can you tell us why you were following me?" The man scowled and said nothing.

"I see. You should know that the men who now have you in their grip are Siccori, assassins. They have been led to believe you are turning people over to the Romans whom you claim are plotting against Caesar."

The man's eyes grew as round as hen's eggs. "They are…I am not any such…you tell them I am not."

"Why should I do that? You see this man here?" Loukas waved in Gamaliel's direction. "He is a very important person in the Sanhedrin. You know what that means? It means that if he agrees with that assessment, that you are a danger to the Nation, you will disappear into the wilderness and never be heard from again."

The man turned to Gamaliel. "Sir, I swear to you, I am only a merchant here on business."

Gamaliel put on his fiercest expression, one he'd seen the Pontius Pilate use on another occasion. If he got it half right the man should be near collapse. "If you are, as you say, only a merchant, you must explain why you were dogging the heels of this man. Why were you following him yesterday and again today?"

Gamaliel guessed at the last part. He had no idea if the man had been following Loukas the day before or not.

"Yesterday? No, no, not him yesterday. It was the other one."

"Other? What other one?"

"The man who calls himself Ali bin Selah."

"The Assyrian physician?"

"I don't know about physician, but I know that he conspires against my king."

"And now you follow this other man. Why not stay with the Assyrian?"

"He has slipped out of sight. I hoped your friend would lead me to him."

Gamaliel had one skill that some claimed was unique to him. He could tell when someone lied, shaved the truth, or just twisted it a bit. And he knew the man lied. Not entirely, a kernel of truth lay in there somewhere, but on the whole the man had tried to cover his real intent with a plausible lie.

"I am sorry to hear that. You are, of course, not telling me the truth, and I am afraid I will have to give leave to these men to take you away. You do know that an attempt to walk out of the wilderness without water is nearly impossible. Those few who did make it out alive lost their minds in the process. Very sad."

The man gulped. "I swear to you—"

"Swearing is forbidden."

"Pardon?"

"I see you are not from these parts so your indiscretion may be pardoned. But our Law specifically forbids the use of an oath. It disobeys the Lord's Command."

"I didn't know, but surely—"

"Enough. Either you speak the truth, or you will disappear." How much farther Gamaliel thought he could take this foolishness he couldn't say, but he hoped Loukas, who'd created the pretense in the first place, would step in. He did.

"Rabban, I have an idea that may save this man's life and bring us the truth. I have in my purse a potion that, if drunk, will force the truth from him. We will have this man, who claims to be telling the truth, drink it and we will be done here."

"Very well. This man assures us he tells the truth, he should have no objection to drinking it. Is that so…what is your name, by the way?"

"My name?"

"Yes. What do they call you?"

Again, Gamaliel thought he heard wheels spinning. This man had more than one problem with the truth, it seemed.

"It is Aswad Khashab."

"Aswad Khashab?" Loukas said, "Well, Aswad Khashab, what shall it be? You will tell us the truth, drink the potion and tell us the truth, or travel with these men into the wilderness?" The man's eyes darted from Gamaliel to Loukas to his captors. "I must tell you, Aswad Khashab, if that is your name, that if you insist on telling lies, the potion will cause you difficulties later in the day."

"I will tell the truth. The man—"

"No, no, drink up." Before Khashab could protest, Loukas had forced the vial to his lips and forced its contents down his throat. "Now you may speak."

Khashab babbled something about a wool merchant who had money to pay mercenaries to fight against the King of Bithynia. Gamaliel did not believe any of it. Also, he realized that the two "assassins" Loukas had recruited would soon be missed at the wine shop and would want to be gone.

"Very well Khashab, you may go, but rest assured that if your information proves to be false…" he left the threat unsaid. The men released their captive who instantly raced away.

Loukas paid the captors who smiled, thanked him, and walked away to their shop.

"You know he lied about everything."

"Bithynia does not have a king, I know—hasn't for many years, and he will pay for that bit of mendacity."

"Pay? How?"

"The potion I poured down his throat is a powerful purgative. His bowels will be reminding him of his perfidy for the rest of the day and well into the night."

Chapter XII

Gamaliel watched in silence as the man scurried away though the crowded street. He puckered his lips and exhaled. The sound that emerged turned heads and produced a few scowls He did not intend it to signify disgust, as some must have thought, but consternation. Loukas turned to him.

"What do you think? Shall we see our friend again or are we done with Aswad Khashab?"

"He did not strike me as a subtle man. Oh, we will see him again but not right away, and not because of your medication. He will need to find some subterfuge so that we will not know him. You should be ashamed of yourself, by the way."

"Oh, I am."

"Yes. Well, he is a liar and a bad one. King of Bithynia… do you believe that? Travelers come to our city and see us as different in important ways and assume the difference must be because we are stupid."

"You are too harsh. This one believed we wouldn't know our history or geography. He has reason to believe that way you know. Israelites are considered the most parochial people in the Empire, Rabban. You, in fact, sometimes seem typically insular and then you surprise me with the breadth of your knowledge."

"I will take that as a compliment, I think, but surely everyone knows there has been no king in that part of Anatolia in a century."

"Everyone except our tracker. And you say we have not seen the last of him."

"No, he will report back to his employer that he has been found out and will be replaced by another for a while and this one will lay low, but rest assured he will surface again. The next one in will be better, but he will be out there somewhere. At least I think so, don't you?"

"Yes, except it would have been nice to know what he was after. We should have pressed him harder."

"Loukas, neither you, nor I, nor our erstwhile 'assassins' have the stomach for the sort of violence needed to extract information from him. Now, if you really did have a truth-telling potion in that sack of yours, it might have ended differently."

"Ali bin Selah would have had something of the sort. He seems to have a potion or powder for everything."

"I am concerned about your friend, Loukas."

"Ali? Why? He left the city and will be well on his way home by now."

"Are you sure of that? I ask because too many coincidences seem to be piling up since yesterday morning, when the body appeared in the Temple. Here's a man whose identity has been removed by terrible burns. Burns, you tell me, inflicted after death. At the same time your friend from far away Parthia or, as he prefers, Assyria, just happens to appear on your doorstep in time to share an opinion about the dead man's last moments. He, in turn, is being followed by another man who may or may not be from the same area, Bithynia notwithstanding. This man loses track of Ali and then decides to follow you. Oh my, and then there is the business of the cord and…it is too much, you see?"

"I do not see the connection between Ali, this man we just interrogated, and your murder, Rabban. Why do you think they are connected?"

"You tested my Latin earlier. My turn to test yours. It is an example of *lex parsimoniae.*"

"You've lost me, what?"

"*Lex parsimoniae,* the notion that the simplest answer is to be preferred in solving a puzzle. At the very least, it should be sought. Simplicity in all things. One of the Greeks you so admire must have said that sometime or another. At any rate, it may not seem so now, but my sense of the thing is that all these strands will eventually weave together and then we will know all."

"It is too much for me, my friend. I will return to my home, consult with my patients, and when I have time, I will inspect your dead man again. I will not, however, entertain the notion that Ali bin Selah is in any way connected to the dead man in the Temple."

"I hope you are right. Well, goodbye, then. I will call on you later and you can tell me what, if anything, the dead man has revealed to you. My students will be wondering what has become of me."

Loukas stepped away and then turned. "I can find no reports of someone missing, important or otherwise."

"Keep trying."

Gamaliel walked across the broad stone pavement of the temple mount toward the upper entrances to the Hulda Gates. They would take him out into the city closer to his home than any of the other five exits he knew about. The wind shifted and again, as the day before, his nose was assaulted by the stench, Holy notwithstanding, of the smoke rising from the altar area. He stopped in his tracks.

Smoke. Incense. He veered sharply to his right and went searching for Jacob ben Aschi. He found him seated as usual near the vestry.

"Jacob, greetings in the Name."

"Ah, Rabban, you are back...and so soon. I am glad, I have been thinking about your question and have had another thought, but you first, what can an old man tell you this time?"

"How is the Holy of Holies cleaned, Jacob?"

"Cleaned? What makes you think it needs cleaning? Oh, because of the dead man. He might have left something, you think?"

"It is a thought. He may have brought something in with him, and assuming he entered on his own, it might still be in there."

"You should ask," the old man said, his rheumy eyes focused in the distance somewhere to Gamaliel's right. "I was going to tell you this very thing. You can climb into the observation tower, but with only the dim light of the slit windows, it is difficult to see much of anything in the Holy of Holies. A body you can see, but without the candelabra lit, it is impossible to know what lies on the floor."

"Then how does one know when or if the area needs cleaning? I know *Ha Shem* could manage it if He wished, but I believe He'd prefer leaving it to the *kohanim*."

"Yes, probably so. To answer your question, there is a long pole with a hook attached to it. Like a very large shepherd's crook, you see. One slips it under the Veil and moves it about. If there is anything on the floor that does not belong there, it will collect it, you could say, and the person holding the pole will pull it free."

"That strikes me as rather inefficient."

The old man shrugged. "If the Holy of Holies is untidy and the Lord doesn't complain, why should we?"

"Still, I would like to have the surface of the room searched with that marvelous pole."

"Ask Daniel. He is the senior *kohen* with this group. He can arrange it."

Gamaliel thanked Jacob and went in search of Daniel. The senior priest greeted Gamaliel and listened to his request. Convinced that further defilement might still remain behind the veil, he put two of his people to work scraping the floor. The veil muffled any sounds the device might make so they had to wait until it was pulled through to discover if it had captured anything. The first pass produced a shred of the Veil. Daniel guessed the inner layer must be rotting and there would be more fabric forthcoming. He was correct. Each pass brought more scraps of dusty material to light. On the fourth pass a bronze bowl caked with what might be dried blood came out with the cloth.

"What is this?" Gamaliel bent to retrieve it.

"It is the bowl the high priest uses to carry the blood of the sacrifice when he enters on *Yom Kippur*."

"This bowl? Are you sure?"

Daniel inspected the bowl. "I am not sure. It looks like what I have been told he carries, but I have never worked on the day, so I couldn't say for sure. It is the same type and style. I do know that."

The hook produced another item on its last pass.

"And this is?" Gamaliel asked.

"Incense pot, I believe. The high priest must fill the room with burning incense when he enters. It is to obscure his view of The Presence while he pours the blood on the stone. One must never look at the Presence."

"So I've been told. Then one might assume that finding these items in the area indicates the dead man entered believing he was the high priest and was performing the *Yom Kippur* ritual?"

"It would seem so."

"Yes, it would...seem so, that is. Thank you, Daniel. You have been very helpful."

Chapter XIII

Seek the simple answer. Gamaliel had said that to Loukas and he believed it. But what do you do when faced with two simple but conflicting solutions? Loukas insisted his evidence pointed to a man murdered elsewhere and inserted into the Holy of Holies. Until this moment, Gamaliel had agreed. The discovery of the bowl and incense pot clouded this theory. The notion that a man, out of his mind perhaps and who, in the grip of the idea of himself as the high priest, had entered the Temple expecting to perform the *Yom Kippur* ritual, now acquired a new life. Without the bowl and incense, Loukas' theory won, hands down. To affirm it now meant conceding that the killer introduced the two atonement symbols into the Holy of Holies to convince the doubters otherwise, and to divert questions to the contrary. That, in turn, assumed a killer with a level of premeditation beyond anything Gamaliel would willingly accept. The situation made less sense every time he looked at it.

He made his way home with the two items under his arm and was startled to see his students, disciples some would say, waiting patiently for his return. How long had they been standing there? He greeted them, invited then to come in, and sat at his table.

"Here is a problem for you to solve," he said. "It is not, strictly speaking, one associated with interpreting Torah. By now you have all heard of the blasphemy in the Temple. I will tell you the facts as we currently understand them and then pose a question."

Gamaliel placed the bowl and pot on the table and laid out the two theories about the dead man currently in circulation. He omitted the parts about Ali bin Selah and the man who'd followed them. That part of the story, if indeed it was a part, added complexity. He wanted to keep it as straightforward as possible. He wanted to hear reasoned responses to the obvious. The obscure he would deal with in his own time.

"Now you tell me what happened and why."

The five men looked first at Gamaliel and then at one another. Some composed their faces into expressions into serious contemplation. One only smiled as if to say, you already know, so I won't embarrass myself by suggesting an answer that might make me seem stupid. Gamaliel did not hold out much hope for him. He was the son of a very influential Sanhedrin member. A political favor, no more. The fifth student, Saul, opened a scroll. Saul raised his head and stared at Gamaliel for a moment.

"We read in the Kings scroll," Saul read,

> *Solomon turned out Abiathar from being priest of the Lord. He did so because he desired the Lord's Word to be fulfilled concerning the house of Eli in Shiloh. When Joab heard the news, he fled into the Tabernacle because he had turned on Adonijah, but not on Absalom. Joab went into the Tabernacle and grabbed the horns of the altar seeking sanctuary. When Solomon was told what Joab had done, he sent Benaiah and told him, 'Go, fall upon Joab.' Benaiah went to the Tabernacle and said, 'The king says you are to come out.' Joab replied, 'No, I will as soon die here.' When Benaiah told this to the king, he said, 'Then do as he requests and fall upon him. When you do, you remove from me and from my father's house the blood of the innocents that Joab shed.*

Saul rolled the scroll up and fixed his gaze on Gamaliel.

"I see, and what I am to make of this, Saul? Are you suggesting that the dead man was somehow acting out Joab's murder in the Tabernacle? Why would he do that?"

"I am suggesting, Teacher, that we are in a time in our history in which the past and the future seem to be merging and the Nation is in great danger of losing its identity. We see the Temple built by an apostate king who nurtured an unacceptable relationship with our oppressors as Joab did to the enemies of Solomon. I think it is possible *Elohim* has sent this madman to the Temple posing as the high priest to alert us to the decay in the Nation and to warn us to mend our ways and return to the strict obedience of the Law."

"That is a unique take on the thing, prophetic even. I will think on it and thank you. Are there any other suggestions?"

The student who'd previously seemed content to let the exercise pass without comment turned to Saul.

"Why did not the Lord strike Joab and then Benaiah down when they entered the Holy of Holies as he did Uzza when he touched the Ark?"

"An excellent question, but one for another day," Gamaliel said. Perhaps there was hope for this boy after all.

The remaining students knew better than to attempt to top Saul who, they all agreed, stood out as the brightest. "Well then, I will dismiss you today with this assignment…meditate on Saul's words and on the problem I have set you and bring me an exegesis when next we meet."

The men filed out and Gamaliel went in search of his lunch.

He spent his midday meal mulling Saul's recitation from the Kings scroll. Saul, he knew, was a bright student with prospects. He had an offer to join the staff of the high priest. Gamaliel did not know if he had accepted, but it would be a signal honor if he had. At the same time he also knew that this young man from Tarsus had a gloomy and rigid world view. He complained about the lack of discipline in the enforcement of the Law. Saul, he decided, might be an inspired student of the Law, but, until the day came when he was brought to his knees by something larger than himself, he would always be a study in contradictions.

Yet the words from the other student, the slow one, nagged at Gamaliel and he couldn't say why. *Why did not the Lord strike*

Joab and then Benaiah down when they entered the Holy of Holies as he did Uzza? he'd asked. Indeed, why not? One must conclude that *Ha Shem* did not always accede to our need for a consistent deity. That line of thought, he realized could only lead him into areas forbidden to the faithful. Still…

At about the eleventh hour Gamaliel made his way back to the temple mount and the guard's assembly point. He needed to speak with the night captain. If the guards were involved, it would be those assigned to the night watch. Zach ben Azar'el turned out to be a burly, red-faced block of a man and, if Gamaliel guessed right, given to bullying and bluster. He could be difficult if he decided to protect his men rather than risk an inquiry. The captain stood at the entrance of the guards' headquarters barking orders to his shift. He glanced skyward to check the position of the sun and then at the peak of the Pinnacle. A shofar would sound, the changing of the guard would soon commence, and it wasn't clear to Gamaliel whether he had a full company.

"Where are Ezra and Hadar?" he shouted. "Gomer, where is your brother and his shadow?"

The man Gamaliel took to be Gomer started to say something and then looked toward the Hulda entryway as if he could will someone through it or, failing that, flee through it himself. He seemed more than worried—fearful. The wind shifted and the last wisps of smoke from the Temple fires drifted toward them.

"Pardon me, you are Zach ben Azar'el?"

Zach spun on his heel and seemed prepared to snap at Gamaliel. He stopped when he recognized the robes Gamaliel wore as belonging to someone of importance. Whether he recognized the man wearing them was less clear.

"Who asks?" he blurted, and then, apparently thinking his tone might have been interpreted as rude, added, "Sir?"

The man called Gomer stepped forward and started to speak.

"Not now, Gomer," Zach snapped.

"But—"

"I am the rabban of the Sanhedrin," Gamaliel said in his most officious voice. Best put this man in his place quickly. He would need him cowed if he hoped to squeeze information from him. "And I need you to answer a few questions."

"Sir…" Gomer shifted his weight from one foot to the other and held his hand in the air.

Zach silenced him with a raised fist and turned his attention back to Gamaliel. He tried, but failed, to appear humble. Gamaliel read in his eyes that little if any cooperation would be forthcoming and even that would be grudging unless he leaned on him.

"Rabban, what is it you want from me?" Zach managed to keep the edge from his voice but still managed to sound rude.

Gamaliel took a deep breath and made a mental note to speak to Zach's superiors sometime in the future. "You are aware of the desecration here in the Temple two nights ago. I would like you to tell me how such a thing could have happened with your guards posted and in place."

The guard glowered at Gamaliel for an instant and then lowered his eyes and studied the laces of his sandals instead. He looked up and exhaled. It was the sound of a man betrayed.

"You heard me ask about Ezra and Hadar? It's possible they might have been bribed. They are absent, as you can see. I suppose they heard they had been exposed and are hiding or have fled. I only hope they received enough money to last a lifetime because they will never work in this city again, and if I find them, they will be flogged within a hand span of their lives."

"But they are not here?"

"No, they are not. Gomer may know. Where is your brother, man? The rabban of the Sanhedrin wishes to speak to them."

"I was trying to tell you. He is missing. No one knows what has happened to Ezra and no one knows where Hadar is either."

Chapter XIV

Hadar and his partner in crime, Ezra, were missing. No surprise there. It is an *axiom*, Gamaliel thought, borrowing the term from Loukas' Greek, that those who abet criminals in the hope of gaining something for nothing must be stupid to begin with. Of course the two men were missing—missing and no doubt lying dead somewhere in the wilderness or in a drainage ditch covered with two days worth of daily waste. Gamaliel shook his head.

"Captain, in as much as these men were in your charge and were on duty during the time the desecration took place, I will hold you responsible for finding them, or what is left of them, and once that is done, for tracking down who they met, talked to, or received money from."

"Sir, I have no experience doing the sort of thing you ask of me."

Gamaliel waved him off. "And I expect to report to the Sanhedrin that you have performed this duty with alacrity and determination. They will not look favorably on your continuance in your present position if they feel you have been derelict in this duty. You do understand that?"

"Sir, I…Yes, sir, I understand."

"Fine. I expect you to call on me by this hour tomorrow and report your progress."

"Sir, as I said, I have no experience, I—"

"No? Well, neither had I until very recently, but it will come to you, I promise. You might start by querying your guards. It is unlikely that only those two men were approached. At the very least, it's likely that one of those still on duty will have information that will take you to the next place, or produce a name, several even."

Gamaliel left the guardsman standing in the doorway mumbling. He did not look happy. Well and good. As the captain of the night guard cohort, he had responsibilities beyond merely posting men. A major scandal had occurred on his watch. Of course he should be less than happy. Gamaliel hoped the threat to his livelihood and his future would guarantee action, movement—perhaps not as much as he would have liked, but something. Anything would be better than nothing. It came as no surprise that two guards had been bribed. That had always been a given. How else could anyone—alive or dead—have entered the Holy Place unless someone looked the other way? But at least he had names and felt sure that Zach would extract more information one way or the other. He did not envy the night guard cadre. Zach would have testimony from them even if it involved the application of physical pain.

Evening settled on the city like a soft blanket. Gamaliel made it to Loukas' house as the first star appeared in the eastern sky. Loukas had him wait in the courtyard while he finished seeing his last patient. Gamaliel used the time to mull over what he knew, what he suspected, and what he wished. The last took up most of the time. He thought there ought to be a pattern. A murder of this complexity usually involved other violence. A pair of missing guards, probably dead at the hand of their briber, for instance. Would there be more? Had the murderer adequately distanced himself from the deed to have become invisible, or would another corpse or two appear with their dead fingers pointing in his direction?

Years before he had visited the sea shore after a violent storm. Ships had been sunk and their crews lost. Days passed and yet the bodies kept washing ashore. Gamaliel wondered if more bodies, figuratively speaking, would wash up on his beach before this was done, a depressing thought.

"I am sorry to have kept you waiting, Rabban. My patients were slow in responding today. So what have you discovered since last we spoke?"

Gamaliel filled him in on the problem of the missing guards and the items found in the Holy of Holies. "The items found there suggest either more than a corpse had been inserted in the space and a high level of premeditation went into the murder, or it was not a murder, irrespective of what the indicators say. As to the guards, I should have interviewed them the day all this happened. Since they were only reported missing today, I suspect they were alive then. If only I had not overslept. It is your fault, you know. If you hadn't plied me with so much of the wine I admire, I would have been alert and available yesterday."

"With respect, Rabban, it does not become you to blame the wine or the wine's provider for your failure. But if it will make you happier, I have a genuinely terrible wine among my stores which I promise you will not drink to excess, if at all. I will fetch it for you."

"That will not be necessary. I am not one for making jests, as you may have noticed, and you have just had proof of it."

"An admission gratefully received. I knew it was an attempt at humor, as was my answer. So, tell me, where were these missing guards posted on the night of the crime?"

"I forgot to ask. How stupid of me. Of course, the bribes had to go to the men who could let someone or some people into the Holy Place."

"And?"

"Those persons or person had to know the layout of the guard postings and…"

"And…what were you about to say?"

"Had to know about the cord on the ankle and have access to the bowl and incense pot, but not know that the cord policy had not yet been used and might never be."

"So we are looking for persons with a connection to the Temple and its practices but not completely familiar. A hanger-on of some sort or—"

"A relative of someone working inside would do. If we could only determine which of the alternatives actually occurred—the person entered and died, or a dead man was brought into the Temple."

Loukas stared at the wall for what seemed a very long time.

"Loukas, you have thought of something?"

"I think you may be wasting time on that part of the problem. I believe you need to move past the details of the death for the moment and try something else. The man in the Holy of Holies was either alive or he was dead when he arrived, yes? To solve the puzzle you should accept both states and move on to the more important aspect, which is who he was."

"Wait, you're saying I should accept that the man was both alive and dead? Loukas, that is an absurdity."

"Our masters would say *reductio ad absurdum*, but it is not absurd, it is a paradox, and you should embrace it. Your information as to which choice is correct is insufficient in either case. Meanwhile, he is most certainly dead now and time is flitting away. His killer and the trail to him grow more obscure. If, you accept he was alive, well then, you still do not have what you need to find out why he would, in effect, commit suicide. You will only find out which of the two states he enjoyed, that is dead or alive, when he entered the Temple, after you find out who he was and why he had to die."

"I don't understand."

Loukas placed a sack on the table in front of Gamaliel. "Very well, I place this sack on the table and I say that in this sack is an apple or a pomegranate. Until you open the sack, it is neither one nor the other and by indirection, both. To discover which, you must open the sack which in this case is a very simple act, and the fact of the sack being opened changes the nature of the problem, you see?"

Gamaliel shook his head. "Loukas, this is nonsense."

"No it is not. In the case of your intruder into the Holy of Holies, it is not easy at all. You cannot peel back the veil at the time of the act. Thus, you must move on from the endless speculation of which—alive or dead— and try to gather the information you need to pull the drawstring."

"I should assume the man was both alive and dead for the time being in the hope—"

"Expectation."

"The expectation, then, that when I find out who the dead man was, I will know in which state he arrived and have my answer."

"Exactly."

Chapter XV

Ali bin Selah did leave Jerusalem, as he said he would. He joined a caravan headed north to Damascus by way of Jericho. Ali had no intention of finishing the journey. A wide stretch of cleared land that bordered the Jordan River provided the caravan's first stopover. Travelers hobbled their animals and made camp. Another caravan headed south to Jerusalem had arrived earlier. Space to set up a campsite posed a problem. Ali, however, had no difficulty.

Dawud, his servant—more than a servant if truth be told—waited for him among the southbound travelers. No one noticed, there being so many people coming and going, that Dawud had been at the camp site for two days. Ali pitched his tent next to his and they shared a meal. After dark, Ali switched clothes with his servant-friend. An application of nut stain darkened his skin and his beard. He donned a pair of boots with a heel that made him taller. The next morning Ali would abandon his place in the northbound caravan and join the southbound. Dawud would wait a day and follow him. No would one notice or care. With an early morning start, the caravan was scheduled to be in Jerusalem by mid-morning. He need only avoid Loukas the Physician and his friend, the rabban. He felt certain the disguise would fool the rabban—they'd only met that one time and then only briefly— but Loukas would be another matter. He'd have to take his chances that the physician would not frequent the places he intended to visit. Either way, at whatever the cost, he had unfinished business to attend to and that included Dawud.

Loyalty is a precious trait when it is present. When it is doubted, it becomes a liability.

"But, Loukas, where do we begin? I can understand your suggestion to let the business at the Temple rest for the time being, but how on earth am I to discover the man's identity? People go missing in this city all the time. Bandits abduct them, the Romans arrest them and they are never heard from again. This man could have been anybody, and you told me your inquiries led you nowhere."

"Rabban, this man was found dead in the Holy of Holies. He is no ordinary missing man. Consider the following: Obviously he is not the victim of Roman justice. They are a brutal race, but not an imaginative one. The notion of inserting someone in the Temple would not have occurred to them. No, they would simply crucify him in a very public place. He is not the victim of banditry, either. Brigands would simply murder their man and leave him to bleed to death in the wilderness or on the road. Either way, neither Romans or bandits would have left him in the Temple. In a ditch or in prison, yes, but not the Temple, not in the holiest place on earth. No, you must find a family, a friend, a business associate, who is wondering about one of their own. The mere fact that I have turned up nothing suggests that this missing person is involved with something they wish to keep hidden."

"Or, suppose this man is only a trader from Tarsus or Antioch and suppose he tells his family he will be away for a full cycle of the moon. Will they miss him yet? How long before they send someone to search for him? Another cycle? And suppose, just suppose, they believe he is in some other city—what then?"

"Then? Then they will never know what happened. I am suggesting that the nature of this murder rules out a nonentity like that. Merchants and traders, if they are murdered, are found in public places more often than not. The very nature of this murder precludes the banal. "

"Which brings us back to the beginning point."

"Maybe this will help. I have studied our dead man in greater detail. Not as much as I would like but a bit more. I can tell you something about his dress, and his occupation."

"From inspecting the corpse, you can tell me what he did as a profession? I don't believe it. No one can do that."

"Perhaps not, but I can try, with your help, of course."

"My help? I know nothing of men and their professions."

"Suppose I told you that this dead man has a callus in the middle of his palm, his right hand palm."

"A callus? Sorry, I have no idea. I don't know what to do with that. Perhaps he threw a spear. Does one throw a spear with the palm of one's hand?"

"I rather think not."

"Very well, we have a man who presses on things with his hand. Sorry, no inspiration yet."

"No? Well, he was badly burned, as you know, but I did have a look at the lining of his nose."

"His nose? The lining of his nose will reveal secrets? What can a man's nose tell you?"

"There, you see? You take things for granted. You friend Jacob ben Aschi is blind, you tell me. Ask him if his nose doesn't tell him a great deal."

"I see, yes. When we first talked he recognized the aroma of the burning sacrifices. He called it holy smoke."

"And?"

"And he knew it was bulls that were being offered, not rams, not doves, not grain."

"There you see? No, the nose is a particularly sensitive area of a man's anatomy."

"A woman's as well if the popularity of perfume is reckoned."

"I meant both. Good, now you are beginning to understand. Did you ever notice that when rheum collects in your nose, your food is tasteless?"

"Yes. So?"

"Most of your taste is determined by your nose, not your tongue. Men who've lost some or all of their tongues will tell you they can still 'taste,' although it is different."

"Consider me properly educated on the wonders of a man's tongue. Now tell me why being so is important, and then what any of this has to do with the dead man's nose."

"Patience, my friend, patience. I told you I had occasion to inspect the man's nasal lining. It suggested something to me."

"I cannot imagine what."

"Of course you can't, but I can. His lining was inflamed—very red due to the blood vessels being enlarged."

"From the fire, of course."

"Not so quickly, wait. If he was struck down by holy fire, as some suggest he might have been, there would have been no opportunity for him to inhale and therefore no inflammation. But if he burned in the fire elsewhere, he would have."

"There, you see. Fire death somewhere else?"

"It is one possibility, but the inflammation had no particles."

"No particles? Loukas, is that supposed to mean something to me?"

"If he inhaled, he would have had particulate matter in his nose, you see?"

"Do you think he was dead before he was burned?"

"Precisely. If he was dead first, then once again, he could not have inhaled the smoke."

"So, why was his nose inflamed?"

"He had frequent exposures to some irritant. There is no question it was of long standing, this inflammation."

Gamaliel shook his head, in frustration. "He has a callus... and had been in contact with something irritating. So?"

"I was going to suggest a smith of some sort, you know a jeweler who has to push—"

"Explain the nose redness, then."

"I can't. He must routinely come into contact with strong odors or powders. I understand acids are used in preparing gold. And you know stone masons have inflamed noses."

"I didn't know that. Acids…that's a thought. What of his other hand? Did it also have a callus in the palm…anywhere? If he did, he might have been a tent maker. They regularly inhale the tannin used to cure the leather."

"You grasp of some things is amazing and then…Never mind. The other hand? Let me think. No, if anything it was remarkable because there were no marks or indicators on the palm."

"Good, then we rule out stone mason, who definitely would, and jewelers, because all the ones I know use acid very sparingly if at all, and he wasn't a tent- or a sail-maker either."

"How do you figure that?"

"If he were either of those two, or something similar, his other hand would have complementary calluses on the thumb and forefinger from handling the rough cloth or leather. No, one clean hand and one rough…from pressing on a rounded… would you say rounded?"

"Possibly, yes."

Gamaliel's eyes sparkled. "He was an apothecary."

"He was?"

"From the mortar and pestle. He holds one in his right hand and grinds away. Many of the powders you use are very irritating in their raw state, are they not?"

"Yes, but…"

"It is not much, but it is enough. I could be wrong, but tomorrow I will scour the city and find out if such a man is missing. Oh, and you must tell me more about this drug your friend Ali gave you—the one you said was made from poppy sap."

"It's called *hul gil.* The joy plant."

"It is commonly used in medicine?"

"Oh, yes. But I am not sure what Ali left me is the same thing. The pain relieving in this mixture is greatly enhanced."

"So it is not *hul gil?*"

"I don't think so. I will ask Ali the next time I see him."

"That could be months."

"Or never."

Chapter XVI

Ali worked his way slowly down the Street of the Herbalists. He felt reasonably sure his disguise would not fail him. He'd been on this street in the past, of course. His brother had moved to Judea two years previously in what he assured Ali would be a profitable enterprise. Ali had expressed his doubts then, particularly as it had been made clear that the Egyptians were determined to stay. As he expected, their displeasure had turned violent. He had doubted his brother could manage on his own in the first place and now Achmir was dead. Ali could only wonder if a similar fate awaited him. He assumed someone would try, but who and when only Mazda knew.

He nearly ran into the rabban of the Sanhedrin. He did not know why this strange old man should be in this place. If he guessed right it meant trouble. The sons of Moses had forgotten their origins. They no longer understood that the concerns of other nations were not theirs, that disputes were settled privately, that Hammurabi's code provided all that was needed to deal with disputes among families, clans, and even nations if necessary. Only if and when the issue became an international concern, threatened power or the throne, were authorities expected to step in. Yet, here was the old man, moving from one store to the next, asking questions, nodding, probing, and interfering.

Ali leaned against a wall. Not all of the shops were open, fortunately, or Gamaliel might very well discover what drew so many people to one of them. The rabban left. His posture and puzzled expression suggested he had not had a successful foray into the street's secrets and intended to return later. That meant Ali had only a few hours to do what needed doing. Then he, like the rabban, would move about the city seeking answers. Gamaliel and his position in Jerusalem allowed him to be straightforward, even blunt in his questioning. Ali, on the other hand, must be careful, discreet. He could not reveal who he was or why he asked—a much more difficult assignment. Still, it had advantages. It might take longer, but he felt sure his information would be more accurate in the end. People with the information he sought would feign ignorance or dissemble with the rabban, but not so with Ali. A question carefully put after a suitable exploration of the subject would give him what he sought—the people he sought.

◇◇◇

Unseen by Ali or Gamaliel, a tall man wearing a checked red keffiyeh shared the shadows a few doors farther along the street. He, however, showed no interest in the rabban. His eyes were fixed, unblinking, on Ali. When the physician moved, so did he. He'd nearly missed him. Ali bin Selah was a clever man and had nearly fooled him with the change in his appearance.

He rummaged around in his beard as if he might have lost some valuable in it at some time and had just remembered what it was. He frowned and signaled a bearded man at the street's other end. He, in turn, worked his way through the crowd to him without once looking at Ali bin Selah. They met, conversed, and then, a decision made, the new man drifted back into the crowd to follow the rabban, his beard and face now covered with the keffiyeh's long end. The first man stayed in place keeping watch on Ali. He would have to make his move soon: his was one of the two names written on the bit of papyrus that had arrived the previous week from Alexandria, and just in time.

◇◇◇

Ali watched the old rabbi leave and then made his way into one of the shops where the rabban had questioned the owner.

They chatted about herbs and their uses. Ali finally elicited the information he needed. The rabban was on the trail of an apothecary. How would he know to do that? Loukas, of course. Loukas, must have said something, but what? The Greek was clever, certainly, but how could he have made such a connection and so quickly? It was a puzzle that Ali dearly wished to solve, but knew he probably never would. Not without revealing his presence in the city or his interest in the dead man. He did not wish to do either—not yet.

When he approached the doorway of a second, closed shop, he sensed he was being watched. By whom? Them, of course. How had they found him out and how so soon? He shuddered. Had they gotten to poor Dawud before…? He wondered, not for the first time, if he wouldn't have been better served staying with the north-bound caravan. He could have come back later with more men and a better plan, and then he would not have had to use Dawud. Too late for that now.

The rabban could be a problem. How well did he know Loukas? Ali realized he'd need to find out. Loukas was an important source of information and something of a friend even, but… Ali allowed the thought to hang in the air.

That the men he believed were now on his trail were connected to his brother's murder was, of course, a given. That said, they all shared the guilt equally and they were all subject to retribution, not just the one or two who had committed the act. Everyone acknowledged that in a blood feud, all offending parties are liable without distinction or difference. He slipped into the shop and waited, standing to one side of a tapestry next to a sandalwood chest, which screened him from sight. When the stranger entered, he gave the tapestry a flick. The movement caught the man's eye. Ali watched as he unsheathed his dagger and crept toward the fabric. He had the weapon poised to strike when Ali's own knife entered just under the intruder's rib cage and up where he knew a heart beat. The man died before he hit the floor.

A knowledge of anatomy is always a useful thing to have.

Ali dragged the body into the shop's rear room and covered it with straw. Then he set about the business of erasing records, inventory, and indeed the very presence of its proprietor. It took just under an hour. Some of the inventory was too valuable to destroy, and that he packed in a sack which he would carry away, like a peddler. Had he done enough? What would people think when they found a body in the building? Did he care?

He bent and removed the keffiyeh from the corpse and wrapped it around his own head. People, if they remembered anything at all, would recall the keffiyeh before the face. Two men in, one man out—the one wearing the checked keffiyeh left, therefore the first one must have perished. He piled whatever would burn into the center of the room. When he was finished, he added both straw and bitumen from a pot to the corpse and set the whole on fire. An eye for an eye, a tooth for a tooth—the ancient code, the code he lived by.

Ali slipped out of the shop and made his way from the street to the next one below and into a small shop where secondhand merchandise could be purchased. If his first disguise had been penetrated, he'd need a new one. On the Street of Castoffs one could buy anything, even a new identity.

Chapter XVII

An irritated Gamaliel left the Street of the Herbalists. He'd discovered nothing he didn't already know or couldn't have guessed and had felt it necessary to purchase a sachet of leaves which, the shopkeeper assured him when steeped in hot water, would be both refreshing and stimulating to the mind. Also, the fact that half of the shops were not yet open increased his annoyance even more. The only useful information he gleaned from his foray into the market with its pungent aromas and exotic denizens concerned a single shop apparently run by a person with the unlikely name of Hannah. Is it truly Hannah? Hannah is a woman's name. The prophet Samuel's mother was named Hannah. It meant beauty or passion. Why would anyone label an apothecary's shop after the prophet's mother? Perhaps this man used Hannah as a descriptor, not a name. Surely a woman would not be peddling herbs and cures on the street. Then again, did it matter?

None of the several people he interviewed could remember having seen or heard from this Hannah person for several days. The importance of that scrap of information lessened significantly when diluted by a follow-up statement that this person frequently disappeared for days at a time and the puzzling addition that in the past there had been a different man running the store. Apparently the store had changed hands. Therefore, this most recent absence did not raise any eyebrows. However, hearing who some of his customers were did raise Gamaliel's eyebrows.

"Who? Are you sure?" Gamaliel had asked a tall cadaverous shopkeeper whose name he could not remember.

"Well, you see, sir, most of the men and women who visit this area are known to us, regulars you could say, cooks from the palace and other eating places, or they are mixers of potions and poultices who come to buy particular items with special properties."

"Like?"

"Oh, well, cooks want pepper from India, spices from beyond there, and you know about mustard, yes?"

"Yes, I see. So, what marked his buyers as different?'

"They were uninformed about what we sell here. You know, people who come to this street are seeking specific herbs which they name. Some are for cooking, some are for mixing or compounding medicines. The buyers are usually one or the other, occasionally both. But the men of whom I speak were neither. They came and asked for that shop, not for anything specific. They made their purchases and left. Many were foreigners, people from far away, beyond Parthia even. Maybe they traveled from beyond the Indus, if such a place exists."

"It exists. Anything else?"

"Some of the customers came from the Roman barracks and some from the palace itself."

"Roman soldiers and the king's servants, you say?"

"They wore shabby clothes to cover who they were, but yes, I am sure."

Gamaliel knew then that he would have to return later in the day and visit this Hannah person, or whatever he called himself. He would bring some Temple guards with him. He did not like the thought of legionnaires or palace thugs needing disguises to visit a shop. Accosting them in that state could be embarrassing. Also, he didn't like the look of some of the other consumers on the street. Herbalists seemed a strange lot.

He had his house in sight when he again sensed someone behind him. That made it twice in two days. Well, not exactly. The other man had been following Loukas, not him, as it turned out. Still…close enough. He paused as if he might have forgotten something and turned half way round. Only a few people were walking the street in this residential area. He caught sight of the man, who seemed familiar, although he could not think why. That man had also stopped and, obviously out of place, knelt to adjust his sandal laces. He wore a dirty keffiyeh, and had most of his face wrapped in the same material.

Yes, definitely, he would bring guards with him when he returned to the street. He pocketed his sachet and headed home.

Gamaliel finished his noonday meal and proceeded to gather the items he would need for a second assault on the Street of the Herbalists. Benyamin announced that Loukas had arrived. Gamaliel had not expected him.

"What brings you to the house of the rabban?" he asked. "Usually it is I who calls on you. Are you certain you can weather a visit into the center of orthodoxy, Physician?"

"I will risk it. I came to tell you something about the dead man from the Temple that I believe is important."

"Good, and then I will tell you where the idea of a man who is simultaneously alive and dead has taken me. What of our dead man?"

"He was only recently rendered a member of the faith."

"Sorry, you will have to be more specific than that. What do you mean, 'only recently rendered a member of the faith'?"

"His circumcision is recent and probably post mortem."

"What?"

"I said, his—"

"I heard you. He is not a Jew?"

"Evidently not…unless…"

"Unless what?"

"It is farfetched, but it is always possible that our killer wants us to think that and…ah…renewed the procedure."

"Would you care to speculate on the possibility of that being the case?"

"No."

"Neither would I. Such a move requires more premeditation than I can imagine. It is possible but unlikely. The more reasonable explanation would be the killer—and now I accept we are looking at murder—wanted us to bounce around the 'insane zealot in the Temple' notion and not look farther. So, your idea that we skip that part of the investigation and search for the man's identity is now officially blessed. It raises more difficulties for us, however."

"As long as it confirms my belief that the man was murdered and brought to the Temple, I am content."

Gamaliel paced to the slit window that gave light, but not access to his tiled front room. "Yes, but now what?"

"We continue searching for that very thing—his identity."

"I have a possibility." Gamaliel described his visit to the Street of the Herbalists and the conversations he'd had with several shopkeepers, and repeated his observation about the peculiar clientele the street attracted.

"Now, before you go any farther," Loukas interjected, "you should recall who I am and what I do. I am one of those peculiar people you noticed. It is a trip I make at least once a month. It is the source of most of the items I need to dose my patients."

"My apologies. In that case, perhaps you will accompany me back there this afternoon and help me locate an apothecary who is missing, is possibly our victim, and who, it now appears, has reluctantly and only lately become one of us."

"Certainly. I need a few things, as it happens."

"I plan to take a few guards with me as well."

"Guards?"

"Yes, there is a certain aura of menace on that street and I would protect myself from it."

"From people like me, you mean."

"No, no, I didn't make myself clear. A question for you—why would palace personnel and legionnaires need to wander the street in disguise?"

"Palace personnel and Roman soldiers wander the street? Is that so odd? Many people go there for materials they use for cooking or curing."

"These men, I am told, are neither cooks nor healers. They visit one particular shop—in disguise, mind you—and leave. They do not shop at the other stores. They do not bargain. They visit this one shop, buy, and leave. I find that intriguing, don't you? Something not right is going on there. I was followed home, by the way."

"Followed? By whom?"

"I have no idea, but I think…no, I am sure I saw him first mingling among the herbalists and dealers. He was in conversation with another man also wearing an odd keffiyeh and—"

"Stop. Wearing a what? An odd keffiyeh? The streets are full of strangers attired in all sorts of dress including keffiyehs of all shapes and sizes and, to my eye, all odd."

"Yes, I suppose that is so, but the second man reminded me of that fellow you purged yesterday. You are correct, of course. I do not travel about that part of the city as you do. Still, he did follow me. I am not brave enough to confront such a man, so I will take guards with me."

"If you wander into the Street of the Herbalists with guards from the Temple or the palace, you will learn nothing. Half of the shops will slam their doors and the remaining proprietors will lie."

"Then I must rely on you to keep me safe. Why does that not make me feel any better?"

Chapter XVIII

Thick acrid smoke filled the street, then lifted away with a passing breeze. It caused Loukas to cough. Gamaliel wound his shawl across the lower portion of his face and said nothing.

"How can you stand this?" Loukas barked.

"As my friend Jacob says—"

"It is holy smoke, yes, you told me. That was not my question. I asked how can you stand it?"

"It is a part of the city. We expect it as a sign that we are faithful to *Ha Shem* and he will be faithful to us in turn. You insist on dressing in the Greek style, though I can't imagine why, and so you suffer. See, I have only to cover my face and the smoke is nothing. Don't you have a remedy for coughing, Physician?"

"Not on my person. When we get to the Street of the Herbalists, I will find one."

"They will have a potion?"

"Or the ingredients, yes. I mix mustard with honey. It works well enough."

"Mustard is useful herb, I take it."

"Yes, it is particularly useful for problems associated with breathing and so on. One makes a poultice of it with the whites of an egg or some other carrier—water if nothing else is available—and applies it to the chest. It is also useful to relieve pain, runny noses, and rheumatism."

"I see. You did notice, I hope, that we are being followed."

"By the same person who tracked you to your house?"

"It appears so. There is that ridiculous headdress, you see."

"He must not have anything better to do. He will learn nothing from following us that he did not know already."

"Which is?"

"Where you live, that you know me, and you are interested in the goings-on at the Street of the Herbalists."

"Do you suppose that is important?"

"Who knows what he thinks is important?"

"Perhaps he waits for instruction and none comes, so he stays on the last task assigned,"

"An interesting thought, Rabban. You amaze me. How did you figure that out?"

"I merely guessed at—not deduced—one possible solution. It may also be that he has something specific in mind that can only be accomplished at a certain time, or place, or circumstance."

"Like what?"

"Oh, I don't know. Maybe he wishes to cut my throat and a busy street would allow his escape. Maybe it is your throat he covets, Loukas."

"I do not find this line either comforting or reassuring. I prefer your original idea—he has nothing better to do."

"Then so be it. Pause at this jeweler's shop while I walk on and see what he does. I will wait for you around the corner."

"Shall I accost him?"

"No, we have had that pleasure once this week already. All it will accomplish is to create another substitute. Let's stay with the one we know. Here is the shop."

Loukas turned into the shop and Gamaliel continued down the street to the corner. Their shadow hesitated and then continued following him, glancing quickly into the shop, and then as quickly averting his gaze. Loukas waited until he felt sure the stalker had moved far enough along the street and then started out the door to catch up with Gamaliel. That was when he noticed the second man—another follower it seemed. Following whom? Gamaliel or the man wearing the "ridiculous headdress?"

He waited another beat and then he took up a position behind the newest member of this growing parade. Were they all going to the herbalists? What could possibly warrant such attention?

An amused Gamaliel waited for him around the corner. The first of their entourage stood on the opposite side of the street feigning nonchalance by inspecting his nails. A bit farther down the street and better hidden, the other man fondled some fabric at a stall.

"This is turning into to be a Greek farce, Rabban. Did you know we now have two followers?"

"Two? No. Where?"

"The man at the cloth peddler's booth is on our trail as well."

"Is he really?" Gamaliel glanced toward the man in question. "He looks vaguely familiar, somehow."

"His back is to me now. How familiar?"

"You know how it is. You are introduced to someone and later, maybe much later, they cross your path but they are not wearing the same headdress, or the hair is not the color you remember, or the salient feature that registered with you when you first met is no longer there?"

"Yes, of course. And you think you may have seen such a person?"

"I am not sure. It was a passing thought. We should be off. If the oaf who has been following us does not know by now we have uncovered him, I daresay he can pose no real threat. Let him follow. Should we invite him to walk with us?"

"Do you think he would accept? If we do that, shouldn't we ask the other man as well?"

"This is becoming much too complex. Just wave to the first one to dispel any lingering doubts he may harbor about his invisibility and then let us be on our way. How's your cough, by the way?'

"Better." Loukas waved an open palm at the man across the street. "There, you see, now he realizes that we have tumbled to his presence and does not know what to do. This trip is moving more and more toward comedy."

"Except that it has all been prompted by a dead man who is or is not an apothecary and, according to you, was or was not dead when he entered the Holy of Holies and has put this all into motion. Besides, the first man and the other are both carrying daggers under their tunics."

"You saw them?"

"Not them, the bulges they make. What else could they be?"

The two set off with one very confused and another very determined follower in their wake. The streets were crowded, and they both had difficulty keeping up, a situation made more difficult by the deliberate bobbing and weaving Loukas and Gamaliel did as they made their way down into the Souk.

At the entrance to the Street of the Herbalist, they were brought short by a crowd of people. Thick smoke billowed from one to the shops.

"That is not your 'holy smoke,' I don't think."

Gamaliel frowned and squinted his eyes against its sting. "No, it is not but I fear it has one thing in common with it."

"Sorry, you've lost me again." Loukas also peered in the direction of the smoke. A few flames flickered here and there, but the fire seemed nearly spent.

"Burning flesh, Loukas. You can't mistake it if you smell it once. Someone or something has been incinerated in that fire. This cannot be good."

He elbowed his way through the crowd with Loukas in his wake. An official-appearing person stood to one side of the smoldering shop asking questions. He challenged Gamaliel when he shouldered his way up front.

Gamaliel told him who he was and why he was there. It was then he discovered that the shop was the one called Hannah and that a body so badly burned as to be unidentifiable lay in the ashes. Presumably this would be the man who used the name. It was very confusing. Why not call the shop by one's own name?

"It appears we are at a dead end," Loukas said.

"Really? I am not so sure. By the way, our followers have both disappeared. Now what do you suppose that means?"

"Either we are no longer interesting to them, or they are fearful of the authorities milling around here."

"Or they have completed their task. Are you sure the second man followed us?"

Loukas shrugged. "How else?"

"Might he have been following the follower?"

"Of course, that is a possibility, but to what end?"

"I have no answer for that, but more interesting is why did he remind me of someone I knew? We should leave here and find some shade in your back court and think about this turn of events."

Gamaliel paused, then bent and studied the body. He picked up a stick that had somehow escaped the fire and poked at the burnt flesh. He lifted the man's hands and grunted. He straightened and smiled at Loukas.

"Bitumen, if I am not mistaken. Another murder. Now, perhaps you will find more of your very fine wine, which will sharpen our wits as we consider this latest addition to the growing number of corpses our investigation seems to have spawned."

"We are responsible for this, you think?"

"Possibly—or not."

Chapter XIX

Inside the city's walls the streets teemed with people hurrying this way and that, busy with important matters, or so they thought. Buildings embellished with gold and silver, marble and alabaster, soared skyward and at their center, Herod's contribution to Jerusalem's glory—the Temple. Outside the walls, Jerusalem presented a different face to the world. The pace slower, movement less purposeful, and buildings modestly reflecting their inhabitants. Gamaliel, who'd never lived anywhere but inside the walls, found his visits to Loukas almost therapeutic. He would not admit that to his host as the code of urban living insisted that in every respect inside the walls was superior to any alternative, anywhere, and most particularly outside the walls. Loukas poured the wine and sat opposite, waiting.

"I think we need to begin at the beginning," Gamaliel mused.

"Very well, a body is found in the Temple—"

"No, not that part. We have discussed that *ad nauseam*. The part before that—a person persuades two, at least two, guards to accept a bribe and permit someone or more people entry into the Holy Place. We stipulate that they planned to carry in a corpse. Presumably those corrupt guards received enough coin to enable them to pick up and leave the area if they had to, or they were paid a pittance, but were led to believe the activity they agreed to ignore was trivial, no more than a practical joke. Later, when the awfulness of the deed became surfaced, they fled, never to be heard from again or, more likely, were eliminated before they could protest or speak."

"Which, do you suppose?"

"I believe the latter. I believe their bodies now adorn a dung pile and the chances of finding them are slim to none. Their availability notwithstanding, we must begin there. Second, now that we know the victim was a gentile, we need to discover the connection he or his killers had with Temple protocols. How did they come by faithful replicas of a cup and an incense holder? Who provided them with the information about how things were done? Does this suggest our killers were Jews?"

"How likely is that, Rabban, given the presumed consequences which must follow such an egregious act of blasphemy?"

"Indeed. What sort of Jew would willingly risk his life that way? Even a faithless Jew would think twice before tempting the wrath of the Lord, particularly when there are dung hills and wadis aplenty for the disposition of bodies. Also, please note that whoever it might have been, he did not know the complete story—thus the cord on the ankle. Someone truly informed, a *kohen* would not have used it."

"Nor the high priest."

"Yes, nor Caiaphas. Good point."

"On the other hand, had they not used the cord, we might not have discovered the body for days or weeks until the smell...."

"And from that we deduce...?"

"Whoever put it there wanted it found."

"Exactly, which brings us full circle. Who wanted it found?"

"It is a muddle. What you have just laid out is but preamble. The story that follows will be difficult to read."

"Loukas, you say it is a story. Maybe yes and maybe no, but you are correct. It will not be easy. It would be useful if we knew who the victim was." Gamaliel frowned at the patch of ground that bordered Loukas' wall, which contained herbs of various kinds. In one corner Loukas had planted mustard.

Loukas waited for what he assumed would be more explanation. When none came he said, "Well, you deduced he was an apothecary. That was a start, and now it appears another practitioner of that trade has been killed. Surely, the two sharing a profession cannot be a coincidence?"

Gamaliel stared at the city wall just beyond Loukas' entryway.

"Is it possible," Gamaliel said after what seemed an eternity, "that that dead man did not own or operate out of that shop?"

"Did not…? Then who or what?"

"I am struck by the man who followed me home. Why follow me?"

Loukas shrugged. "Because someone told him to?"

"Someone else stalked the street this morning and saw me. He asked around and discovered I had questions about a missing apothecary, and he decided he needed to know why. But then I left the street. Suppose he had pressing business at the place and could not leave it. He would have dispatched an accomplice to run the more trivial errand. Later, when that man returned to the street in our wake, he could not find his contact to give his report. He asked around, while we were doing the same and he discovered…"

"What?"

"I think he might have discovered that his chief had perished in the fire, which, in turn, would send him rushing away. If this man is related somehow to the person we questioned…what's his name…"

"Aswad Khashab"

"Yes him, and…wait…I lost it."

"Lost it? Lost what?"

"Nothing. Let it go. Something…a memory or, I don't know, something, but it's gone. So, it would seem that there are several persons tangled up in this business, and by now they are in a panic. Ah yes, that must be it. If so, then let us assume that our first dead man, the one found in the Temple, was this Hannah person. He must have had associates? Are they, like us, on the trail of his killer?'

"Gamaliel, really…"

"Stay with me. Another thought—who traded with him, was he killed for a sale gone wrong? Why was his shop destroyed after the fact? You would think his death would be enough. Why attempt to erase all traces of him?"

"To complete a cover-up."

"But why this second dead man? It is an easy enough matter to set fire to a deserted shop, but this man was murdered and his identity, like that of the man in the temple, deliberately obscured. No, we are missing something important."

"Something important? Of course we are, but…" Loukas sighed and pulled a face that Gamaliel knew meant his friend probably needed a break from any more speculation but he couldn't break his train of thought just yet. Loukas would have to hang on a bit longer.

"One last thing, Loukas. That man had been coated with bitumen and set on fire. That is something more than mere arson with consequences. Our killer wanted to send a message."

"To whom?"

"Ah, now there you have me, Loukas."

"We need to find the man who followed us."

"That would be useful, but I think it would be more useful if we found the other one—the one who, I now believe, must have been following him. That man will have information that could unravel the whole."

"Well, if you say so. How do we go about doing that?"

"I have no idea, but I am sure his seeming familiar is very important." Gamaliel sighed and glanced down. "My cup is empty, Physician. Would you be so kind?"

Loukas poured another portion into the rabban's cup. "You will drink me out of my supply soon, Rabban. My well is not filled with this wine. Next, I will serve something local."

"Sorry about that. It's just that…By the way, speaking of mysterious elixirs, were you able to pick up the ingredients for your cough tonic?"

"Yes, I was. Curious, that. When I told the herbalist what I intended to do with the mustard and honey he said something odd."

"Odd? How odd?"

"He said that our dead man twice over had his own formulation. A particular cough tonic he said, and it had a special ingredient of some sort which people were convinced bordered on the miraculous."

"Had your herbalist tried it?"

"I don't think so, but he said people from all over came to buy it."

"People from all over and we hear that Romans and palace people in disguise were his regulars as well. Now, don't you find that interesting? I think I need you to tell me about that pharmacopeia as you promised. What sort of things do people seek from apothecaries?"

"Ah, for that we will need more wine."

Chapter XX

As evening approached, Gamaliel made his way homeward. The mixed aromas of roasting meat and spicy stews reminded him he hadn't eaten. He felt exhausted from a day traipsing about the city. Worse, another death had been added to his list of things to cope with. But at that moment, all he wished for was some peace and quiet, a meal, and an hour or two to return, however briefly, to his studies. The last person in the world he wanted to see would be the high priest. Yet, he it was who waited for Gamaliel in his atrium.

"High Priest, to what do I owe the honor of your presence?"

"I am here to check the progress of your investigation."

"My investigation? Yes, well I am now certain that the dead man in the Holy of Holies was not—"

"Dead man in the…Don't be absurd. There is no investigation needed there. The situation is obvious. The man crossed through the Veil and was punished for his blasphemy. There is nothing more to be said."

"But I thought you asked me about my investigation. If not about that, what?"

"The rabbi, of course. The rabble rouser, the irritant to the eyes of *Ha Shem,* that's what. Have you found him out? I asked you to study him and find a reason to close down his movement."

"You asked, but I never agreed to it, High Priest. You will recall when we had this conversation before…was it only two nights ago? Yes, it was. I told you then that I could find no fault in his teaching beyond what other self-appointed teachers of his kind proclaim. He is radical, I grant you, but he is also clever. He never quite crosses the line and breaches the Law."

"He breaks Shabbat law."

"Does he? How?"

"It is reported he healed a cripple on Shabbat."

"Reported? By whom?"

"It doesn't matter by whom. The fact of the matter is, he did."

"I see. It raises an interesting moral question, if true."

"It is true. The man was questioned. Interesting moral... what? What do you mean it's an interesting moral question?"

"Well, put yourself in the cripple's position. Should you refuse to be healed because receiving this sign would break Shabbat law?"

"I am not speaking of the cripple."

"Ah, but you must. If this Yeshua did, in fact, cure the cripple, both are guilty of the same transgression. The cripple should have refused the help and trusted the Lord to provide relief at a better, holier time."

"That is nonsense."

"Nonsense? High Priest, it is you who overreach. I am charged with interpreting the Law. If I am not mistaken, that is why you are here. You wish me to catch this rabbi out. Well, sir, you cannot have it both ways. If the rabbi broke Shabbat, so did the cripple. Now, will you condemn him as well? You know you won't because you are single-minded in this pursuit of this Yeshua person. I do not know why, and I cannot persuade you to change. So, I ask only that if you are serious about destroying this man and others like him, you must stay within the Law's boundaries and punish all who break the Law equally. In this instance, that would include the cripple."

Caiaphas could barely control his anger. "But he blasphemes," he shouted. "Listen to this: he says, and I am quoting him as exactly as I can, he says this, 'The kingdom of the Lord is like a mustard seed.' A mustard seed? That is idiotic. The Lord's kingdom is as grand as Rome, as wise as Greece, and as holy as Jerusalem. A mustard seed? Hah!"

"Yet it is an interesting simile, is it not? Mustard is not as simple a thing as I was always led to believe. It has great curative properties, for example. So, to compare the kingdom that way would be a compliment, don't you think?"

"Curative? He says it starts as a small thing and will grow to be like a tree where birds may build their nests. The Kingdom is tiny but may soon be a large shrub with birds in nests at its top?"

"Did you know that gardeners are reluctant to plant mustard? It grows so fast and it is nearly impossible to root out once established. Now, I would take that to be a rather good representation of what we hope for, don't you?"

"We hope the Way will grow and encompass the world? I think not. The Lord has his people. They were the chosen out of Egypt. If He wanted more, He would have them. His kingdom shall be like the cutting placed on a high holy place and it will grow and be tall and grand for all to see."

"You do understand that Ezekiel spoke that piece while in exile in Babylon?"

"No matter, it is appropriate. We do not grow, Rabban, we cultivate."

"Do we? Is that all, then? Perhaps you are right, but to wish to punish this Galilean for disagreeing with you seems a bit harsh."

"He has followers and their number grows daily. They say he is the Messiah."

"He is not alone in having that honorific. Others have before him and still others will after him, and as for as his numbers increasing, good for him. But consider. How long will they follow after they grow weary of similes and wish rather for action? Has he an army? Can he free us from bondage? Can he lead us like Father Moses to a promised future? Can he reestablish a kingdom free of outside pressure like David? You know he doesn't and he can't. Failing in that, it is only a matter of time before his followers turn to a new leader, a new Messiah, if you will, one with at least the illusion of power. In the meantime, I tell you with respect, you are wasting your time on this. Help me with the more serious matter of the defilement in the Temple."

"That is a dead issue, Rabban."

"Yes certainly, dead and scorched."

"Don't be coy with me. You know what I mean. There will be no investigation into the death."

"Deaths, pleural…there has been at least a second and the consensus is there are two guards lying dead somewhere as well."

"That is as may be, but as far as the *kohanim* are concerned, the facts are as they seem and no more need be done. In this, I believe the Sanhedrin will agree with me."

"The defilement was outrageous. Where is your anger? Justice, High Priest. We must have it. *But let justice roll down like waters, and righteousness like an ever-flowing stream.* Justice, High Priest. Surely we cannot turn away."

"I have never liked Amos. He is too simple-minded."

"Nevertheless, he is a prophet and speaks for *Ha Shem*. Listen to yourself. Either we fulfill our calling to be the Lord's chosen and stand for the Perfected Way or we are just another religious sect, no better or worse that the Greek and Roman pantheons, the followers of Mithra in his several manifestations, or even Ba'al-Zebuwb."

"Now you blaspheme."

"The truth cannot blaspheme, sir. Now, I am tired. I have had a very busy and confusing day. My head has been crammed full to overflowing with facts and speculations. I have been followed by criminals, witness to a murder, and I have not had my evening meal. So, I will bid you goodnight. If you want your radical rabbi, you will have to catch him yourself. I have no interest in the process."

"You will be remiss in you duties as rabban."

Gamaliel bit his lip. "Yes, yes, good night, High Priest."

Gamaliel escorted the still fuming Caiaphas to the door and saw him into the street. Two Temple guards he had not noticed when he came in stepped forward to accompany the high priest away.

"And, so that you do not hear it from one of your informers," Gamaliel yelled after him, "I will continue to study the business of the dead man in the Temple. It is certain that there is more to that death than anyone realizes or, perhaps, wishes to be known."

Caiaphas wheeled around. "You accuse me of complicity in this?"

"Not at all. Are you?"

The high priest scowled, turned, and marched away, his bodyguard and dignity in disarray.

Chapter XXI

That night Gamaliel dreamt again. The man in the mask appeared, as he had done before as did the body, and the burns, but instead of the wild dancing and alterations in its expression, the figure wheeled and turned his back. Then mustard plants, the wild sort they call black mustard, popped up from the ground one after another and the plants, growing, budding, leafing, first here then there, flowed toward him like a river. Seeds flew from their casings, hit the earth and sprouted, producing new shrubs. There seemed to be no end to this inexorable march of the plants. The man spun and tried to flee, but disappeared into the sweep of plants and drowned as they caught up and enveloped him. The burned body, everything, disappeared into the roiling green and yellow stream. Gamaliel woke sweating and fearful. What did all this mean?

As with the earlier dream and less reluctantly, he determined to take this new version seriously. *Ha Shem* intended for him to find some meaning, to understand. Why else visit him with these bizarre images of the masked man, a corpse, and now an invasive, tidal wave of plants? It had to do with the murder, certainly…but did it? Would the Lord waste time on such trivial matters? Would the murder of one out-of-place gentile concern the Creator? People might wish the Lord intervened in their petty affairs. People prayed it to be so, but would He concern himself in anything so mundane, here or anywhere else? It was not likely, no matter how nontrivial it might seem to the persons involved. No, this was not the stuff to place at the Lord's feet.

Perhaps this dream was to be understood as a warning of something greater. Was there a great calamity to be visited on the Nation soon? Rome ruled with an iron and cruel hand. What worse thing could happen beyond that? No, something else had to be behind the dream—that is, if it meant anything at all. His last conversation with the high priest related to the rabbi from Nazareth. But it seemed unlikely that the maunderings of an insignificant country rabbi had anything to do with the dream or would hold any interest for the Lord.

He replayed his conversation with the high priest in his head. Kingdom like a mustard seed. Caiaphas had objected to the simile. People's understanding of the future, of end times, varied from one end of the array of possibilities to the other. What one wished for told you much about the speaker, but those wishes were rarely ever congruent with Torah. No, the future must remain a mystery except when the Lord wished to move his people toward a new place in history as he had done in Egypt. Gamaliel held to the notion that Israel's history began with Moses, not with Abraham as others believed. This dream must be a warning, but of what sort, and in what way did mustard, plants—plants with medicinal properties—relate to the events of the past few days, much less to the future?

He rose and washed and prepared for his morning meal. Benyamin brought him his usual pitcher of cool goat's milk, a wedge of cheese, and the end of a loaf of bread—his milk meal.

"Benyamin, how do you treat a cough?"

"Pardon? Did you ask me how I treated a cough, Rabban?"

"I did."

"You have a cough that needs treating?"

"No, it is a hypothetical question."

"Ah, like the one about how would I go about murder, I see. Is the person coughing me or someone else, hypothet…whatever?"

"Is there a difference?"

"Indeed, yes."

"I don't understand."

"There are treatments and there are still more treatments. If the coughing is from a child, there are things one does that would not be done for an adult and the other way round, you see?" Gamaliel opened his mouth to speak but Benyamin kept talking, so he filled it with bread instead. "And if it is an adult, what sort of cough it would be makes a difference."

"There are different remedies for different coughs?"

"Oh, certainly. For the cough that follows the stuffiness one experiences after getting a chill, one simply sips warmed wine that has cinnamon or some other spices or fruit in it. If there be no wine available, or if wine is part of the sufferer's general problem, well, you could do nothing as that sort of cough usually takes care of itself."

"I see, and the others?"

"There are tonics and poultices available. Some are very sharp and bring a quick relief, but will often, if improperly applied, burn the skin, or the throat if imbibed. Of the tonics, there are some that make you sleepy and you will be of no use to anyone for hours and—"

"I take your point. May I assume that the majority of these concoctions are mustard based?"

"Yes, but some formularies add other items. Pepper is sometimes used to promote sneezing. Some healers believe sneezing will help the body to expel the bad humors quickly. And there are other ingredients that the apothecaries keep secret. One usually finds the formula that works best for oneself and then stays with it."

"I see. Thank you, Benyamin. That will be all."

Alone again, Gamaliel turned his attention back to the dream and its possible significance. Nearly an hour of concentration brought him no closer to comprehension than before he'd started. His students began to arrive and he put aside his worries about dreams, mustard, and the mysterious Hannah, who seemed to turn up every time he rolled one aspect or the other of it over in his mind. Did that mean the Lord had an investment in the problem of murder in the Temple after all? No, not likely.

But who was Hannah?

Ali bin Selah, in his latest disguise, arrived in time to see the seven young men he took to be the students Loukas had told him about enter Gamaliel's house. If he understood the arrangement right, the rabban would be engaged for the rest of the morning and part of the afternoon. If he were going to make his presence known to Loukas, now would be the time to do it. Yet he hesitated. He knew the physician, but was it enough? Could this philhellenic healer be trusted? Or would he go to the Jewish or Roman, authorities? Ali needed to find out exactly what he knew. If he knew too much and if that knowledge should happen to uncover the solution of the death…Ali would have to deal with that, but how to do so would not be easy.

He was about to slip away when a familiar figure skulked down the shadowy side of the street and planted himself in the entryway of a small alley. The rabban interested someone else, it seemed, but probably not in the way he did. Ali's only wish was to avoid the Jew. This man apparently wished to confront him. Confront might be too strong a word. At the very least he had to have designs on the old man. What could they be? Did Ali care and if so, why? Whoever he was, he clearly did not know his prey, and whatever it was he wished to do had would have to wait. Gamaliel would not emerge from that fortress of a house for hours. Ali started to leave when another thought struck him and he stepped back into his hiding place.

What if Gamaliel was not the person of interest, but some other man? After all, didn't the students just arrive? Maybe one of them had a secret. Ali would delay a visit to the physician for now. He settled into his own shadowed hiding place to wait.

Chapter XXII

Gamaliel greeted his six students and set them a task to unravel, a text—some lines from Amos, the high priest's least favorite prophet, or so he said. The rabban had tossed off a line or two the night before about justice which had irritated Caiaphas. In the morning he decided to see how these bright minds would interpret them. Once he'd made the assignment he turned to the seventh man.

"Zach, I assume you have a good reason for arriving here in a plain robe rather than properly dressed as a Temple guard and accompanying my students at that. Forgive me if I do not consider the latter a coincidence."

"You would be correct, Rabban. I waited for them so as to blend in. The same reason dictated my leaving my armor at home."

"Then you must have something important to tell me… perhaps it is something you do not wish others to know you are telling me."

"I have been ordered by those above me, and they by those above them, to cease my inquiries into the matter of the bribes and…you can see how that would work. Whatever or whoever is behind the man's death in the Temple, it is certain that important people wish the matter to stay hidden. I received instructions to speak to no one, especially not to you."

"But you didn't stop?"

"Not right away. I kept asking questions, but I added a warning. If any of my guards spoke to anyone else about what I was doing, they would soon be looking for a job as a shepherd—and lucky to get that. Yesterday I stumbled onto something I think is important enough to pass on to you, and dangerous enough to persuade me to be much more discreet."

"Ah, in that case you'd better sit down." Gamaliel pulled a bench away from the wall and gestured for the guardsman to sit. "Benyamin, bring us some wine."

The guard sat and glanced around the room. "There are no windows here? We cannot be seen or overheard?"

"We are quite private here. Why do you ask?"

"I am sure someone followed me here. I made a point of joining your students. Everybody knows they arrive here at the third hour and most know their number varies. I thought seven men instead of six would not attract much notice. I guess I was mistaken."

"This man might have started following you before you merged with the students."

"That is so. But I felt sure I was alone up until I met up with your six. I am usually pretty good at that. My friends say I have a hawk's eyes because I can see things well off to either side."

"That must come in handy. Did you consider the possibility that it was not you, but one of the students who was being followed?"

"No, I did not. I supposed that, because I came across this knowledge, I must be the target."

"One last thing before you tell me your news. If what you know is so dangerous, why would the man only follow? Isn't it more likely he would simply get you aside and kill you on the spot?"

"I served briefly as a legionnaire in one of the cohorts assigned here. Many people know that and they know that I am not so easy to kill."

"I see. Well, here is the wine."

Benyamin placed two cups and a ewer of wine on the table between them. He glanced at the guard and his expression left no doubt as to what he thought of a palace guard sharing wine with the rabban of the Sanhedrin.

"Benyamin, I have a small task for you. Find some reason to exit to the street and walk west toward the Upper City and then circle around and approach the house from the east. Keep alert and see if you can tell if there is anyone lurking in the street as if he is waiting for someone in here. Also note if you are followed. Oh, and wear this man's cloak. Do not pull it all the way round you, just enough to cause someone to notice."

Benyamin's furrowed brow suggested he had second thoughts about his master's sanity, but he left. Moments later, the sound of the great front door banged shut.

"We will have a report in soon enough, but Benyamin is a slow walker. Now, tell me your news."

Ali saw the man exit. For a moment he thought it was one of the students, but it was an older, stooped man, a servant perhaps sent on an errand. The man hesitated and peered nervously up and down the street, then toddled off toward the Upper City. Ali sank further into his shadows. The watcher on the other side of the street stepped forward as if to greet this new arrival. Then he, too, hesitated and stepped back. What to make of that? Ali watched the old man disappear.

He had begun to think he could use the time to better advantage elsewhere. The errand runner, though running did not describe the old man's pace, soon returned. But from the east this time. Now that was odd. Either he had multiple errands to perform and the last at some location on the east side of the city, or the errand in the Upper City had failed and he'd been sent elsewhere, or he had been sent out for some other reason. What? To scout the street for people like the man across and himself? Did Gamaliel believe there would be someone out here with a less than innocent motive? How did he arrive at that? Ali shot a quick look at his counterpart. If his posture meant anything, that man was as confused as he.

The old man disappeared through the great door.

◇◇◇

Gamaliel sat back and tried to process what Zach had told him. He tapped his foot and waved one hand about, silently ticking off points in his mind and arranging them in columns in the air. The guard waited, unsure of what was expected of him.

"Rabban? What does it mean…beyond the obvious, that the palace is somehow involved in the man's death?"

"The palace? Oh I think not. Someone from the palace surely, but it is more complicated than that. The king would not condone it. The king and his government are away in Tiberias. Only a few low-level functionaries remain in the city. No, what you tell me leads elsewhere.

"But…"

"I have sources in the palace. If the king or anyone near to him were involved, I would know about it."

A very annoyed Benyamin entered the room. If he were a person of rank and privilege, a person whose facial expression would be important to read, thunderous would describe his features best. He shed the guard's cloak with an air of disgust. As he found himself downwind from the garment, so to speak, Gamaliel had to admit that it did smell a little ripe.

"So, Benyamin, what did you learn?"

"Aside from this man's poor sense of cleanliness and maintenance of his clothing, only two things that would interest the rabban."

"And they are?"

"There are two suspicious men in the street, not one. One tallish, lean person stands in the shadows across from the front door, and a shorter, stocky man likewise to the west in the alleyway. That one seemed very interested in the cloak, which I suppose means he is interested in your guest."

"And the first one?"

"He is just there. He could be simply an idler, or someone expecting to be joined later, or he might have followed the first. It is impossible to say."

Gamaliel stood and paced the floor. Three turns across and back and then he turned and faced the guardsman.

"Zach, I think it would be safest for you to linger here. I have no doubt that what you told me is the reason you have acquired a stalker. I am also persuaded that, given the chance, he will put a knife in your ribs."

"Not without a fight. It is just as likely I will put one in his."

"Brave words, but foolish. I do not want either to happen. As long as you tarry here, the man who seeks you will as well. That is one combatant neutralized. I must be off to Loukas and tell him what you told me. The more people know it, the safer you will be."

Chapter XXIII

Ali bin Selah had had enough. That the servant, the would-be errand runner, had been sent out on a scouting mission and had spotted him and the man across the street seemed obvious. How or why Gamaliel had tumbled to one or the other or of them or even why he bothered to look would be a question to address another day. As much as he wanted to know what that other lurker sought, he did not want to be found out even more. When the rabban's front door slammed shut, Ali joined a crowd of passers-by and set off toward the Sheep Gate and thence to Loukas. He had hoped to avoid a visit to the physician at any cost but circumstances had changed and not in his favor. After the events of the past few days he felt he needed to act promptly. His limitations were significant. Not only was he acting alone, but just finding his way in this strange city was difficult even in the best of times. Now it meant he must approach Loukas and discover what he and the rabban knew. He had no other choice, and then, if his friend and the rabbi had uncovered some things…well, that could pose other problems, but first things first. He needed to speak with Loukas.

As he was not as familiar with the streets of Jerusalem as he would like to have been, and because it was important to avoid the Temple mount, he took a more circuitous route through the city. Also, in an effort to confuse and lose anyone who in the off chance might have picked up his trail, he doubled back several times. For those reasons and because his hunger required a stop to purchase and eat something, he took longer than he might have otherwise to find the right gate to exit the city, pass through it, and make his way down the slope to the physician's house.

How could he have known that Gamaliel had also decided to consult with Loukas, had taken a direct route, and arrived ahead of him? Loukas would not be the only person to be surprised at Ali's unexpected arrival.

Loukas greeted Gamaliel and offered him a bench. He raised his eyebrows and jerked his head toward the room he'd had carved in the hillside where, because of its natural coolness, he kept his wine, among other things—including corpses when necessary. In fact, the body of the dead man still lay in it, but this odd usage was not something either of them spoke of.

"If you are offering me wine, the answer is no, thank you. I need a clear head. If you are suggesting we discuss our dead man, the answer is yes. I have learned something in the last hour which is disturbing but at the same time revealing." He frowned and sat. "Why do I have the feeling I may be sinking into that sand they say is found in the great Egyptian desert that swallows people up?"

"It is that serious?"

"It is."

"Then I will have the wine even if you will not."

Loukas went to fetch refreshments. The courtyard gate rattled as if someone sought to gain entrance. It was bolted as usual. Loukas was hospitable but not stupid. An unlatched gate was a license to steal.

"Who seeks to come into the House of the Physician?" Loukas asked, very formally, his normal address to patients, current or aspiring.

"Ali bin Selah, Loukas, open up quickly. I have need of you, and I do not wish to be seen in the street."

Loukas strode to the gate and unbolted it to allow his friend entrance. He glanced at the person outside and began to swing it shut.

"No, no, truly, Loukas, it is I, Ali. I have changed my appearance that is all. I will explain why later, but now please let me in." Ali squeezed through the gate.

"I don't understand—"

"I did not wish to involve you in this affair, my friend, but you see my brother—"

"Ali bin Selah, we meet again it seems," Gamaliel made his presence known. As much as he wanted to hear bin Selah's reason for his unusual appearance and the circumstances that forced him to it, he felt certain that Ali might not be inclined to share it so freely if he knew he had a listener other than Loukas.

Ali whirled and took in the courtyard, Gamaliel and Loukas. "How….? I just left your house. You could not have…you were not there? I saw your students enter. Seven of them and then the servant came out and—"

"Six."

"What?"

"I have six students. The seventh man was a Temple guard. He came to tell me something about the night of the murder in the Temple. I came here, obviously by a shorter route, to confer with Loukas, and that, I assume, is what has brought you here as well."

"You have the advantage of me."

"So it would seem. If you wish to consult with our friend and my presence is inconvenient, I will retire. But I must tell you I am more than curious to know why you went to such extremes to hide yourself."

Ali seemed momentarily lost in thought, eyes closed in concentration, brow furrowed. "Six, you say, and the seventh was a guard with information about the body in the temple. Did you know that your visitor was followed to your house by someone who seemed interested in him, and not in the best of ways?"

"I did. Being tracked and trailed by a variety of villains seems to be the occupation in which half this city engages lately. Loukas and I were subject to that the day after you and I met. That man said he had been tailing you and having lost sight of you, hoped

Loukas would lead him back. Now, the guard has a follower. I can only guess that your radical change in appearance is due to your suspecting something of the same. I knew there were two men watching my house and now I know you must have been one of them. Would it be too much to ask if you will tell me why before I leave you to confer with Loukas in private?"

"I will offer just this—I intended to visit Loukas. The reasons are not important—"

"Not?"

"For the purposes of answering your question, no. I guessed you and he were engaged in this murder business and you could well be here when I called. I slipped around to your house to find out."

"You know where I live?"

"One only has to ask anyone in the street for the location of the rabban's house."

"But you didn't come here,"

"If you will allow me to finish. I saw your students arrive. I assumed, incorrectly, that there were seven not six, and as I turned to leave, the other man arrived. He had a familiar face. I stayed to find out, if I could, what interest he had in you. As I said, I thought all of the men entering your house this morning were your students."

"And what prompted you to leave?"

"I guessed if he were waiting for you, I could come here and speak to Loukas in private. But it seems I took too long in coming, so my plans were foiled."

Gamaliel stared at Ali for a long time. Finally he sat down again and placed his hands on his knees. "Loukas," he said. "I will have that wine now. No doubt our visitor from Parthia will join us."

"Assyria."

"Pardon, my mistake. For some reason I got it into my head it was Parthia."

"I see. No, I am from Assyria, I assure you."

"Very well, Assyria it is. Sit, Ali bin Selah, and tell me first why you withheld from your friend, Loukas, that the body in his store room was your brother. When you have done that I would like a lesson on the compounding of cough syrup."

Chapter XXIV

Loukas stared blankly at Gamaliel. Ali seemed dazed. His eyes darted first to Loukas, then to the fig tree, and then to Gamaliel. A small bird lit on one of the tree's branches. Gamaliel did not know much about birds. This one had a thick beak which led him to believe it fed on fruit and nuts, not insects, but he realized he could be mistaken. One has to be careful at jumping to conclusions based on assumptions.

Loukas poured the wine for himself and his two guests. He seemed ill at ease, which should have been no surprise given he had the rabban of the Sanhedrin in full interrogation mode and Ali bin Selah in what could only be described as fugitive mode. He sighed and sat. A breeze ruffled the leaves of his fig tree, and the scents from his herb garden drifted across the courtyard to the trio.

"As I said earlier, if my presence will disrupt your talk with Loukas," Gamaliel said, "I can retreat either temporarily or permanently. However, I do have things to report to you, Loukas, and will need your thoughts."

Finally, Ali turned to Gamaliel. "Loukas says he trusts you. He says you can unravel difficult riddles. I will trust you as well. I must think how to put it to you, but first tell me what you meant about my brother."

"I think your brother is, or I should say was, the man Hannah. What I am not clear on is when exactly he died and why."

"And the compounding of cough mixture?"

"Ah, that I think, has a great deal to do with what is going on, why the Palace seems to be involved in the Temple murder and…well the list goes on."

"You think my brother is someone called Hana? Why would you think that?"

Gamaliel hesitated. Ali's Assyrian or Parthian accent shortened the name. Was that important? Something did not smell right here and it wasn't Loukas' herb garden. He sensed—an assumption to be sure—that Ali was not yet ready to be forthcoming. He shook his head.

"His shop was burned to the ground and a body lay in the ashes. Even as we speak the authorities are attempting to ascertain the cause of death. They may have difficulty doing so as the body had been badly burned, like our dead man in the Holy of Holies. I wonder, do you suppose that could be a coincidence?"

"How can I say? I am a stranger to the city and to your murder. How does this relate to my brother again?

Gamaliel watched as Ali's eyes seemed to go opaque, like a snake's do from time to time, particularly when they are about to shed their skin. Whatever he had on his mind it would not be articulated anytime soon. Gamaliel guessed that this Assyrian would soon shed this most recent persona like the snake and reinvent himself once more.

"You see, my brother's name is Achmir, Rabban, not Hana. He is dead, murdered in fact, but not lately. Some weeks ago to be exact. Why would you think that the man in Loukas' cave is my brother?"

"Achmir, you say. Then I am wrong and I beg your pardon."

"But you have yet to answer my question."

"And you are in a disguise. Shall we discuss that instead?"

Ali stood and glanced at the gate. "I must go, Loukas. I will call on you another time." He bolted to the gate and dashed through before Loukas could reply, much less protest.

"What was that all about?" he said.

"I think you will find that your friend, Ali, has a secret which, like a landslide, started as a small disturbance at the top of a hill and has now grown to a life-threatening event. One that might bury us all."

"A landslide destined to kill? You do not often wax poetic, Rabban. Why did you believe this Hannah person was Ali's brother?"

"A stab in the dark, I confess. There was something…My friend, Jacob, is blind and he sees, he tells me, with his ears. I thought I heard something in Ali's voice and, like blind Jacob, made a guess as to what it meant. I was wrong."

"Really? That is not like you—to guess, I mean, not the business of being wrong."

"Yes, well, tell me about cough mixtures."

"If you promise to tell me what the guard told you."

"Of course."

◇◇◇

Gamaliel had many scrolls and bound sheets of papyri. Most of them dealt with the Law, its proper interpretation, and application. He also had holy writ, commentaries on it, and opinions from others like himself on a variety of subjects, almost all related to interpretation of Torah. He rummaged through the stacks of scrolls and volumes in search of one of the few pieces he owned that had only a glancing relationship with the rest of his collection. He found it in the very back of a dusty shelf with the few other items that did not connect with his studies or students either. He carried it to a table and unrolled it, taking great care not to crack its edges. It had not been opened for years.

He spent the next hour reading and taking notes. When he finished, he sat frowning at the scrap in front of him. It made sense in a way, but why would one fight and fuss over such a trivial thing, much less kill for it? Was *hul gil*, the joy plant, really so important? Why should an ingredient found in tonics compounded for coughs, aches, and assorted maladies precipitate so much interest? If his sources were correct, and he had no reason to doubt them, then the late but not lamented

Alexander the Macedonian must shoulder some of the blame for this mess. Perhaps that would explain the palace's interest in his investigation. But would it also explain the army following all of them— him, Ali, the guard, and who knew who else?

Furthermore, Ali bin Selah dramatically changed his appearance and he had lied. Why? From whom was he hiding and what secret drove him to his present state? Did it have something to do with this substance? Why would he need to disclaim any knowledge of Hana or Hannah? Gamaliel felt certain the two were related and closely so. Something Loukas had said tweaked at his memory, but he could not get his mind around it. Something about Draco, the ill servant currently at death's door. Whatever Loukas had said, it would not come. Most days Gamaliel was comfortable in his advancing age, but there were other times, like this one, when memory and words failed him, that he experienced a small stab of fear. Age is not a comfortable cloak to wear.

Benyamin tapped on the door.

"Yes, Benyamin?"

"I did as you asked and followed the guardsman. The man was indeed waiting for him and took up his trail immediately."

"Were you noticed?"

"I do not believe so. As I said, the tracker stepped out onto the street. Our man slipped around a corner, and the shadow followed. When I arrived at the corner, I found the latter doubled up on the ground with a very large bruise on his head and no sign of the guard."

"Zach said he could handle it. He must realize that another will find him, and if the plan was to kill him for what he knew or they think he knows, they will not stop trying until they succeed or the need goes away."

"And how will that come about?"

"If I can sort through the tangled threads of this business and find a killer or two, it might. Of course, I may not do that in time. My worry now is for Ali bin Selah."

"Who?"

"A friend of Loukas the Physician and a player in this drama. I fear he could be the next and unnecessary victim. As the saying goes, one reaps what one sows."

"Who says that?"

"Lots of people, Benyamin. I am surprised you have not heard it."

"It must be from the areas where cultivating crops is the major occupation. Almost no one sows in the city."

"Very true. One wonders what sorts of mutual understandings we could construct if the people in the city sowed and the country people traded."

Chapter XXV

After his meal, Gamaliel retired to his room to read. Once again he added more oil than usual to his lamp and read on into the night. As curious as he was to sort through the bits and pieces of the murders, feeling certain they were connected, he did not wish to abandon his studies altogether. He'd done that once before and it had gone hard with his spirit.

The next morning, he awoke late and groggy. As a rule, when he arose it would be to the cooking aromas emanating from the kitchen. Not this morning. Benyamin had let him sleep and had waited. He rose and washed his face, said his morning prayers, and headed to the center of his house, a large naturally lighted atrium. He sat at table and called for his servant. Benyamin poked his head around the corner and scowled.

"You would eat now?"

"Only some cheese, and bread, and water."

"You're sure that's all? It is not enough to sustain a child."

"It is enough for me."

The servant reappeared with the end of a loaf of bread, a pot of honey, cheese, and some figs.

"I did not ask for all of this."

"You will need it. A messenger just arrived and said the high priest requires your presence at once."

"At once, he says. We shall see about that, but you are correct, under these new circumstances I will need sustenance."

Gamaliel dawdled over his meal and considered what Caia-phas wanted from him this time. Surely he didn't intend to pursue his obsession with the Galilean rabbi. Perhaps, at last, his ire had raised the level of righteous anger. Perhaps he would act to unmask the perpetrator of the worst desecration to the temple since Nebuchadnezzar's hoards descended on the city and looted Solomon's Temple and carried away its people. Perhaps, but probably not. There was something not right about the high priest's reaction to the whole situation. Gamaliel would like to know what brought it on, but dared not ask. There are answers to some questions you do not want to know.

His meal finished, he retired to his study to pray, as was his custom unless something urgent occurred that required his atten-tion. His morning prayers, a visit to his *mikvah*, and a change of clothes completed, he set out for the house of Caiaphas. The high priest lived near enough to him to make the walk almost pleasant. The view from Caiaphas' forecourt across the Kidron to the Mount of Olives might be the finest in the city, except possibly that from the roof terraces at the palace. If he were allowed to do so, if the Law were not so specific on the issue, Gamaliel would covet that view. He imagined one could sit there in the cool of an evening and feel very close to the Lord. He wondered if the high priest ever did—feel close to the Lord, that is; not sit there.

For a change, Caiaphas had something other than Yeshua ben Josef on his mind this morning, and it did concern the Temple, but outrage at the circumstances was not it.

"You have been stirring the pot," he said without preamble or greeting.

"Greetings in the Name to you, too, High Priest. What pot, or should I ask whose pot, have I been stirring? And why should I care?"

"I have come from the Palace. You know how I hate that place. A filthy lair of licentious living. And the queen, well…"

"Is it the queen's or the king's pot?"

"Not the king's, no…well, possibly. It wasn't made clear to me. The king is still in Tiberias with the queen, unlike the prefect, who is in residence at the fortress, for some reason. Do you know why that might be?"

"I had no idea Pontius Pilate graces our city. Does he?"

"Yes. But to the point, not the king but his consul, minister, whatever that pompous man who curries favor with foreigners is called, took me to task. I do not like the King's underlings scolding me, Rabban. No, I do not like it at all. And then to be summarily dismissed by the little…? I will pass a serious complaint about this rebuke along to his majesty, you can be sure of that."

"What problem did this court functionary feel he needed to report to you? More importantly, how does it apply to me?"

"You have been poking into the death of the impious man, against my advice I should add. You have been asking questions. Some of the legatees from the west have reported they were displeased and discommoded by it."

"They were…You did say discommoded? How is it that a dead man in our Temple is the business of legatees from the west or anywhere else, for that matter? Where in the west, by the way?"

"I am not sure—Egypt, I think."

"The Egyptian ambassador is upset that I am curious about a man in…Now that is strange indeed, but consistent with what I was told yesterday."

"Yesterday? What were you told yesterday? Never mind, I don't want to know. For your own good, I insist you to drop your investigation. The events surrounding the man's death are clear and the conclusion obvious."

"Clear to you, perhaps, but not to me. The man was not, I repeat, not a madman who burst into the Holy of Holies on some misbegotten mission to cleanse the Nation or have a few private moments with *Ha Shem*."

"Rabban, you blaspheme!"

"I am being irreverent, perhaps, but blasphemy comes at a higher cost. A reminder, High Priest, as you noted, I am the rabban and I will be the judge of blasphemy—mine or anyone else's. I repeat—the convenient story you have adopted will not serve. Our dead man met his end elsewhere. His killers or their accomplices brought him to the Veil subsequently. They then introduced him into the Holy of Holies as you saw that morning." Caiaphas opened his mouth to protest. "Do not interrupt me, High Priest. We have determined that your madman had two things about him that should convince you of this if nothing else does."

"And they are?"

"He was only recently circumcised and he traded as an herbalist or an apothecary."

"You know this for a fact?"

"Ah, if it is facts you seek, ask yourself this. Why would an emissary from Egypt care a Galilean fig about a dead man in our temple? Find me the facts behind that and I will tell you the facts of the dead man. You will not find them, by the way. The Egyptian will insulate himself from inquiries by you and anyone else."

"Why would he?"

"That, High Priest is precisely the point. Why ask? Why not be forthcoming and say, 'I wish your man to cease his inquiries into the death in your Temple, which, by the way is no business of mine in the first place, because…' because why, do you suppose?"

"You vex me with these supposes and perhapses. The king could ask."

"He could, but he is, as you pointed out, not in the city and he would be wasting his time. The mode of speech among diplomats is at best, mildly dissembling and at worst, unabashed lying. Do you really believe the Egyptian will reveal to our King the reasons for his wish to suppress an investigation as I have described it?"

"No."

"No, indeed. Even if he mustered the courage to do so, the emissary would not tell him."

"It makes no sense." Caiaphas paced the room twice—up, turn, back, up, turn, back. "Rabban, hear my advice. Whatever you may believe to be the circumstances of the occurrence, you will be well advised to accept the evidence that a man, a gentile you now claim, entered the Holy of Holies and confronted an angry Lord of Hosts."

"High Priest—"

"Hear me out. You have ruffled the feathers of the court once already and although the king seems not to mind the meddling, the queen still seethes at the very mention of your name and insists you be removed from office. The last thing you need to do now is create another reason for her to pressure her husband. The king may not be able to withstand her harping forever."

"There are two reasons why I cannot take your advice, excellent as it may be. On the one hand, there is, as I said before, the need to see justice done and as this murder is so intimately tied to the Temple, this need goes beyond the merely theoretical. It is absolute. On the other hand, the very fact that a foreign power has intruded into it suggests that this is no random killing, but rather one that may involve the Nation at the highest levels."

"You believe that?"

"I do."

"You will not stop?"

"I will not."

"Then I hope for your sake you survive this sally into international politics. I do not relish breaking in a new rabban, but..."

"But?"

"It would give me great deal of pleasure to see that officious monkey of a palace minister put in his place."

"We are at least agreed on something."

Chapter XXVI

Caleb, a Samaritan traveling from Jericho to Jerusalem, detoured from the main path to avoid a group of obnoxious youths intent on ragging on another despised visitor from the land where the Lord was worshipped on Mount Gerizim rather than in Herod's Temple. Even though Herod's predecessors had destroyed Gerizim, Caleb and his coreligionists still preferred the ruins to the extravagant Temple in Jerusalem. His path took him through a narrow declivity into a wadi. At first he thought the shapes piled in its bottom must be someone's goats which had wandered away or had been chased by a lioness and had fallen into its depths. A second look made him think otherwise. He scrambled part way down the steep bank and stopped a few cubits away from the tangle of limbs and torsos. The stench nearly knocked him over. It seemed evident that some animal, maybe several, had found and feasted on the remains since they had been deposited there. Why some had been spared this second assault and not others would be a question for someone familiar with the beasts of the wilderness to sort out, certainly not Caleb. He retreated and managed his ascent up the wadi's steep bank considerably faster than his descent.

He stopped the first patrol he met on the road. For all their faults, and he could think of many, the Romans did a fair job of keeping travelers safe on the roads. The patrol listened to his story and asked the location of his find and then dismissed him. They would do nothing else. They had no interest in dead men whom they assumed were just a few more Judeans foolish enough to stray from the main road and fall into the hands of the area's bandits. They might have been more concerned had the Samaritan mentioned that two wore the garb of Temple guards. As Caleb did not frequent the Temple, he wouldn't have recognized the uniforms even if he'd looked.

The innkeeper where he stopped for the night listened to his story as well, nodded, and said that since the patrol had been notified, nothing more could be done. He also stated there was no room in the inn for Caleb even though the obvious lack of patrons indicated he lied. His actual words to Caleb were, he had no room for *his kind*. The Samaritan did not complain. Why bother? Samaritans had come to expect this abuse. The citizens of Judea and Perea, as well as those up in the Galilee, looked down on him and his people, insisting their brand of Judaism, formulated as it was after the repatriation from Babylon, represented the only Way and not the bastardized version practiced in Samaria. Things never changed. Of course there was that strange woman and her story of the rabbi at the well, but who could trust someone like her?

Satisfied he'd done his duty he settled in for the night in his sleeping blankets beside the goats. It would be pointless to speak more about those dead men.

Had Gamaliel any knowledge of the carnage in the wilderness he might reconsidered his intention to expose the killer of the Temple man, as the murdered man had now come to be called. People who dispose of their victims in the wilderness do not do so to hide them, but rather to hide the fact of murder. Missing persons do not attract the attention bodies do. The killing of Temple guards could cause a panic in some quarters and create difficulties. Dropping them into a remote wadi or garbage heap tended to lessen the impact. What people did not know could not hurt them, the saying goes. Of course the victims and their families might disagree. And if the victims included representatives from other lands and cultures, well best let that stay hidden as well. Rome would not be bothered if a few residents of Judea thinned the population that way. But if too many visitors turned up dead, that could only spell trouble.

As it happened, Gamaliel did not know, and it would be several more days before anyone else did, either. By that time he would have solved the mystery. The report of those multiple deaths would only confirm the outcome.

As it played out, he left the high priest more determined to piece together the bits and pieces of the Temple man's last days than before. He felt certain he needed to find Ali bin Selah. How to find him posed another problem entirely. Would Loukas have any ideas? The only connection he had to the self-proclaimed Assyrian would be through Loukas. Gamaliel knew Loukas, and Loukas knew Ali. What he wished to know now was the connection between the Street of the Herbalists, Ali, and the murdered man. After Ali's odd visit, the possibility that one existed seemed strong.

He needed to concentrate on this murder business and get it over with. And he needed to find Zach the Guards Captain again. In the light of the warnings from the high priest, Gamaliel needed to quiz him more closely. And then there was the problem of the hands on the dead man found in the apothecary's shop. They were not the hands of an apothecary. So who was he? He left a note for his students telling them that their studies were suspended for a few days.

Ali bin Selah's plan to visit Loukas had been interrupted by that meddling Pharisee. He spent the remainder of the day looking for a place to hole up while he weighed his, by now, dwindling options. His search for shelter brought him to the village of Bethany and a shabby inn on its periphery where the relative lack of business between High Holy Days forced the innkeeper to ask fewer questions of potential lodgers than he might have otherwise. So Ali moved his meager possessions into a tiny room which had access to the roof, a feature the inn keeper described as limited and special. Why that should be true eluded Ali until another guest asked if he would take money for switching rooms.

"Why would you wish to do such a thing?" he asked.

"Why? Where else would you sleep in the heat? In the rooms a man might roast like a sheep on a spit. Don't people sleep on their roofs where you come from?"

Ali shrugged. The thought never occurred to him. He supposed some of the poorer citizens in Nineveh might do so. He really didn't know. His house had a central fountain and atria designed to circulate the air throughout the various rooms and cool it. Sleeping on the roof with its minarets and finials would be difficult at best and unthinkable in any case. As much as he had learned from Loukas during his visits, Ali realized he had more to learn about this nation's odd customs and problems. At the moment he had a bigger fish in his net that needed to be brought into the boat. Access to the roof appealed to him not so much for the chance it afforded for a cooler night's rest, but because he saw the advantage of a second exit from the building it offered, should he need one. His funds were running low and the money would have been useful, but he declined the offer to exchange rooms. He had funds available in letters of credit, but to cash them meant coming out of hiding and presenting himself in public, which, of course, was what he did not wish to do. Not just now. Not until he had to, and not until he knew what Loukas, and by indirection, the rabban, knew.

For his part Loukas spent the day, the portion not filled with patients, reviewing everything Gamaliel told him including the latest—the Palace's attempt to suppress the investigation. He did not possess Gamaliel's intuitive skills. For Loukas, problems were solved by assembling facts, arranging them in logical order, and then reading them like a scroll. The problem's narrative would then unfold and the solution an inevitable conclusion. Accordingly, he sorted through all the facts he had, added Gamaliel's bits and pieces that he had not heard personally, added in the odds and ends Ali had mentioned when he'd analyzed the body and, after a half hour of intense concentration, came up with exactly...nothing.

He thought back through everything, this time more slowly and rearranging some of the parts. He asked himself, what would Gamaliel do had he been in Loukas' place? Except for examining the body, a thing Law forbade, the two of them had done and seen nearly everything together. True, he had not accompanied Gamaliel on his first trip to the herbalists, but Loukas had seen the burned out ruins and the body in the souk. Gamaliel had not seen Ali's reaction to the body. Did that mean anything? Could either be important? Did either matter? What had Ali's reaction been at the sight of the Temple man's body? Gamaliel would have noticed something, but what? An *anamnesis*, he thought, I will have an *anamnesis*.

He was still attempting to relive the moment when his new servant, who'd been tasked to watch Draco, cried out. Draco was dead. Well, at least Ali bin Selah's potion had made the passage easier. He covered the poor man's body with the bed sheet and turned to leave. Arrangements had to be made. As an afterthought he picked up the vial of pain relief. Empty.

"Draco said he could no longer stand the pain. He must have downed it all at once," the servant said.

Draco had indeed drained every last drop from the small flask. Loukas had warned him not to self-medicate. Apparently, he'd found the strength to reach the vial and do so anyway. Well, a blessing however you looked at it. Loukas retrieved a second vial from the shelf where he'd stored it earlier. He would add this useful elixir to his other medicines.

Chapter XXVII

Gamaliel woke the following morning from a dreamless sleep. He rushed through his morning prayers, ablutions, and breakfast, then set out for Loukas' house on a bright and crystal-clear morning. He had one stop to make on his way. The night guards would be just now assembling to turn Temple security over to the larger day shift. If he hurried, he should be able to catch Zach ben Azar'el. He needed to pinpoint the source of the comments the guard made concerning the palace. Did he mean the palace as in the king, or the palace as in its many lesser functionaries? The king was not in the city and so it was difficult to assign royal annoyance to the investigation. It must have come from a lower level, but from whom? Either the high priest had it wrong or Zach misspoke. Gamaliel was hoping the high priest had made the mistake, but he needed to be sure.

As he expected, the night guards, all looking a little worse for wear, had been just then dismissed and were headed toward the Hulda tunnels to the South Wall and the lower city. Yehudah, the captain of the guards, had dispatched the day shift to their posts.

"Rabban, greetings in the Name. You heard then?"

"Heard? What might I have heard? I came to talk to Zach ben Azar'el."

"Then you haven't heard. The captain of the night guard has gone missing. That makes three from the night shift unaccounted for now."

"I knew about the first two. Zach believed they took a bribe to turn a blind eye to the events of the other night and have fled or paid for their indiscretion with their lives."

"Well, he is missing. I have no idea why or where. Can I help you with anything?"

"I am afraid not now. When was Zach reported missing?"

"He failed to report for duty last night. His second in command roused me and I stood Zach's watch. Now, I must stand my own."

"You have my sympathy. I do not think your companion missed his shift of his own will, however."

"You believe he is sick? Why not send word?"

"Not sick, Yehudah. I think it is worse than that."

Gamaliel shook his head and hurried across the platform toward the north exits and the Sheep Gate.

"You believe he's dead?" Yehudah called after him.

Gamaliel raised his arm in a parting gesture and kept walking. The sacrificial fires, which had been banked for the night, were being stoked as he strode past. Soon the hiss and sizzle of burning flesh and hide and the resultant acrid smoke would once again grace his city.

A few of the *kohanim* greeted him as he passed, but he ignored them. His mind, like an overlarge wine cask, began to fill with all the pieces of his puzzle. As they fell in, everything else was forced up and out to spill over and away to wherever it is that thoughts go when they are no longer one's immediate interest. He neither heard nor acknowledged the people who had to dodge out of his way as he bore down on them. Zach missing…probably dead. Where was Ali bin Selah? What would he have told Loukas had he stayed instead of bounding off like a frightened gazelle? More importantly, what might Loukas have told him? Gamaliel stopped abruptly in midstride. Was it possible Ali had another purpose in mind when he barged in yesterday?

"I have become suspicious of everyone," he said aloud and attracted the curious stares of the crowd on the mount. "I practically accused the high priest of staging a murder. Did I only mean to annoy him or did I think there might be some truth in it?" He shook his head angrily. "No, of course not. Still, one should never rule out anything."

A passerby, unfamiliar with who the rabban of the Sanhedrin was, a pilgrim no doubt, pulled up beside him.

"Are you all right, Father?"

"What? All right? Of course I am all right. Who do you think I am? Do not call me father as if I were in my dotage, sir. Foreigners!"

The poor man stepped back and started an apology but Gamaliel barreled off, still muttering to himself. "Of course I could be completely wrong about all of this. It might still be an elaborate ruse to discredit the guards or the priests or…or what? Why tempt the Lord's wrath in such a way? But the dead man was only recently circumcised. Now there is something we must reckon with, and soon."

His headlong rush took him into the path of a youth equally oblivious to his surroundings hurrying from the opposite direction. The young man barreled into Gamaliel, caught his balance just in time, and snapped at the old man.

"Watch it, you old fool."

Gamaliel spun around and gave the boy a tongue-lashing he would remember until the day he died. Had the young man known that it had been delivered by the highest laic member of the Sanhedrin, he might have felt suitably chastised instead of angry. As he did not, he made a rude gesture and continued on his way.

◇◇◇

Gamaliel burst through his gate to find Loukas arguing with the crew of *kohanim* assigned to burials. The final disposition of the late Draco apparently posed a problem for them.

"No matter what else we may discover from here on out," Gamaliel groused without the usual greeting in the Name, "We are most definitely looking at some sort of conspiracy. Who is this?"

"These are the agents assigned to manage Draco's burials rites. We have a problem."

"I see. Well, a conspiracy, Loukas."

"You say that with great finality. It raises two questions. What sort of conspiracy and by whom? Also, how did you arrive at that conclusion?"

"That is three questions, and the answers in order are 'I don't know,' 'I don't know,' and 'what possible alternatives do we have for piecing together what we know thus far?' Wait, Draco is dead and these are agents sent to bury him? When? And what problem could he pose now?"

"Draco died last night. I am quarreling with these men over burial practices. They say because Draco was not of the faith and his manhood had been mutilated as well, he cannot rest among those who are of the faith and intact. I do not know what the situation would be if he were one, but not the other. Either way, I contend that dead is dead and who, except possibly *Ha Shem* Himself, could possibly care. And I seriously doubt that He does. This man's response is that He does care and the Law is the law. As rabban, can you enlighten me here?"

"I see. I am sorry for the loss of such a faithful servant, but you said death would be a blessing."

"It was a blessing from, and now an inconvenience to the Lord. I wish him to be placed in a tomb, and these men say he cannot because his corpse will somehow defile the ones already there."

"I will have a word with the priest." Gamaliel took the young man aside and they spoke briefly. The *kohen* seemed intimidated in the presence of so notable a person as the rabban of the Sanhedrin, but still remained stubborn. Finally, Gamaliel said something that satisfied the priest. He nodded and departed.

"He will arrange for the body to be picked up shortly."

"Draco will be entombed? How did you manage that and do I want to know?"

"As it happens, I have an empty rolling stone tomb and your Draco will inhabit it until such time as his bones can be collected and placed in an ossuary. At that time you may find him a place on the Hill of the Dead."

"Your tomb? What happens if you die before his bones can be collected?"

"Then he and I, both of us, will be someone else's problem, won't we?"

"I see. Thank you. Now, you came crashing in here with talk of conspiracy. What did you mean?"

"I did? Oh, yes I did. I have been thinking. On my way over here I had a chat with Yehudah, you know, the captain of the Temple Guards. It seems the night shift captain, Zach ben Azar'el…you know the one who told me about the interference from the Palace? Zach has gone missing." Gamaliel paused and wiped his face with a cloth he pulled from his sleeve. "Is it my imagination or are young people ruder than they used to be?"

"Are they? Sorry, how does that question relate to the missing guardsman?"

"There was a young man who nearly ran me down on my way over here. He called me an old fool. Do you believe the effrontery?"

"You told him who you were, of course?"

"No, I told him who I thought he was."

"And?"

"He made a rude gesture. Appalling, what has the world has come to?"

"Indeed. You did say someone is missing and there must be a conspiracy?"

"Oh, yes. Here it is in a nutshell."

Chapter XXVIII

Gamaliel finished his narrative as the Temple shofars sounded the third hour. Loukas had listened, at first patiently, and then with increased agitation. Gamaliel paused and took a breath, then shook his head. "I have listened to myself speak and now realize it cannot true. Have you ever noticed, Loukas, that sometimes a thing which you have convinced yourself must be true, vanishes like the morning dew when you speak it aloud?"

"Often."

"Really, to suppose the palace, the Roman authorities, and the high priest are somehow connected in a vast plot to eliminate one lone apothecary is absurd."

"Of course it is." Loukas said and shook his head in apparent frustration. "I am at a loss. You just spent the better part of an hour describing in elaborate detail a bit of chicanery in high places and now you say it meant nothing?"

"I didn't say it meant nothing even though in retrospect, it is. I ask you instead, what doing so does for our investigation."

Loukas threw up his hands. "I am clueless. What does it do?"

"It tells us that, once again, an illusion has been created to lead us astray. It is a very elaborate and deliberately crafted illusion. You, I, and who knows who else, have been lured into another trap. We have been set to wasting valuable time looking for connections where none exist. The question I put to you now is, why is that?"

"To cover the reality of the thing, I suppose."

"Close enough. First we were stuck in the Temple trying to connect the death and the apparent facts of the murder to an angry *Ha Shem*. Then, because we assumed our dead man practiced as an apothecary, we went to the herbalists and looked there. Now we hear from two differing sources that the palace and the Romans must be involved. It is like the Oracle at Delphi—all smoke and mirrors."

"You've been to the Oracle at Delphi?"

"Only vicariously. I have received reports. The illusion of other worldliness has to do with polished reflective surfaces set at differing angles, torches, and a great deal of incense and its smoke. One has no idea where the message comes from or how many people are delivering it, who's there and who is not. Very clever, if I do say so, but that is beside the point."

"Not holy smoke then?"

"For the Greeks, possibly, for Israelites, never. We have been led by the nose like a bull going to slaughter."

"Or to be sacrificed up on the Temple mount?"

"Exactly. We are being served up, you could say."

"By whom?"

"There you go. You have put your finger on the quintessential question. Who indeed? You were quite correct in suggesting that we ignore the facts of the body in the Holy of Holies. Alive and simultaneously dead, you said."

"And that led us nowhere."

"No, no, do not be so pessimistic. It was a good start. We just didn't go back far enough."

"Now you have lost me. I have to say, Gamaliel, that I have always considered myself to be reasonably astute. I can solve complex problems and diagnose disease as well or better, if modesty permits, than most of my contemporaries. But at this moment I feel as confused as a student at his first geometry lesson—with Euclid himself as tutor."

"I suppose I should be flattered. I have no knowledge of either geometry or Euclid, so I cannot be sure. Forget what I just said.

In a nutshell, the conspiracy, the real conspiracy, is that there is no conspiracy as we imagined—well, as I imagined. You have different thoughts?"

"Let me see. All of the clues and actions taken in the execution of this murder were intended to lead us farther and farther away from the central core of the thing. And that is…what is it?"

Gamaliel shook his head. "I haven't figured that out yet, but I will."

"Of course you will. You will?"

Gamaliel closed his eyes and tilted his head back as if to take the sun on his face. "In truth, I feel the way a man must if suspended over a chasm supported only by a fraying rope. For the sake of argument, let us suppose that the dead man in the Temple represents a second murder. That there had been an earlier one, a more significant one, but the fact of the body being placed where it was has diverted us. What then?"

"What other murder? I don't recall an antecedent murder."

"Neither do I, but if we posit that there was one, where will we be led?"

"Is anybody of importance missing? I think we would have heard if that were the case."

"Must it be someone of importance? Suppose it was someone whose death would be unremarkable but for his connection to something of importance."

Loukas rolled his eyes. "Why do you do this to me? What thing of importance."

"I don't know, but I have been considering two facts. First, your friend Ali arrives for a visit, but not at his usual time, and then he leaves in a hurry—heading north, he says. Then he suddenly reappears as someone else without explanation. What shall we make of that?"

"I make nothing of it. Are you supposing that Ali bin Selah is somehow mixed up in these murders?"

"For the time being, I am. I have only the thinnest of reasons to do so, but, yes, I believe he is connected somehow."

"I don't believe it. He told me he searched for an acquaintance he was to meet elsewhere and came here on his trail."

"Yes, I know. And he brought you wine and a potion for Draco. Do you still have that mixture?"

"I do. Why?"

"Have you tested it yourself? Am I right in assuming that Draco took it regularly and it eased his pain greatly?"

"Yes. In fact he seems to have downed the whole vial in his last moments."

"Is it possible it might have hastened his death as well as given him relief from pain?"

"I don't think so, but I suppose it might have, given his fragile condition."

"So, there is none left to test?"

"I have a second, full bottle."

"I would like to see it."

"Now?"

"Now."

Loukas ducked into his chambers and emerged a moment later with a vial filled with liquid. Gamaliel admired the delicate Roman glass, but wondered whether placing such a tonic in something so easily broken would be considered prudent.

"You test it, Loukas, but be careful. Just a taste on a fingertip should do for a start."

Loukas broke the wax seal on the vial's neck and pulled the stopper. He placed a finger over the opening, tilted the bottle over and back and replaced the cap. He touched his finger to his tongue and ran it around in his mouth.

"I am impressed and not a little dismayed," he said. "Even this small dab has numbed my tongue and the rest of the mixture burns."

"Numbs, you say? Could that be *hul gil*?"

"If it is, it is not what I am used to. This is a mixture of mustard, this numbing substance in wine as a carrier, and honey, if I am not mistaken."

"Aside from the substance that numbs, is it a common admixture?"

"Yes, I would say so. Except for this substance..." Loukas wetted the end of his finger again and repeated the tasting process.

"*Taste and see that the Lord He is good.*" Gamaliel chanted. "*Blessed is the man that puts his trust in Him.*"

"What?"

"One of King David's songs. Is the second trial any different? Have you discovered anything new?"

"No. I am curious about whatever it is that has such a powerful effect on the senses. I must ask Ali when he comes again. Do you think he will? Why do you suppose he has disguised himself?"

Gamaliel frowned. "Why does anyone disguise himself? He wishes not to be discovered. That being the case, the more important question is why did he break his anonymity and come here?"

"To talk to me."

"Yes, but he could have done that any time. He could have done it without pretending to be someone else. No, something has happened between the time he left and the time he showed up again at your gate."

"What happened, and why did he come to me afterwards?"

"I am not sure about the first part, but I think he came to find out what you had discovered about the Temple man or, more likely, what the two of us had deduced since he last talked to you."

"Why would he do that?"

"Why indeed? If we knew that, we would be halfway home. That assumes I am correct in suspecting your friend's involvement. Remember he said his brother Achmir had been murdered not so long ago."

"And...?"

"Didn't I suggest an antecedent murder? So, what if it were Ali's brother, Achmir?"

"How...? I am at sea, Rabban. Please explain."

"I wish I could."

Chapter XXIX

Obviously Loukas did not share Gamaliel's suspicions about his friend, Ali bin Selah. Whether that reflected a sense of loyalty to an acquaintance, a belief in the essential innocence of mankind in general, or distrust in his friend's powers of deduction, Gamaliel could not say. But Loukas was having none of it. Gamaliel sighed. He did not want to lose his friend's good counsel.

"Of course, I could be completely wrong in this, Loukas. It's just that one has to consider all possibilities."

Loukas' face lost its stubborn look and he nodded. "There is the fact that he said he would leave the city, didn't, and returned in disguise. I suppose we should explore that, but his brother? It is a reach."

Gamaliel opened his mouth to respond just as Loukas' new servant stepped out into the sunshine of the courtyard

"Master," he said addressing Loukas, "there is a man here who insists on speaking to you. He says it is urgent."

"Is he a patient? Tell him to wait in the anteroom and I will attend him shortly."

A stocky man wearing an apron and a headdress made from some sort of animal hide pushed his way past the servant. "I am not a patient, sir, at least not today. I have knocked at the door of every physician between here and Bethany and you are the first and only one at home. I require your assistance immediately."

"But you say you are not a patient. What then?"

"There has been an accident."

"An accident? What sort of accident?"

"Not an accident, precisely. A guardsman from the Temple has…he is…"

"He is what, man? Speak up."

"I am afraid he is dead and perhaps worse."

"Worse. What can possibly be worse than dead?"

"He fell on his sword and the Law is strict about those things."

"Gamaliel, what is this man raving about? What law would apply to a man who accidently fell and killed himself?"

"I do not think this man means the dead man actually had an accident. He means the man committed suicide and the Law is strict in condemning that."

"The Law forbids suicide? And what, pray tell, is the punishment for that? Is it a capital crime? That would demonstrate the seriousness of the act, surely."

"Don't be facetious, Loukas; it doesn't become you. It is always a matter between the Creator and the created. The punishment is not at issue. *Ha Shem* expects obedience to the Law, no more, no less."

"Wonderful. I will think on that for a while." Loukas turned to the messenger who, in his impatience, shifted his weight from one foot to the other. "Where is this dead guard that you require my presence to certify? That is why you are here?"

"Yes, sir. Bethany."

"You did say Bethany, yes, I see. So, you came all the way from Bethany to talk to a physician? Why?"

"The town Elder thought that since the dead man was attached to the Temple and because there has been talk of a mighty sign occurring there some days ago, we should have some official pronouncement about—"

"Has anything been done to the body?" Gamaliel interrupted.

"No, sir, the Elder said no one should touch or move the body. He lies where he fell."

"Good. We should be on our way, Loukas. It appears there has been a new development in our mystery. Let us hope it moves us forward."

"Development? Do you believe this suicide has something to do with the death of the man in the Temple? How?"

"The dead man, our suicide, is a Temple guard. That alone speaks to a connection and, unless I am mistaken, this new corpse is our missing guardsman, Zach ben Azar'el, a fact that, if true, will add to our fund of knowledge but poses a question."

"Just one? You disappoint me, Rabban. What sort of question? Wait, I see. Why would the person who sought to uncover the briber of the guards on his watch and who accused the Palace of involvement turn around and kill himself?"

"Exactly, and additionally, what drew him all the way to Bethany of all places? We must hurry."

Bethany sits on a hill across the Kidron Valley and beyond, about two miles from Jerusalem. Gamaliel had made the journey on occasion, but, as a "man of the city," not often and then only during the week. Except during the Passover and High Holy days, when pilgrims cover the hills in and around Jerusalem, Bethany was beyond the permissible Sabbath day's journey and considered another camp. On those special days, the borders of the Jerusalem encampment—an archaic term gleaned from Exodus—would be extended and the two entities would theoretically overlap. But this was neither a feast nor holy day and the exception did not apply. Gamaliel, of all people knew that. As Shabbat did not begin for another six hours, he felt it safe to make the trip. If, however, he could not complete his investigation by nightfall, he would be stuck in Bethany for a day, and he knew enough about Bethany to not want that.

"We must hurry, Loukas," he said again.

Loukas waved at the messenger to lead the way and they departed, but only after Loukas had given instructions to his servant regarding the removal of Draco's body.

"Bring that mixture with you, Loukas."

"The pain relief? What for?"

"I am not sure but I think it is important that you have it with you at all times."

"I see. After two miles, most of it uphill, you expect to be in great pain, my friend?"

"That is a distinct possibility."

A need to blend into one's surroundings is paramount if keeping watch on a house or a person is the task set for you. Two such people watched the three men leave the physician's house. One of them followed the trio down the hill into the Kidron Valley and thence up the Mount of Olives and on to Bethany. The other lingered and considered his options.

The physician's servant had closed the door. How many others were lurking about? Would this man allow him to enter? What kind of information would he find if he were to enter the house? Unless there was more than the one servant he knew about, he should have no difficulties. He could always dispose of him should he suddenly find an allegiance to his employer greater than his willingness to cooperate, but that would have to be a last resort. Killing always provoked questions. Better leave the scene as you found it. He was about to step out from the shadows and knock on the physician's door when a group of men bearing a stretcher marched down the street and stopped at Loukas' door. He joined them. This would be easier than he expected.

The men had been sent to remove the body of a dead servant. The servant died? How fortunate. None of the group questioned his presence among them, assuming that he belonged to the household. The young man who opened the door to them accepted that he was with the party of men. One servant only—perfect.

While the men wrapped the body of the grossly disfigured man, he searched the room, the house and, with the servant's acquiescence, the storage unit carved into the hillside.

The men finished their preparations. He would have to leave with them or stay and work on the young man. But what would he know? Not much and in the end, he might have to dispatch him which would only raise the stakes higher. Instead, he slipped out of the house with the funeral party and resumed his post opposite. Tomorrow was Shabbat, therefore, the healer would return before nightfall.

There was time.

Chapter XXX

The guardsman lay sprawled on his back in a cramped, cluttered alleyway behind a rundown inn. Crates and several broken amphorae partially blocked the entrance and prevented a crowd from entering and disturbing the site. The location also provided the reason it had taken so long for the body to be discovered. A serving girl sent out to get rid of some rubbish had chosen the alley as the spot to drop her armful of trash, even though the innkeeper had directed her to take it to the community dump.

Gamaliel was puffing when he and Loukas arrived. They were greeted by the man introduced as the Elder, although Gamaliel had no idea what the title meant or how the old man came by it. He had succeeded, however, in keeping the morbidly curious away and the scene, except for the recent addition of a pile of fetid straw, had been reasonably well preserved.

"It is as I thought, Loukas. This poor man is Zach ben Azar'el, late of the Temple guards. What do you suppose he had in mind when he journeyed to this out of the way alley?"

"It is an odd place to choose if one has made up one's mind to commit suicide."

"This isn't a suicide, my friend. This is another murder."

"Gamaliel, I have always admired your ability to see the truth of things when others cannot, but how in the world do you know this is not a suicide? Look at the man."

Zach ben Azar'el, his face pale and set in evident surprise, sprawled on his back, legs apart, arms flailed out and his short sword protruding at an acute angle from a point just below his sternum.

"The sword is at an angle," Loukas lectured. "The correct angle is important. There are two efficient ways to stab a man to death. One is downward in the angle of the neck on the left side…here. He pointed to a spot where his collar bone joined his neck. To do that one must stand close to the victim or behind him. The other, more common way, is at this angle up under the center of the ribs. Straight in won't do. Up and in and you will die instantly."

"That is fascinating, Loukas. If I ever decide to become an assassin, I will remember that. Knowledge of anatomy must be quite useful to someone in that line of work. So, he did not fall on his sword."

"When a man decides to kill himself in this fashion, he holds the hilt of the sword against the point where the ribs meet and angles it upward. Then, when he is ready, or his desperation overcomes his fear, he pulls it in. That will penetrate his heart and then he falls."

"I would think he would fall forward. Otherwise one cannot say he fell on his sword."

"You are being too literal. It is a figure of speech, Rabban. He might as easily have fallen backwards."

"You are the expert and will not dispute the point, but I am willing to bet, were I a betting person, which I am not, that the fall is usually, nay almost always, forward—thus the expression. Anyway, this man did not kill himself."

"And you come to that conclusion how? Certainly not because he fell the wrong way. What do you see?"

"What do I see? It is not so much a matter of what I see, as who this is. Zach served as a captain in the Temple guard. Men selected for that duty are vetted for their knowledge of the Law and their absolute devotion to it. Nothing less than total adherence is tolerated. He knew the Law. He would never have killed himself. Therefore, someone did him in and made it look like suicide."

"There are no exceptions? Come now, what about King Saul who did precisely what this man must have done. You call that... something I can't remember, but I am sure there is an exception."

"The Talmud says, *For him who takes his own life with full knowledge of his action, no rites will be observed—no rending of clothes, no eulogy.* You are thinking of *anuss* which is the condition attributed to Saul, who, after his defeat at the hands of the Philistines, realized what would have happened to him if he were taken alive. He impaled himself on his sword. More importantly, he finally understood that he had disobeyed the Lord and, in the moment of his defeat, realized his sin. There was no other recourse left to him."

"I am going to suggest something here, friend, and you can tell me why I am wrong, if I am. I don't think so, but you have a way of turning the world on its ear. So, suppose it was Zach, the guard of the Holy of Holies, not his subordinates, who took the bribe. He goes through the motions of seeking the culprits, reports a highly inventive tale about the Palace and duplicity in high places, and then hears that you have gone to the high priest. He guesses his story is about to be disproved. He comes to this lonely place, realizes the depth of his sin against the Lord, and, like King Saul, kills himself. End of story."

"A very plausible account. You are to be congratulated. I am impressed."

"Then you see the possibilities?"

"Oh, yes, certainly. But it won't wash. The high priest did not refute his story, he confirmed it. This man was murdered and his death made to look like a suicide."

"And you can say categorically it is?"

"Yes. Look, to plunge a sword into one's own chest cavity takes strength and leverage. Here take this stick." Gamaliel handed Loukas a stick he retrieved from the ground. "Now, position it as if it were a sword and you were going to shove it into your innards. There, you see? Your shoulders are hunched forward in order to grasp what would be the hilt, and you are leaning forward. That is the natural way one would stand if he were attempting to kill himself in that fashion. When the sword goes in, he will fall forward on his sword and it is the fall that insures the wound will be lethal. As you can see, this man, who, by the way, is an orthodox, practicing Jew, is lying on his back. Someone dispatched him and then borrowed his sword to finish the business."

"For the moment I will concede to your version but...how was he, as you say, dispatched?"

"A very good question. There are footprints here."

"Well, there would be, the girl who found him, the old man who sent for us. Any number of people could have come in here."

Gamaliel scanned the ground with the diligence he would an old papyrus scrap, seeking a clue, a hint to its origins or authenticity. His gaze moved to the inn wall and finally climbed to its top.

"How does one get to the roof? Innkeeper, I need to walk on your roof."

The innkeeper bustled over and led them into the interior. "There are several ways to the roof. It is a feature of the inn. There is the main ladder over against the wall. I keep watch on that. Access to the roof is a privilege for which a guest must pay."

"I see. And the other entries?"

"Two of my guest rooms over on that side have a separate means of climbing up. Guests pay extra for a separate room and more still for a roof way."

"People sleep on the roof on hot nights?" The innkeeper nodded. "So, innkeeper, did anyone go up on the roof by way of your ladder?"

"No, no one."

"You're sure of that? Very well, who occupied the rooms with access?"

"It was a slow night. I rented one to a merchant from Gaza, one to a gentleman like yourself, and the last, the one with no access, was used by a man who, I believe came from the Galilee, but I can't be sure."

"Did any of these men have a visitor, or did any of them seem to know one or the other?"

"I can't say. Many people crowd in here during the night for company and refreshment. People are leery of walking the streets at night except when the patrol comes by. Then they will walk behind them to their house or wherever. Until the patrol comes along, they stay here. It is very good for business."

"No doubt. So, you can tell me nothing about the men with access to the roof, what they did, what they said, to whom they talked?"

"Sorry, no. It is something we are trained not to do, if you follow me."

Gamaliel snorted in disgust and rolled his eyes. "Very well, show me your roof. Come along, Loukas. You wanted to know how our guard was dispatched. The answer is on the roof."

Chapter XXXI

That the inn's roof had been used the night before seemed obvious. Mats had been drawn up from below and one or two lay scattered in the center, evidence of at least one person using the space for sleeping. The tops of the inn's walls rose up from the surface and formed ledges which circumscribed it. The roof sloped toward either side wall which was punctuated periodically with holes to allow the rain or the infrequent snow's melting to drain away. Against the ledge that was formed by the wall facing the alley where Zach's body was found, two cups and the scraps of some loaves evidenced that at least two people shared a meal there. Gamaliel picked up the cups and held them to his nose. He dipped his finger into each in turn and tasted the dregs.

"You said Ali's wonderful mixture was composed of something akin to *hul gil*, mustard, and wine as a carrier. Do I have that right?"

Loukas straightened up from peering over the edge at the dead man, his body now covered with a cloak. "Yes. That is correct as near as I can tell."

"It is the mustard that causes the burning sensation?"

"Yes."

"And that would limit how much of the medicine anyone might consume at one time. Too large a dose would burn one's mouth and the person taking it would probably spit it out?"

"Very likely unless, like poor Draco, the pain in his body superseded that in his mouth, or he was desperate for death and ignored it. But, yes, a normal person's dose would be regulated by the mustard."

"If the mustard were not included, would the other substance be distasteful?"

"I don't know, but assuming you are correct in implying it is a variant of *hul gil,* no, it would most likely be undetectable and therefore dangerous to use as a medicine except under the strict supervision of a care giver. All this is leading up to something. Are you going to tell me what that is?"

"Yes, I will shortly, but note first the ledge in front of you and compare it to the ledge on either side. What do you see?"

"Here in front the tiles are relatively clean whereas on either side…" he spun and took in the other three wall tops. "They are variously dusty. Someone sat here."

"Our guardsman sat there. He drank from this cup, went numb or suffered a dislocation of place and time. A shove sent him over the side. He wouldn't have felt a thing and the fall likely broke his neck. At the very least he would have been stunned. Once on the ground, he did not rise and his murderer needed only to slip out the door, borrow his sword, and make sure he would never speak of what he knew."

"Or his murderer thought he knew."

"Very good, yes, or thought he knew."

"So, he *was* murdered."

"As I said. Now, we must hurry back. It will be Shabbat soon. We must get back to Jerusalem and have this man in the ground right away."

Gamaliel clambered down the crude stairs and began barking orders. Within moments, a messenger had been sent to the Temple. Stretcher bearers assembled and the body was sent on its way to Loukas' cave/storeroom, and the two friends were speeding as fast as Gamaliel's by now weary legs could carry him toward the city.

Loukas slowed to keep pace with Gamaliel, "You asked the question earlier. What was Zach doing way out here?"

"He had been ordered to end his investigations, remember? And he told us he intended to continue them anyway. It seems certain someone offered to help him."

"Who?"

"It is just a guess, mind you, but I think it was either you or me."

"What? I never."

"No, of course not, but suppose someone dressed as a rabbi or who posed as your or my friend, met Zach with the offer to help. Wouldn't he go almost anywhere?"

"Ah. And our stalker can do that?"

"Why not?"

They were within the boundary set for the Jerusalem Shabbat journey just as the third star twinkled in the sky. They slowed their pace.

"Where to, Rabban? I mean, the body will be temporarily interred and, with you allowing the Law to be stretched a bit, safe enough for now."

"If you will humor me, I would like to see to the body and then I hope you will accompany me to my house where we can consider this new development. Also, I want you to test the dregs in this cup and then we will discuss whether another visit to the Street of the Herbalists is in order."

"It will be late when I return home."

"Probably. You should not be out and about on Shabbat night. You may spend the night with me and in the morning return home."

"I do not want to put you out."

"It will be my pleasure to have company. Since my wife died and my children grew up, it is lonely in my house. I will welcome the change."

"Then it is settled."

The man standing in the shadows had counted on Shabbat to insure Loukas' return. He also assumed, incorrectly, that the rabban would go directly to his own home. He watched as the men carrying a dead body climbed the hill and entered Loukas' courtyard. So, they would stow it in the hillside for the time being. Next, Loukas and the rabban arrived. The Jew seemed out of breath. That fact brought a smile to the lurker's face. Not much of a smile—a smirk, in point of fact. Now it would be just a matter of time. The rabban would leave, then the bearers would leave, and Loukas would be alone except for the servant. He would wait.

As he expected, the bearers, their task done, retreated into the city to seek lodgings. They could not return to their homes. That is, those who lived in Bethany could not return until this time tomorrow evening. He watched as they scattered. When they had cleared the street, the man assumed the rabbi and the physician would be essentially alone. There was the possibility of the servant, but that should pose no difficulty. He started to cross the street to the courtyard wall. He would vault that, if the gate was locked, and deal with one or both as needed. He had taken only a half step when the house door opened yet again. Loukas and the rabban stepped out and turned and headed up the slope toward the Sheep Gate. What now? He guessed that if he had to accost the physician and his meddling friend in the street, so be it. He needed to have done with this. He loosened the knife from its sheath and took another step. The best plan, he thought, would be to make his move before his prey entered the city. Run up, a quick stab in the neck on one and slash on the throat of the other. Shabbat or not, the streets in the city would be crowded. Best to do it here. He picked up his pace to overtake them.

Within two or three cubits of the rabban's broad back, Gamaliel raised his arm in greeting. A column of Temple guards wheeled around the corner and immediately surrounded the assassin's targets. He turned away, waiting to see how this would play out. He had no compunctions about confronting a physician and an old rabbi, but a half dozen armed guards was another matter. The two groups fell into animated conversation as together they made their way to the Sheep Gate and the city.

The now familiar itch on the back of his neck prompted Gamaliel to pause and gaze back down the road toward Loukas' house. A man stood motionless in the street staring back at him. His appearance labeled him as one of the Nation, yet there he stood with the gates about to slam shut and with no apparent intention of returning to his home to keep Shabbat.

"What sort of Jew have we here?" he wondered.

"Rabban," the Captain of the Guards said, "we must hurry. They are closing the gate."

"Yes, yes, coming."

The party marched through the Sheep Gate and it banged shut behind them. For the residents of the city Shabbat had begun. The appearance of the star and the sound of the shofar from the Pinnacle may have marked the official start of Shabbat, but, for the practical-minded, the closing of the great gates into the city made the day a reality.

The sound of massive doors slamming—those close by and those far away—echoed across the city. Except for one lone man, the street was empty. The sky darkened as the sun dropped over the western wall. He stamped his foot in frustration. The rabbi's angry god had foiled him again. He cursed his luck and strode back down the road toward Bethany, his fists in tight white balls. Shabbat had no hold on him, and he was also sure that the stupid innkeeper would not care where he came from, when, or how, as long as he had money to spend.

Chapter XXXII

Gamaliel and Loukas said their farewells to the guards and assured them they would talk again after Shabbat. From now on, no work could be done until the next evening. Investigating murders, except those described in holy writ, would be work.

"What then will we do for the next twenty-four hours?" Loukas kept Shabbat in theory rather than practice. He had convinced himself that if he moved slowly and his actions were not overtly selfish, he had satisfied the conditions of Shabbat. The fact that no shops were open, nor were merchants willing to transact business that day, made it impossible for him to do much anyway. His very thin piety was shared by a large percentage of the country's rural population. Inside the city, not so many.

"We will contemplate the greatness of the Lord. Do not make a face at me, Loukas. It is a very useful way to pass the time. You should try it. You might be surprised at the results."

"With respect, Rabban, I do not see how the solution to a murder, multiple murders which, in fact, may or may not be connected, can be forthcoming by shuffling through old sheets and singing psalms. There are facts to be analyzed and sorted. How does the death of this man Zach relate to the Temple man? Who is following us and why? And, once again the nagging question, why put a corpse in the Holy of Holies?"

"I have found Shabbat to be the single most useful time in which to accomplish exactly what you suggest."

"So, you are not going to waste a day contemplating the mightiness of the Lord?"

"Quite the contrary. That is exactly what I will do. I discovered over the years that often the best way to solve a problem is to ignore it for a time. Somehow, that part of my mind that I cannot control and which is silent most of the time seems to churn through details without any conscious effort on my part and the next day or the one after that, the answer pops into the part of my mind I do control. The beauty of the Lord's commandment that we keep Shabbat is because we need it, not because He wants it. Our minds need it, and certainly our bodies need it. So, tomorrow we will rest and contemplate other things. We have food and drink set aside for us. We may stroll here and there and resist thinking about our problem. You will see, Loukas. You will see."

"Not even reading?"

"Well, I think it might be permissible if we were to read selectively."

"Selectively? As in what?"

"You might wish to start in Kings. My student Saul thought the murdered man might have some connection with the story of Joab. You do recall the story of Joab and his perfidious relationship to King David? No? Then you should start there. Personally I don't think Saul is on to anything, but he is an astute young man and I always listen to him even when I don't agree with what he is saying. You must meet him sometime. Then there is the story of Uzza and the Ark, and if you have time, take a peek at Exodus and the directions *Ha Shem* gives for the construction of the Tabernacle. You might find that useful."

"I don't have any alternative, do I?"

"None at all."

The two men ate their evening meal of cold lamb, beans spiced with pepper, and bread. They read until the light failed and then slept. For the morning, Benyamin had left them cheese, boiled eggs, another loaf, and goat's milk that had been kept cool in the basement.

"The Tabernacle, Gamaliel, there is a disjunction between what the Lord wished for and what King Herod produced." Loukas said after they had settled in the atria near the small fountain.

"Herod, Zerubbabel, Solomon, and David, if he had had his way. Men seem to think that the Lord will be pleased with us if we try to improve on his designs. It is the arrogance of humanity and it invariably ends in disaster."

"You think this Temple an extravagance and will end in disaster?"

"I didn't used to, but now I have my doubts. It is so large and ornate. The money spent on its construction would pay for who knows how many meals for the poor. It annoys me when our high priest turns a blind eye to the extravagance of the Temple party and obsesses over the teaching attributed to some rabbi or another. Oh well, there is no use in complaining about it. For better or worse the Temple will be finished as Herod planned for it to be. I hope that if I am correct in my thinking that it is overreaching, the Lord will forgive me for my too human vanity and let it pass."

"If He doesn't?"

"I will not allow myself to contemplate that possibility."

"Very well then, here is another question for you on this most unusual Shabbat. Why is it so important for the high priest and the *kohanim* to hold to the notion that the Temple man died at the hands of the Lord?"

"You have crossed the line, Physician. I said we must not try to work on our puzzle this day."

"This is only peripheral to the puzzle, Rabban. There is no way the high priest's version is the answer. Thus, my question is to a different point entirely."

"Ah? Very well. The simplest answer I can offer comes from scripture. *Fear of the Lord is the beginning of wisdom.*"

"I don't understand."

"Add Proverbs and maybe Job to your reading list."

When Shabbat ended at the twelfth hour, Gamaliel lit some lamps and pulled sheets of papyrus from the stack on his writing table. "Now," he said, "we can find out what the silent portions of our minds have uncovered for us."

"I must confess that I didn't hear anything from that part. I regret that the noisy part that I control, as you say, stayed busy all day. I am sorry. I do not have your self-discipline."

"No matter. You tried. For now it is enough. What conclusions did your undisciplined mind discover?"

"I think I want to know what was in that cup that you found on the roof. I want to know if it is the same substance that Draco drank, and if it is, as I suspect, I think the next thing we should do is to return to the Street of the Herbalists."

"Do you think we will be followed?"

"I don't know. There is only one way to find out."

"Indeed. As for my unconscious mind, it occurred to me that the innkeeper said something very significant when we asked him who had rented his rooms."

"You think the merchant is our man?"

"No, no, that wasn't what I meant. He said 'he was one of you.' I wondered about that. This morning it came to me."

"I am not following. What?"

"He assumed that because the man dressed like me, he must *be* like me. People mistake you for a Greek, do they not?"

"All the time."

"And that is because you dress in the manner of the Greeks. If you wore robes like mine, they would not think so."

"Of course. I am still not with you."

"As we approached the gate, I turned and looked down your road. There was a man standing there who would be 'one of us', if we were to guess at his nationality and profession."

"And?"

"And he made no move to treat the day for what it was, or was about to be."

"Sorry…?"

"He did not seem to be preparing for Shabbat, as his appearance suggested he ought. You see, we make sweeping assumptions based on what a person looks like. The fact that the innkeeper said his boarder was one of us meant we dismissed the idea that he might have been anything or anyone else."

"You think he was from another country?"

"No, no, you miss my point. He wasn't one of us at all. By dressing a certain way, our killer or killers could be hiding in plain sight."

"And you conclude?"

"I think I have had a look at our killer—several looks, in fact, and so have you."

Chapter XXXIII

Benyamin entered the atrium with a plate of fruit and the news that the captain of the Temple guard waited in the foyer. At least he thought that was who waited at the door. Since the caller had dressed for the street rather than duty, Benyamin confessed he couldn't confirm it. Gamaliel ignored the fruit and motioned Loukas to follow. They met the guard and three of his subordinates at the door. As Benyamin had said, the guards were not in their usual dress. Instead, they had donned the clothes of working men and could pass for anything from drover to laborer, anything that is except what they were, four very fit and tough young men, including their captain.

"Splendid, you are ready."

"As you requested, Rabban. You said we could help you find the killer of our comrade and the perpetrator of the obscenity in the Temple, and here we are."

"Indeed. Loukas, we will have company on our foray back to the Herbalists."

"So it would seem, but won't we be a little obvious? Six men who obviously have no place on the street careening around asking questions?"

"We will not be together. These men will shadow us. If we are followed, they will be watching. If there is danger, they will intercede. You and I will be asking the questions."

"As to that, Rabban, you have the brains we need to solve

this puzzle, but your very presence is intimidating. If you start asking questions, I doubt that you will get the answers you seek."

"How then?"

"First, I think you should, like these men, and our killer if you are right about him, wear something other than your rabbinical robes and certainly remove your chain of office."

"I can do that."

"Good, then you should let me do the questioning. I will ask in Greek, as that is how I am known on that street. They may or may not know and certainly won't care if I am of the Faith, but they expect me to address them in Greek."

"Will you know the questions to ask?"

"You will tell them to me."

"It is not as easy as that, my friend. I think I shall be a contemporary of yours from…where shall I be from? Gaza. The innkeeper said one of his boarders came from there. They are enough like us for me to be one, but different enough to not raise suspicions."

"You were on the street some few days ago. As a man from Gaza or not, you are unmistakable. No, Rabban, on second thought, you are too hard to hide."

"I take your point. Yehudah, have you a suggestion?" The guardsman raised his eyebrows and shrugged.

"Can we acquire a sedan, do you think?"

"A sedan chair? You mean one with curtains?"

"Exactly. I will sit in it. I will be your client from afar who wishes to remain anonymous, a person of mystery but possessing few scruples. You are making inquiries for me. My carriers here," Gamaliel waved at two of the larger guards, "will park me near enough for me to hear. If I need you to pursue a particular line of questioning I will cough. You then will 'consult' with your patron."

"That will work, but first we must find a sedan."

"A far easier problem to solve than the murder of several guards and an invader of the Holy of Holies, I should think."

They found a curtained chair and with Gamaliel ensconced within its depths, the party made their way to the souk and the Street of the Herbalist. It wasn't really a street, more a cul-de-sac off a larger street, but time and custom had declared it a street and so it was. Gamaliel had cautioned Loukas to begin the questioning slowly, and the term he used was glancingly, by which he meant that Loukas should try to avoid the obvious. Loukas shot him a sour look.

Loukas spoke literate Greek, rather than the *koiné* heard on the street, and Gamaliel, much to his distress, could not always follow him, particularly as he remained confined in his chair and out of sight. In addition, the sun bore down and he dared not open the curtains, which increased his frustration. But by the time they had made their way halfway down the street, several items had become clear. The place he'd always thought of as Hannah was in fact called Hana. The pronunciation of the word by Ali had not been a reflection of his accent. He had pronounced it correctly. The word, one of the herbalists who hailed from the north somewhere— Gamaliel did not hear where—and said it was of his tongue, meant bliss.

Bliss? Not beauty or passion, but bliss. Were they all that different? After all, when shifting from one language to another certain nuances of meaning can be lost. Could Hana, unlike its Hebrew cognate, Hannah, be a man's name? Now that would be something he'd like to know, but who to ask? Gamaliel coughed.

"Ask him if Hana is a man or a woman," he murmured to Loukas.

"Rabban, that does not make any sense. What pretext shall I use to ask it? We are in the middle of discussing the various proportions of *hul gil* and mustard—"

"Find a way. Tell him your client is not quite right in the head, I don't know, but find a way."

"Not quite right in the head. That part should be easy enough." Loukas returned to his questioning. "Yes, I see, one to ten for small children. By the way, before it slips my mind, I am told there is an apothecary on the street, a woman, named Hana. Is that correct?"

The shopkeeper grinned widely and displayed a set of extremely crooked teeth. "No, no, Hana was a man's name. The person who kept the shop which is burned to the ground— you see over there—called himself Hana. I do not think Hana was his real name. Some of the other shopkeepers might know. He was not a friendly person."

"I see. Is there a reason why he was thought to be unfriendly?"

The storekeeper's eyes rolled to one side. "Aside from the fact he was an Egyptian and, to some of us, an interloper, he had something that some of the others wanted him to stop selling."

"He sold whatever it was to men from the palace and the Romans."

"I did not tell you that."

"No, of course you didn't. And these people who resented the sales, would that have included you?"

"I am a merchant. I do not like to see my business slip away to another, and yes, of course, I wished he would share his secret or stop selling it. I would feel that way about anyone I compete against, but I was not with those who may have felt more strongly, and I do not burn down shops."

"Of course you don't. These others, who would they be?"

The shopkeeper glanced over his shoulder and studied the street and his face became unreadable. "It is not for me to say, but...."

"Yes?"

"They called themselves Assyrians, but Parthia is what they meant, I think."

"Cough."

"Thank you, sir. I will return for some wild mustard in a while." Loukas stepped up to the sedan chair. "Yes?"

"Move on to the next store. Push very hard about this Hana person and what he was selling. Also, find out where he came from."

"I don't need to. We can leave, I think."

"Don't...what do you mean?"

"It is about the *hul gil.* I am convinced that this Hana had a more powerful variety, and he had a monopoly on its sale, or nearly so. Since he did not seem willing to share the secret or the product, he was murdered, you could say, to reestablish equilibrium in the marketplace. I am sure of it."

"But what of his origins?"

"He is said to be from Egypt, but it is confusing. This shop-keeper intimated that Parthians were at odds with him. There is always prejudice in the market and Egyptians are thought to be less than honest."

"Are they?"

"No more so than eighty of a hundred others who sell here. One must always be careful when purchasing anything, Rabban."

"Thank you for that. So, you think we are done here?"

"Yes. And Yehudah is signaling that he has something to tell us. We should go."

Chapter XXXIV

Gamaliel, borne like royalty, or perhaps more like a successful courtesan, left the street in style, carried up by two burly guardsmen and followed by a meager but well set up entourage consisting of the captain of the guard, Loukas the Physician, and one other. Their exit from the herbalists was noted by a few and tracked carefully by one man in particular. When they had disposed of the chair and found a quiet spot where they could sit and have refreshment, Gamaliel called them to order much as he would his students.

"Yehudah, you signaled that you had seen something important. Were we followed?"

"No, Excellency, it's not that. I suppose we might have been, but I saw no evidence of that. What caught my eye was a person I thought I recognized. Then I wasn't sure. It seemed so unlikely. Can a person have a double—I mean of course he could have a twin—but is there another way that could be?"

"Possibly. It is more likely the person who seemed to be someone else is that person after all. You thought you recognized someone and then doubted it was the person you thought it was for some reason. Am I close enough?"

"Yes, you see, this person should not have been on the street, but there he was."

"Why shouldn't he have been on the street?"

"Well, I thought I saw one of the priests. This particular cohort of *kohanim* is still on duty, is it not? If so, he should be at the temple, not wandering the streets of the souk."

"But he was. Anything else?"

"If he was a priest, and if he had permission to wander off from his assignment, why would he be dressed as merchant selling cheap trinkets?"

"No, Yehudah, the question is why wouldn't a man who wished to blend in to his surroundings become the very thing one would expect to see in a certain place? How better to hide in the souk than to be a part of the souk and…"

Gamaliel stopped in mid sentence and stared off into space. His mouth dropped open and Loukas, aware of the numerous flies that buzzed about their table worried one would sail in.

Finally Gamaliel's jaw snapped shut and he stood.

"My friends, I believe we have turned a corner. There is a long journey still ahead of us, but today we have made genuine progress. I must return home and study."

"And I must see to my patients. I have been away too long. My servant is new and will not know how to cope." Loukas rose and dropped some coins on the table.

"Loukas, how long has this new man of yours been employed?"

"A few days."

"How did you come by him?"

"When Ali heard of Draco's condition, he left to pick up the medicine you saw, and he brought a young man back with him. He said he found him standing idle in the marketplace seeking employment. He said he had some skill, and so I brought him in. Ali thought it seemed a fortuitous coincidence."

"Loukas, send him away."

"What, dismiss the servant? How will I manage?"

Gamaliel turned to Yehudah. "Would it be possible for you to loan one of your men to the physician for a few days? I will see to his pay, if necessary."

"Wait a moment, Rabban. I am perfectly capable of paying my help. Why must I dismiss the servant?"

"Call it a hunch, a feeling, a prickling on the back of my neck, Loukas. Do this as a favor for me. If I am wrong, you can have your young man back later. I do not like...what did you say?...'fortuitous coincidences.'"

"Oren can be yours, Physician. He is a good man and has served in a household before he joined us."

"Can he use a sword?" Gamaliel asked.

"Most excellently, sir."

"Use a sword? Gamaliel, what are you getting at?"

"As I said, a prickling—"

"At the back of your neck. It could be too much sun."

"You forget. I was in the curtained chair. No sun in there, just the heat from it."

"I still don't understand, but I will go along. You will explain all this later, I assume."

"Of course, all in good time. It is a matter of perception. We see what we are accustomed to see. A rabbi is a rabbi. We don't ask him to prove it to our satisfaction. We see a man appropriately dressed, teaching twelve or more men in the marketplace or up at Solomon's Porch and we say, 'there is a rabbi.' Whether he is one or is not is never questioned. The same is true with priests, guards, men selling trinkets on the street, and servants, sad to say. Only when something seems amiss do we question our first impression. Yehudah saw a seller who seemed not to be what he pretended. I am convinced it is the clue, the first indication we need to grasp if we are to solve our problem. Go to your patients, my friend. Take Oren and send the boy away. Yehudah, will you see me home and tell me more about this seller of trinkets?"

The seller of trinkets, as Yehudah had made him out to be, followed the entourage for a few streets. He had the feeling that the man who'd joined the party as it left the street had recognized him somehow. He allowed himself to get close enough to see who made up the group. He recognized Loukas, the physician, of course, but none of the others. The tall man who seemed to be in charge of the others, the one who he guessed had found him out, seemed familiar as well. Who or in what capacity he knew this person eluded him at the moment. He felt sure it would come to him later, but now he sensed that caution should be his mode.

He guessed the passenger in the sedan must have been the rabban of the Sanhedrin. Why could he not avoid that man? Would this nation of ridiculously religious people be any the worse off if its meddling rabban were to die? He spun on his heel and melted into the crowd. The physician had to return to his home soon. He would wait for him there. Now there was no mistaking what those two men knew or would soon guess. He had already wasted too much time on this project. More goods and men were on the way to the city from the east and he needed to divert them, which was his way of internalizing the fact that the goods would be stolen and their bearers killed. He might try bribing these men, but past experience taught him that men who accepted bribes were likely to reverse their loyalty for a larger bribe. Either way, people who accepted bribes couldn't be trusted. And, of course, there were always ninnies like the two night guards who, once fooled, had to be eliminated before they ran bawling to their overlords about what they had done and begging for forgiveness. Idiots. Luckily most of the coins he'd tempted them with were still on their person when he finally caught up with them. So, his investment in their willing stupidity had been small. And then there were the regulars to Hana and its predecessor, like his former accomplice who worked for *hul gil* and who also had to be held accountable. Those types were especially unreliable.

But bribery would not remove the threat posed by the rabban of the Sanhedrin and his friend. Either he would have to eliminate them or they had to be sent up another blind alley. This time it had to succeed.

Chapter XXXV

Gamaliel had had a good day, that is, if unraveling the circumstances surrounding a death is the thing one enjoys. Notwithstanding doing so was never his desire, it had been a good day. At last he found a crack in a wall that had up until now had seemed impenetrable. It was all about appearances, and things not being what they seemed. He had a start, but what next? Did he have a reasonable suspect? Yes, he did. Was his suspect a certainty? Not really, not yet. Soon, maybe. The suspect had both means and opportunity. Did he have a motive? The answer to that question still eluded him, but he felt that *hul gil* would be at the center somehow. But how, and more important, why? And what of this rift between the Egyptians and the Assyrians? Not Assyrians, Parthians. Did anybody call themselves Assyrians anymore? He'd had a conversation about that earlier. With whom? He needed to think about that. It was important somehow.

As for *hul gil*, it could be purchased easily anywhere in the streets and most, if not all, healers prescribed it. So how did it become a substance over which men would fight and die?

He'd set a task for his servant before his trip to the souk. He was to call on the one man in the city who Gamaliel knew would have the information he needed to answer that question.

"Benyamin, where you successful in acquiring the scrolls I asked for?"

The servant waved in the direction of a table set in the corner of the room. "Yes, but their keeper did not part with them easily. He only relented when I told him they were for you."

Gamaliel smiled, lifted the cracked and tattered sheaf, and inspected them with a critical eye. "I will guard them with my life."

"I told him as much."

"I will have my evening meal early and afterwards I want to be left completely alone. You understand? No visitors, no interruptions. None at all."

"Yes, Excellency, you wish to entertain no visitors."

Gamaliel made a trip to the *mikvah*, washed, said his prayer before the evening meal, and ate. Afterward, refreshed in body and spirit, he set about reading the scraps of papyrus and scrolls. It would require yet another extra measure of oil in his reading lamp for a long night with his nose pressed close to dusty sheets of papyrus.

The cultivation of plants had never interested him before. Now he found it fascinating—at least one particular plant.

Caiaphas, the high priest, found himself in a high dudgeon. In spite of his warnings, the rabban of the Sanhedrin remained adamant that the body found in the Temple was a murder victim. Even if true, no good could come from an investigation. The man was dead, the Nation would be served best if the reason for his death was what the general populace believed it to be—an irate deity had carried out the fate taught in every synagogue and shule in the Nation. Yet, Gamaliel kept banging on the gong of murder, not the acceptable alternative. In so doing, the rabban had upset palace officialdom in some way. He ignored warnings. But that wasn't all.

Gamaliel, who could waste time on that insignificant death, refused to pursue his official duties. His charge as rabban of the Sanhedrin made him the preserver and maintainer of Orthodoxy, yet he refused to rein in these itinerant rabbis who were confusing the people across the breadth and length of the land.

It wasn't just that one from Galilee, though he was the worst, but the whole phalanx of the misinformed and misguided. True, most of them would yield to the Temple Pharisees' persistent questioning and give up. But a few remained. And Yeshua ben Josef in particular needed to be silenced.

Gamaliel said that Yeshua from the Galilee had become an obsession for him. Had he? Caiaphas shook his head. Not at all. He had a duty! They both had a duty. Why was Gamaliel shirking his? The high priest paced the floor from one end to the other mumbling to himself and grinding one fist into the palm of the other hand. How could he maintain the position that rabbi Yeshua did no harm? People flocked to him, especially since the Baptizer had been killed by that weak king. Did the rabban even listen to him? Mustard seed, he'd said? Outrageous! *Ha Shem* did not choose them because His kingdom resembled mustard plants. What idiocy! The Kingdom is like the cedars of Lebanon…well, maybe not them. They were all harvested by now. The Temple then, yes the Temple, built to last forever, to stand against the ravages of time and conquerors, whoever they were and whenever they came. The Temple would endure forever. Mustard seed—bah!

Having reassured himself of the permanence of the Nation and his position in it, he retreated to his bedchamber and settled in for the night. Outside, people moved about. Some with duties to perform or obligations that kept them out. Some others lurked in corners and shadows with less noble purposes in mind, and at least one with murder in his heart.

But the high priest would sleep well.

Trailing the physician offered no challenge. He felt cheated. He did not consider it a rational thought, but he did enjoy the game and his man refused to play. The physician either suspected no one to be on his trail in spite of his sure knowledge that he'd been followed earlier, or he had a child-like trust in the essential goodness of people. In either case, his tracker had no problems following him to his home. The presence of the other man caused some concern. If he lingered in Loukas' company too long he could become an obstacle. Why were the two of them walking together? He watched as they paused and the physician seemed to peer into the other man's eyes. So, this second man must be a patient. If so, there should be no problem. The physician would treat him and he would leave. Then, the physician's servant would leave the gate unlatched. He would have an easy entry to the house. He could be in and out in no time at all.

The two men disappeared into Loukas' house and the tracker slipped into the deepening shadows across the street to wait. Soon, one more minor difficulty would be eliminated. Then he could find the others, remove them from his list, finish this business, and go home. Too bad about the physician, he didn't deserve it, but with his death the rabban would be forced to shift his attention elsewhere. He waited. The door opened and the servant stepped through. He turned and, arms spread, seemed to be pleading with Loukas...why me? The physician only shrugged and said something the watcher could not make out. Disconsolate, the servant walked away.

Loukas' shadow met him in the street. "What has happened?"

"I have been dismissed. He has brought another man in to take my place. I don't know what to do."

"Dismissed? Did he give a reason?"

"No, only that if I returned on the first day next week he might reconsider."

What could this mean? How could he have made a connection between this boy and..."Come with me. I have a room in an inn. You know Bethany? Good. You can stay with me and we will see what we can do for you in the morning."

The two set off through the Kidron Valley. Something less than an hour later the watcher arrived at the inn in Bethany—alone.

Chapter XXXVI

Gamaliel expected Loukas to join him early in the morning, about the third hour. It was nearly midday when he arrived. He did not look happy.

"Trouble, Loukas? I thought you'd be here sooner."

"And well I might have been had I not taken your advice about my servant. Thanks to you, I spent the better part of the morning attending to an inquiry about that man's death."

"That man? What man is dead, and why were you at the inquiry, and what has any of this to do with advice from me to sack your servant?"

"What man? My servant, of course. You said I should send him away. I did. This morning someone stumbled over his corpse in the brush at the foot of the Mount of Olives. I put him out in the night, as you suggested, and some thief or brigand must have found him wandering about in the dark with no place to go and killed him—stabbed him with a knife."

"And I am to blame because you believe that if you had not taken my advice, or if I had not given it, he wouldn't have been out in the dark and an easy mark for a killer."

"Yes, I do."

"I will accept the responsibility for the man's death, but I will also say that it is equally likely that had you not put him out as I suggested, you, not the boy, might have been the recipient of a mortal knife wound."

"I do not see how."

"No, I am sure you don't. You will have to take it on faith for the nonce. Now, to proceed, I spent the night reading about the cultivation of plants. Are you aware of the intricacies attached to the art of plant cultivation? It is much more complex than I ever imagined."

"What do I know of plant cultivation? I know you plant a seed or take a cutting and if it is watered and in good soil, it grows. What more is there?"

"That, my friend, is not cultivation. That is merely sowing and reaping. Cultivation is the art of improving the plant or its fruit. You cull out the plants that do not bear good fruit, or seeds, in the case of grain, and keep only the best and heartiest. For flowers and spices you selectively breed the most beautiful and aromatic. In time you get a better return from your planting or you get a product closer to what you really want."

"I am impressed with your new-found expertise and I am sure cultivation of flowers and roots is critical to the health and welfare of the Nation. What has any of that to do with murder? We have the Temple man, the burnt storekeeper, Zach the guard, and now my servant, all dead and cold in their graves or soon will be. I realize you believe the first three are related, though there is no evidence to support it. Are you supposing my dead servant is also connected and if so, how do plants, flowers, seeds and their cultivation relate to any of them?"

"You are still angry with me. I am sorry for the young man. I am persuaded that in the end you will see that I was right in my advice to send him away, and, indeed, the murders are related and cultivation of some plants…well, one in particular, is critical to our inquiries."

"How? That is like connecting the moon and the sun."

"If I understand your Greek astronomers correctly, not to mention the odd eastern astrologers who wander through from time to time, the sun and moon are most definitely connected… indirectly, perhaps, but connected. The linkage between the several murders is made through what I spent the night reading."

"The cultivation of plants? My servant, a stranger scorched and left in the Holy of Holies, a clerk of some sort in a shop on the Street of the Herbalists, and Zach the guard are connected by plant lore?"

"You left out the two bribe takers."

"Fine, add them as well, and you insist they are all parts of a larger piece?"

"Exactly."

"I will have to take your word on that. Oh, speaking of Zach? You were right. He was most certainly murdered. I looked at his body this morning and he has a broken neck. He was alive when the sword was shoved in him, and he would have died anyway, but his killer shortened the time."

"You can tell all that from looking at a body?"

"Yes. The broken neck was obvious when I looked and he had bled profusely from the stab wound. Therefore, he was alive, but not for long either way."

"It is my turn to take your word. Well done, Loukas."

Ali bin Selah had spent a restless night reassessing his position and options. He had a decision to make. He could cut his losses and quit the city, this time for good, leaving it to others better prepared to pursue this sordid business than he, or he could press on. The former would leave the decision of who sold what and to whom up in the air temporarily and would inevitably end in a much larger and more violent response in the future. On the other hand, he would be free and clear, able to return to the city in the future with a reasonable explanation for his behavior, should he need one, and able to contact Loukas in the future. However, one thought held him in place—what did the rabban of the Sanhedrin suspect or know? By reputation the man wielded substantial power in the city. If he persisted in his inquiries, things might come to light and that could create difficulties for many people, including Ali and his associates.

Since he'd revealed himself in disguise to Loukas, and by accident to Gamaliel as well, his presence in the city would be known and suspect. If he made a clean breast of it—found some way to explain it all away, he might still be able to finish what he started. That would have serious consequences for the two men. He would have to weigh the merits of each course of action. And then, he had others to answer to and that had to be factored into his decision.

He wrapped the still unfamiliar robe around his shoulders and set off for Jerusalem. He made a point of avoiding the cluster of people at the foot of the Mount of Olives. No good could come from mingling with that crowd. If he hurried he could be at the Sheep Gate by the sixth hour.

◇◇◇

"Very well, you have my attention, rabban. How does the science of plants connect with my dead servant and the others?"

"You remember our discussion about mustard? You mentioned that there existed a difference between the wild mustard and that which you had in your garden?"

"I did?"

"I think you did. Maybe I misremember. Sometimes I cannot distinguish between what someone has told me and what I have just read. Nevertheless, you do remember the high priest's distress at the rabbi's description of the kingdom being like a mustard seed and so on?"

"Vaguely."

"Well it is the same thing."

"There are times, Gamaliel when your thought processes make me manic. You assume that everyone can make these heuristic leaps as quickly and as easily as you do. I cannot. You must walk me through the thing step by step."

"You don't see?"

"No."

"Wild mustard, on the one hand, can be very strong and one mixes it with honey or whatever in a poultice carefully. The sort that most people grow is weaker but more quantifiable. There you see?"

"May the gods of medicine have mercy on me. You are making no sense at all."

"Tut, one must not swear an oath, even to pagan nonentities. I am sorry. Look, it is very simple. Wild mustard is strong, but unruly in the garden. If you plant it, it will take over the garden. It is an invasive and undesirable plant. But through careful cultivation it has been tamed like a wild camel to a form that behaves itself, but in the process of taming its predilection to invade every corner of the bed, it has lost some of its strength. There you see?"

"I see that I now know more about mustard growing than I probably need."

"The process to strengthen the mustard while keeping its noninvasive characteristic would be a good thing, would it not?"

"I suppose so. I still don't see how—"

"How about cultivating *hul gil?*"

"Where are you taking me?" Loukas evidently was not appeased by Gamaliel's half hearted apology and subsequent discourse on the merits of plant cultivation. "And what are you suggesting about the pain reliever?"

"That is two questions. I'll answer the first. You will need to mull over the second. In the meantime, we are going to call on a blind man to ask him what he might have seen on the day of the first murder."

Chapter XXXVII

"A blind man who sees and…I am having great difficulty staying with you, Rabban. Of course, you know that already. What blind man sees?"

"Isaiah tells us, in a somewhat different context, of course, *Then will the eyes of the blind see and the ears of the deaf be unstopped*…Do you remember my telling you about Jacob ben Aschi? He is the old *kohen* who has lost his sight. He comes to the Temple most days and talks, drinks a little wine, and sits in the sun when there is some to sit in. He is blind but 'sees' with his ears. Things you and I might miss, he will pick up because he must listen so closely. An inflection of a person's voice tells him things sighted people do not notice."

"And you think he has 'seen' something…I feel silly saying that. You think he may have heard something important?"

"It is what I hope will happen. I think it unlikely that the business of the body in the Temple is a simple matter of bribing two guards."

"An if he has, you should pardon the expression, seen nothing…?"

"It will not be the end of the world, but it will take us back a step or two."

"I will not be the one to stand in your way. I hope you are right—about this priest and about the servant. So, lead on. But—"

"Yes, yes, but. We will talk on the way and perhaps I can ease you mind on the *but*."

◇◇◇

Jacob ben Aschi arrived at the Temple somewhat later than his usual hour. He greeted the priests on duty as always and felt his way to the stool he occupied nearly every day. The *kohanim* had become accustomed to his presence over the years and would probably miss him if he failed to appear. He recognized Gamaliel's voice before the man himself rounded the corner.

"Greetings in the Name, Rabban. Who have you brought with you this morning?"

"And to you Jacob. This is my friend Loukas. He is a famous healer. We have come to ask you a question."

"A healer and a question, you say. What answers can a blind man give to questions? We do not see what happens around us."

"That is not true. You see into the hearts of men. Eyes are not required for that."

"It is the hearts of men you wish me to expose then?"

"In a manner of speaking. The day before the discovery of the travesty in the holy place, what did you hear? Recalling that day, did anything seem to have been out of place?"

The old man sat quietly for a while, his eyes empty of expression but a scowl on his face. "There was one thing, now that you mention it."

"Yes?"

"Give me a moment to remember. Yes…that was it. Yes, when the priests arrive there is always some commotion, confusion, particularly when it is a new cohort taking up its duties. If new members have been recently been added to the cohort, they must be instructed in the way, you could say. Our scriptures tell us what to do, but not always how to do it. That is true especially in this amazing Temple King Herod has bestowed on us. The instructions in the scrolls, you know, Rabban, are for a tabernacle, for a simpler time and place."

"Yes, it is a significant leap from a tent in the desert to this mammoth building. So?"

"So, it is to be expected that some, perhaps many, of the *kohen*, even those who've served before, will need guidance. So, hearing a fresh voice, a misunderstanding or mix-up or two is not unexpected. But now that I think of it…you know, as I cannot see; I cannot count except by keeping track of voices and there is no real reason for me to do it, but—"

"But you think something was not quite right." The old man pursed his lips. "Do you think there was one too many in the party?"

"Oh, as to that, I couldn't say. There is no fixed number in the cohorts, you know. There might be a rule, but in practical terms, the number will vary from cohort to cohort and day to day."

"Then what?"

"There was…it seemed to me, that is…one of the priests was out of place. He drifted to the edge of conversations, asked odd questions, that sort of thing. Nobody seemed to know him, at least not intimately. That is not unusual in itself, of course. Men are added and subtracted all the time. You take that boy, Josef ben Josef. He has been sent away already for his indiscretion on the morning of the discovery."

"I am sorry to hear that. If he hadn't been, what did you say, indiscreet? If he hadn't, that body might still be lying in there."

"Do not even think it, Rabban. Let me finish. This man's, this *kohen,* you understand, his voice, bespoke not just of inexperience, but of ignorance. You understand the difference? It is one thing to ask 'how' questions and quite another to indicate a total lack of knowledge about anything including the placement of things, areas of responsibility, and so on."

"One of the priests was not a priest."

"I think that might have been so. In the excitement, everybody forgot all about this person and as he has not been around since, there is nothing to remind us about him. Nothing, that is, until you came nosing around."

"Did you happen to mention this to anyone else?"

"I don't think so…maybe I did. Yes, now that you mention it. One of the guards was asking questions."

"One of the guards? Do you know who?"

"No, one of the night men, I think."

"Zach! Ah ha, Loukas, it is as I thought. More than guards. We must go."

Loukas held up a hand. "Wait, Rabban. I have a question for this man."

"You do? Really? "

Loukas scowled at him.

"Sorry, of course."

"Sir," Loukas said, and bent close to stare into the old man's sightless eyes, "what do you see?"

"What do I see? You are taunting a blind old man."

"No, I am very serious. I will rephrase my question. What, if anything, do you see?"

"I can tell you are very close to me, you block the light."

"You see light. And shadows? Shapes?"

"Yes, but not enough to go about my duties. Not enough to buy and sell, to plant and harvest, to read, or recognize you, or anyone else."

"No, but something. Very good. Come with me to my house. I can restore your sight."

"What?"

"Not perfectly. You will still need help with some things. Do you read? Never mind, someone can do that for you, but yes, there is hope."

"Are you a miracle worker?"

"No, but I talk to other healers from all over the world when they visit this city. I am a student, you could say. You have what are called cataracts. They are far advanced and block nearly everything from view. I have seen and been taught by a healer from India how to correct that problem, at least enough so that you do not need to be led from place to place."

"This is true?"

"Yes, more of your sight than you might suppose can be returned to you. Gamaliel, I will be busy with this man for the next several hours. I will rejoin you later."

A stunned Gamaliel could only mutter, "Very well, but be sure that Oren stays close by."

Chapter XXXVIII

When Gamaliel returned home, his mind was still so wrapped around the things that the blind *kohen* had said and Loukas' claim to be able to restore his sight that he didn't notice the three legionnaires stationed outside his door. He nearly stumbled into one of them. He regained his balance and returned his mind to the present. Legionnaires at his doorstep could only mean one thing. He shuddered at the thought. He stopped and spread his arms at his side, palms up.

"You are here to tell me the Prefect, the Honorable Pontius Pilate, wishes me to dance attendance on him, correct?"

The three men exchanged glances. They were not accustomed to having a summons to appear before the Roman Prefect received in such a flippant manner. One, who seemed to be senior in rank, only nodded and waved Gamaliel into line and they marched off.

"Why is the prefect in the city?" Gamaliel asked. He didn't expect an answer. If these men knew why the Roman official, whose visits to the city were normally confined to High Holy Days and special events, had traveled from Caesarea Maritima on this otherwise ordinary day, they were not about to tell him.

They marched around the Temple Mount rather than cross it. Romans were not welcome on the mount, or anywhere else, particularly after the massacre instituted by the same Pontius Pilate near the Temple the year before. The journey took less than a quarter of an hour. Young and fit legionnaires moved at a brisk pace. Gamaliel huffed along in their wake. At the Antonia Fortress, he was passed on to a second group of four, who escorted him through the fortress' labyrinthine hallways to the prefect's quarters. His escorts left him in an antechamber where he was told to wait.

Gamaliel stood in the center of the room for a half hour, shifting his weight from one foot to the other. The prefect might or might not be occupied, but he would not appear until he had made it clear who had the power. Gamaliel understood the wait. It was a trick he had used on occasion himself. He resigned himself to inaction and tried to guess what Pilate wanted.

Finally, Pontius Pilate swept into the room and fixed Gamaliel with a stare that was supposed provoke terror into the hearts of lesser men. Gamaliel had dealt with the Roman official in the past and knew he had no intention of imposing physical violence on him, though he was perfectly capable of doing so had he wished.

"Greetings, Prefect. I am your servant. What may I do for you?"

"Rabban of the Sanhedrin, I thought I was done with you months ago. Now, it appears I must call you to task yet again. Why is that?"

"I am sorry, Excellency, I have no idea. How have I offended you?"

"No offense as such. I am informed you are meddling in an affair the authorities in the palace wish you to avoid and you condone the behavior of a renegade rabbi who may present a threat to the Empire."

"I am guilty of all that? Can you be more specific? You say a *rabbi* threatens the welfare of the state? That seems very unlikely. Most of the rabbis I know are not a threat to doves in trees or flowers in the fields."

"Nevertheless, it has been so reported. And then there is this probing you insist on doing that has upset the king. Why I should care about that royal mouse, I do not know, but as it is my official duty to pursue these sorts of complaints, I ask you, what are you up to this time?"

"First, I need to separate the two questions. Or are you suggesting they are somehow connected?"

"I can't say."

"You have been in communication with the high priest, it seems. Is it he who says there is a seditious rabbi roaming about the countryside fomenting rebellion?"

"You are ahead of yourself, Rabban. Is this Galilean a threat or not? The high priest tells me he is gathering a growing number of followers and they might attempt an attack."

"Is that likely? If it is the rabbi I am thinking of, he has, on a more or less permanent basis, as many as seventy or so followers. Crowds do, in fact gather to hear him—hundreds, some say thousands."

"There, you see. And then what do they do?"

"When he is finished teaching? They go home. Prefect, they are farmers and fishermen, women and children. If they carry weapons, they would be used for gutting fish and pruning trees. I do not think your legionnaires have much to fear from pruning forks, do you?"

Pilate barked. Gamaliel assumed it to be the closest thing to a laugh the Roman could muster.

"Nothing threatens Rome, Rabban. Your men have foolishly been throwing themselves at us for decades. You raid our camps. We kill you. Your attempts at war have produced a nation of women and children. Your best men hang rotting on crucifixes the length of the Palestine. We fear no one. It is not fear of your rabbi I want to discuss. I wish to know if he intends to follow the footsteps of the rebellious fools before him. It is our policy to crush the thought before the act."

Gamaliel's expression did not change but he felt the Nation's pain caused by years of futile skirmishes by Zealots and their supporters, which had, as the prefect noted, reduced the nation's population to the point where sixty to seventy out of a hundred adult citizens were women—and they had children to feed and care for without their men. The men, as Pilate said, lay dead or dying across the land.

"Rebellion, Prefect, is not what that rabbi preaches, I promise you."

"I will take your word for that, at least for now. What then of this meddling?"

"Now, that does present a threat to your Caesar."

"Nonsense. How can it? The legions of Rome have crushed every attempt at bringing us down. Your own experience in this country amply demonstrates that."

"You are correct as far as you go, but you can be defeated and I know how. It is the reason I am investigating the dead man in the Temple in spite of the wishes of the Palace and Temple."

"I do not see how a dead man in your temple can possibly cause any trouble for the empire. Explain."

"I set you a hypothetical case. Suppose there is a group preparing to fall on your men—"

"Pah!"

"Let me finish, please. But, the day before this attack, all of your legionnaires fall deathly ill, are incapacitated, and lose their will to fight. What then?"

"How does it happen they fall ill, Jew?"

"I can think of many ways that might be. We have a powerful Lord who has answered our prayers in the past. A plague on the Pharaoh, locusts, the first born struck down. Why wouldn't he help his people now?"

"Why? Because for decades that is exactly what you people have been praying for and he has remained silent. It seems he is done with you."

"You may hope so, but I said I could think of other ways. We could poison your well."

"It is guarded night and day."

"Good, then you will not accuse us of rebellion when your troops lay down their arms because they have become incapacitated by their own hand."

"What do you mean by that?"

"If I am right in this, if my investigation is on the right path, the means of your destruction could be at hand and we have nothing to do with it, although it might conceivably be the work of the Lord. I must not think that, however. Perhaps that is the meaning of the mustard plants..."

"You are not making any sense, Rabbi. What mustard plants? What agency do you speak?"

"Sorry, the mustard is something else...only a dream. No, there is something in the culture...I do not know what, exactly, but I can guess, and it has the power to destroy your soldiers."

"Really? Then it begs the question."

"The question?"

"If you are correct, why would you stop it? Do you not wish for us to be destroyed?"

"May I speak frankly?"

"With caution, yes."

"I do hope for your eventual destruction. That should not surprise you, but I am not so foolish as to believe that when the effects of this scourge are let loose you will not promptly root it out and then find someone to blame for it other than those responsible, which would be your own people. And, if past practice is precedent, that someone will be us. We suffer enough at your hands. We do not need more. So, it is in the best interests of the Nation to protect you from yourself, and may *Ha Shem* forgive me."

Chapter XXXIX

Loukas met Gamaliel at his doorstep. Gamaliel appeared distracted. Without knowing what was on his friend's mind, he gestured for him to enter.

"Benyamin," he bawled, "we need refreshment. Wait here Loukas, I have just come from the presence of the prefect and I am in need of a trip to my *mikvah* and some prayer time."

"It was that bad? You have had dealings with him before. Why was this any different?"

"He reminded me why I dislike the Romans so much, why we continue to suffer at their hands, and he gave me a momentary, but painful moment when I doubted the Lord and his love for his people. Benyamin will attend to you. I will be back in a moment."

It had been a seriously depressing meeting. Gamaliel rarely succumbed to depression. He trusted in the Lord and anticipated that his Kingdom on earth, the Nation, would be restored. Surely *Elohim* would do a mighty act and lift this awful burden with which Rome had saddled them for so long. Too many of his acquaintances, some very close to him, had given up hope. Almost all despaired at the Lord's silence. They yearned for a Messiah, for a new Moses to deliver them out of this new bondage. And now this arrogant Roman had shaken his confidence anew. Would no one stand for the Lord? Even the high priest, the man entrusted with the soul of the Nation, had been reduced to pandering to the prefect. To save the people, he would claim. To save his position, more like. Gamaliel did not like himself when he plummeted into these dark places. Prayer and a trip to the *mikvah*, then to find out what Loukas had been up to. Could he really restore sight to the blind? Now that would be a sign, wouldn't it?

◇◇◇

Somewhat refreshed and cheered, he rejoined Loukas after his moment in the bath and prayer.

"So, I must know, can you make the blind see? Is the age spoken of by Isaiah upon us? Tell me."

"I do not know about Isaiah. I have read the scroll and can make no sense of it as it stands. It will take a sharper mind than mine to unravel that book. But to answer your question, yes I can and I did. Your friend Jacob has his sight. It is not perfect but it is functional. He rests in my house with soothing cloths on each eye. They must heal."

"It is a miracle?"

"It is a procedure."

"A procedure? That is all you will ascribe to a thing that allows the blind to see? Where is your faith?"

"My faith, good friend, is in the accumulated wisdom of the Lord's creatures. Miracles, in my experience, are the work of men dedicated to solving problems. I learn from such men, they learn from me. The wisdom accumulates and then miracles occur."

"I give up on you, Loukas. I try to turn you from your unbelief and you spurn my efforts. Very well, how did you restore the old man's sight if it wasn't a miracle?'

"It is called couching. I do not know why it is called that, so don't ask. You take a needle, not too sharp, and insert it in the eye just so. Then you push at the clouded part until it falls away. Then, the person sees."

"That's all? This can restore sight to the blind? There will be no more blindness?"

"No, that is overreaching. It only works on this particular variety of blindness—the kind Jacob had. The other kinds are intractable as far as I know."

"Nevertheless, it is a wonderful thing you did. The Lord will be pleased."

"You think? Then he must thank the Indian physician who taught me how to do this procedure. Do you think *Elohim* will? The man who taught me is not of the faith."

Gamaliel rolled his eyes. "As I said, I am finished with you."

"Tell me what the famous Roman said to you that put you in such a state."

Gamaliel recounted his meeting with the Roman prefect and the implicit connection between the high priest, the palace, and the local ruling governor. As he finished, a loud pounding on his door announced a new episode in what had already been a busy day.

"Benyamin, see who that is."

His servant entered the room. "It is a messenger from the high priest. He says you have been summoned."

"Does he, indeed? Loukas, this is what Caiaphas does when he thinks he is the voice of *Ha Shem*. He becomes imperious. He mimics our oppressors. Benyamin, tell the messenger to tell the high priest that the rabban of the Sanhedrin declines the invitation."

Loukas' eyes popped wide. "Can you do that?"

"Do what?"

"Snub the high priest like that."

"It seems I just did. Benyamin, you may tell him that I am not in the mood for lectures about what or where my duty lies with respect to the Nation, Rome, the high priest, or anyone else with a problem they think falls on my head. If Caiaphas needs to speak to me, he can call on me here."

"He will not be pleased to hear your message."

"No, but it pleases me to send it. I have had enough bully-ing for one day. I wish to celebrate Loukas the physician's great accomplishment. Benyamin, send the messenger away and bring us some wine and food."

◇◇◇

Across Jerusalem in the part of it that had come to be called the Upper City, the object of Gamaliel's current anger seated himself with his family to eat his evening meal. He always ate and retired early, believing that mornings should start promptly at the first hour as it was the best, indeed the only, time to start one's day. Neither his children nor his wife were as enthusiastic about that declaration, a fact he ascribed as coming from the darker area of their souls.

He received Gamaliel's response just as he finished thanking the Lord for the blessings bestowed on him and his family, and especially for the food which seemed to overflow the table.

Whatever appetite he might have had, and if it were any normal day it would have been prodigious, quickly disappeared. He left the table and stormed out into the courtyard, yelling for his attendants. They, in turn, had to leave their evening meal, which they scheduled early to coincide with that of their master. He formed them up in two columns and with himself in the center, gave the order to march to the rabban's house.

It took a quarter of an hour to form up and another quarter to make the trip across to the lower city to Gamaliel's home. In all, counting the time the messenger had spent returning from Gamaliel's house with the unwelcome response, the calling of the guard to the court yard, and the subsequent march east, something just less than an hour had elapsed from a rejection by Gamaliel to an intended confrontation by Caiaphas.

It was during that brief span that Loukas came to appreciate Gamaliel's instinct and cunning. By the time an angry high priest arrived and had his guards bang on the rabban's door, both he and the physician were comfortably ensconced in a shop three streets away with wine, various fruits, and a wheel of cheese. The shopkeeper owed the rabban a favor.

In the meantime, Benyamin, with great trepidation, announced to the high priest that the rabban of the Sanhedrin would call on the high priest in the morning at the third hour. Then he closed the door.

Chapter XL

"I told you how I spent the day, Rabban, and you filled me in on the mind of the prefect. Now, can we please return to the basics of this business? You said something about having seen the killer. We spent time with the blind *kohen*. When he spoke to you, and for the life of me I cannot remember what he said, you became excited and seemed eager to do something. What happened this afternoon at the Temple?"

"If I did not already know it, I had reaffirmed for me that things are not always what they seem. I am sure there is a bit of wisdom in scripture to remind us of that, but at the moment, with the prefect's admonitions and the high priest's demands still ringing in my ears, my mind refuses to go there. But didn't you hear what Jacob said?"

"I was too occupied with estimating the condition of his eyes. I am sorry but it is an occupational hazard. I see the disease before I see the man."

"Very well, the meat of the nut is this. Jacob believed, when I probed his memory, that among the newly arrived *kohanim,* this new cohort of priests that had only just arrived, that there was one who apparently did not belong. In the confusion of assuming their new duties, he went unnoticed. Later, with all the excitement, he was forgotten. Do you see what that means?"

"An imposter was in the Holy Place from the outset?"

"Yes, and more than that. He had access to the Temple, the guards, the routine, everything. Who would question a priest as he moved about the inner courts?"

"No one, probably. Didn't Yehudah say he thought he saw a man who looked like a priest in the Street of—"

"Exactly. Can it be that our killer is able to insert himself everywhere and anywhere? And yes, Yehudah's observation was what gave me the idea to talk to Jacob."

"So, bringing a corpse to the Holy of Holies could have been easier than we assumed."

"That and more, if we consider all of our dead men are connected. He could move about the city unnoticed as well."

"You mean disguised as a priest."

"Not just as a priest. No, a *kohen* wandering aimlessly about the city would be noticed."

"How…no, why, then?"

"We see things, Loukas, and we assume they are what they appear because they meet a set of learned expectations or what they signify. You reminded me that I said I had seen our killer."

"Yes, that's right. What did you mean?"

"I meant that if he dresses as a Pharisee might, you know, in a dark tunic and cloak, wouldn't we glance his way and say, just another Pharisee? If he, like you, wears the distinctive garb of a Greek, we think, he's a Greek. People always mistake you for one. You said as much when we interviewed the apothecaries."

"That is true. I am usually taken to be Greek, gentile at least. So?"

"So, our blind man, Jacob, sniffs the air and declares it to be Holy Smoke. He cannot see the smoke but he recognizes the aroma, so he says that is what it is. Suppose he had caught a whiff of the smoke from the burning apothecary's shop. He might have said the same. It would be an assumption based on his past familiarity with the scent, you see? But is it? We ascribe virtues and substance to things and to people because we need to have things in their place. We create taxonomies of the things in our life because we yearn to have an orderly existence."

"Yes, that is so, but why—?"

"We say the smoke from the sacrifices spirals heavenward to *Elohim* carrying our prayers. It is a comforting image. But in the end it is only smoke and only holy because we say it is. In the same way, a man is a seller of trinkets if he looks the part and we say so. But while the smoke stays smoke, appearances can deceive. How a person looks does not make him what he wishes us to believe he is. Our killer is in our midst. He has been tracking us, I am sure of it. Remember, I said that I thought one of the men who followed either us or the other man—we'll never know which for sure—looked familiar. He must have been the man I saw in the street the other night who ignored Shabbat. Was he the priest in the temple? Was he who knows how many other persons who have crossed our path over the past few days?"

"I see. Wait, do you believe the man you describe is Ali bin Selah? Is that why you had me sack my servant and why you were short with him when he popped up the other day?"

"It is a possibility, but I am not prepared to say one way or the other, only that I worry about him because he appeared at your home as someone else after he'd announced his intention to leave the city. I thought that suspicious on its face. Then as the evidence piled up…well, it seemed prudent to act on the suspicion. If I am mistaken about him, and I sincerely hope I am for your sake, I will offer profuse apologies."

"Give them to him, not to me. I appreciate your concern for my safety. I am sorry I snapped at you this morning."

Gamaliel waved the apology off. He filled their cups. "The problem we now face is which way to turn. Do we attack this *hul gil* mystery and let the death in the temple go, or do we concentrate on the dead man and let others better equipped deal with that exotic mixture?"

"I have no advice for you as I do not know what you mean when you speak of *hul gil* as a mystery to be solved."

Gamaliel smiled. "For a man who can restore sight to the blind, you are singularly sightless yourself when it comes to certain critical areas. Very well, I will tell you what I believe to be the problem with *hul gil,* but I must add the caveat that I could be very, very wrong."

Gamaliel then laid out what he suspected, and the dilemma he faced in bringing his suspicions to Pilate. Loukas listened with a physician's ears, nodding now and then. They had consumed the contents of the pot of wine, half the fruit, and the entire wheel of cheese by the time Gamaliel finished.

Loukas stood and turned to his friend. "If you will allow it, I think I would like to use your *mikvah.*"

He sounded and looked very sad, like an important part of his life had been crushed, or a close friend had died.

Chapter XLI

Whatever plans Gamaliel might have had for the morning were swept aside by the arrival of Caiaphas. There could be no avoiding him this time. With his attendants in his wake, he marched into Gamaliel's house like a conquering army, like David against the Philistines, like Julius, the first Caesar, into Rome.

"Rabban," he said in a voice just shy of a bellow, "we will talk, now." The high priest glared first at Gamaliel and then at Loukas. He held his gaze on the latter.

"It is perfectly fine. Loukas and I have no secrets. What you say to me you may say in his presence. What is it we are to discuss?"

"Blasphemy, Rabban, blasphemy. Oh, you will excuse him as usual. You will say he is but a harmless, well-meaning country rabbi. It is shameless how you relieved the prefect's concerns and leave me alone to deal with this…this…this blasphemer."

"Am I correct in thinking you're referring to Yeshua ben Josef? What has he done now?"

"He dishonors Shabbat. I told you before; he healed a cripple on Shabbat. It is unacceptable, as you know full well. This time he must be stopped. It is your—"

"We are back to that? He healed the crippled man on Shabbat. Surely one could argue that—"

"You could argue—you did argue. You spend your days arguing and picking at the Law, but the Sanhedrin does not wish you to argue, it wishes you to rule."

"The entire Sanhedrin has met and come to that resolve? Why was I not there? We could have avoided this—"

"No, the core of the…the leadership was. I need a response from you immediately."

"I see. As a point of reference, how would you define blasphemy, Loukas?"

"This conversation is completely out of my area. If you ask me how to treat a congested chest, the ague, set a broken leg, any of a hundred different sorts and conditions, I would have an opinion, but diseases of the spirit, theological disputations? You'll not get a word from me."

"High Priest, then. How would you define it?"

"You know perfectly well what is meant by it. An offense against *Elohim*."

"Any offense? All offenses? What sort of offenses? You say he breached Shabbat because he healed the cripple, is that the gist of your complaint?"

"It is."

"Ah, I see. Are we to judge the act of healing or the fact it was performed on Shabbat?"

"Rabban, do not bandy words with me. We have a problem and it must be addressed."

"Yes, of course we must. Did you know that our friend the physician, here, can restore sight to the blind?"

"I don't see what that has to do—"

"He has done it just recently. He made Jacob ben Aschi sighted again. Think of it. One of the most respected priests on the roster has regained his sight and may resume his duties. Is that not a wonderful thing?"

"What? Jacob can see? I don't believe it. He has been blind for years. No, it cannot be."

"But it is. Loukas healed him on a weekday, so no offense was directed toward the Lord. But I wonder, High Priest…a hypothetical if you will…how would you feel if it had happened on Shabbat? What if Jacob received his miracle on Shabbat? Is not the Lord served best with a sighted Jacob? Would the restoration of one of his priests not be pleasing to Him? Certainly he would not take offense, do you think?"

"The cripple was not a priest, the rabbi was not a physician, and the question is moot because it did not, in fact, occur on Shabbat."

"That is quite true, but I put it to you that the cases are only dissimilar as to the day, not the effect. And that being the case, I ask again, had Loukas done his healing on Shabbat, how would you deal with it? Would you be here haranguing me, or not?"

"You are the rabban. It is your duty to define the Law. Can you excuse this or not?"

"Tsk. I see that you do not care for my question, but then, I did not think you would. Let me try something else. Blasphemy can be defined, I think, as lying about or to the Lord. I would reduce it to something like that. A man who breaches Shabbat breaches the Law, but he does not blaspheme. There is an important difference between the two, though many do not recognize it. So, has this man simply breached the Law, or has he blasphemed? Where is the falsehood?"

"You are being Greek, a sophist, Rabban. It is not your place to toy with the Law."

"On the contrary," Gamaliel's voice now took on an edge, "I am being the rabban. This is exactly what I do. If you tell me this rabbi broke the law, I agree. It is within the Lord's purview as to what punishment will befall him for that. He will be displeased or he will not. We do not presume to know His mind and there is no authority left to us to punish a breach of this sort. Now I put to you another case—"

"I will have no more of this nonsense. You are not keeping the Law, you are twisting it."

"I am not finished. Take this case. If you know for a certainty that the man found in the Holy of Holies had been placed there by some one—a true blasphemer, in fact—and you still insist that he died at the hands of the Lord, what would you call that?"

"What?"

"It is simple enough. If blasphemy is, among other things, lying to or about the Lord, and you tell such a lie in order to advance a theory about His reaction to anyone who invades the Most Holy Place, what have you done?"

Caiaphas' face turned several shades of red and then, as if the plug had been pulled, the color drained away and he became as white as the marble bench on which he rather abruptly collapsed.

"You cannot mean…" he gasped.

"Loukas, pour the high priest some wine. He looks poorly."

"High Priest," Loukas said as he stepped to his side, "Put your head between your knees and take slow but steady breaths."

Caiaphas did as he was told and moments later he seemed better.

"Are you experiencing any pain?"

Caiaphas tapped his chest.

"Gamaliel, the high priest needs to lie down for a while. Fetch that vial of *hul gil* we brought from my house and mix a small, a very small amount of it with honey and water."

Gamaliel did as he was asked. They half carried him to a couch. Loukas administered the mixture slowly. Caiaphas relaxed and closed his eyes.

"High Priest, you must rest here for an hour or so. Then have your men fetch a sedan and carry you home. Take what remains of this week to rest and I will call on you within the hour. Under no circumstances should you exert yourself."

"I have an appointment with the prefect in an hour."

"Not today, not this week. Send a messenger with your regrets and have him say the high priest is ill and cannot attend him."

"He will be angry."

"He is always angry," Gamaliel said. "He will get over it. You should know by now that no matter what you do to please or placate him, if he feels the need, he will chop you off at the knees and not blink an eye."

Caiaphas rolled his eyes much as he had when reporting his blasphemy. Gamaliel wondered if, in the high priest's mind, he thought speaking against the prefect equated with speaking against the Lord.

"Now rest," Loukas said. "I will send someone to my home for my remedy box. There is a plant I learned about from one of my colleagues from the west the leaves of which he says works wonders with this sort of complaint."

"High Priest," Gamaliel said, "One last question for you. If this had been Shabbat, what should Loukas have done just now?"

Caiaphas groaned, but his color returned.

Chapter XLII

Gamaliel gazed at the retreating figure of Caiaphas as he disappeared down the street in a conveyance cobbled up by his servants—not quite a sedan chair and not quite a stretcher—serviceable if not elegant. He looked miserable.

"You must be careful when you bait the high priest, Rabban. You might have killed him."

"Loukas, surely not. The man is impervious to criticism. Half of the time he simply doesn't listen. The rest of the time he ignores you. He will live forever. Besides it wasn't criticism, it was a critique."

"Enough. You want me to believe that it is your wish he live forever?"

"Of course. I hope you are not suggesting I want him dead. If the high priest were to die, it would be a tragedy…no, a national disaster."

"A national…I think you exaggerate."

"Not at all. As much as we abhor his snug relationship with Rome, replacing him would result in an appointment sanctioned by a crazed Caesar and certified by an obnoxious prefect. Where is *Elohim* in that? It is a prospect no one could possibly want."

"Then, I repeat my warning. You must not bait the man. I have seen the signs he displayed just now many times and, as often as not, collapsing like that—a cold sweat and chest pains—will end in the person's death, sometimes immediately, sometimes after a few days. All I am saying is be careful when you push him like that."

"Arguing with Caiaphas is one of my few remaining pleasures. Now you will deny me even that."

"Yes, yes, I must be off to retrieve my bag and attend to the man. Whatever you had in mind for today's activities will have to wait, that is if they included me."

"In truth, I had not begun to plan how to lure our killer out, but I know that before we are done with this affair, that is what we will have to do."

"What is the problem, then? Never mind, I haven't time to listen. You can tell me later."

"It has to do with motive."

"Motive?"

"Yes, I can't think of any. We have several men whose deaths I am sure are connected, but I lack a real clue how or why they are. You said it yourself, 'a separation, that the dead man was involved in something. Separating him from any hint as to what or who that might be renders him isolated and you with no place to start.' Or words to that effect."

"You have given up on the goings on in the souk then?"

"No, but I can't quite fit that part with the Temple man. It is maddening."

"On that happy note, I will take my leave." Loukas stepped through the door with Oren at his heels.

For the man who had been watching the house and Loukas and Gamaliel and now lay in wait across the street, the problem had become many times more complicated for him as well. He found himself in a deeper hole than he'd ever anticipated. While no one, or nearly no one, would miss a guard, an apothecary, or even a physician, the rabban of the Sanhedrin was a very public figure and therefore a poor subject for a murder. When public figures come to an untimely or a suspicious end, they tend to attract an excess of attention. He could only guess at what may have transpired between the rabban and the prefect the previous day, but if the two were now allied in the pursuit of the man responsible for any of the recent killings, then he was in more trouble than he'd bargained for. And if that weren't bad enough, Loukas the physician, who he believed had no status except for his acquaintance with the rabban, now attended the high priest.

Caution urged vacating the city and his assignment. The problems begun with Hana could be addressed later, after enough time had passed and the deaths forgotten. That would be the conservative move. He rejected it. He'd come to avenge a murder, reestablish his market, and to do a job. He would not leave until he'd finished it.

He moved off down the street, eyes and ears alert to any and all around him.

◇◇◇

Gamaliel sat by the slit window and watched as first Caiaphas in his ungainly carrier and then Loukas disappeared into the growing crowds on the street. He, like the man in the shadows across the street, also considered his options. Somewhere out on that same street, figuratively speaking, wandered his murderer. He would like to devise a trap, but, as he'd told Loukas, to set a trap meant having knowledge of what bait would entice a killer to step into it, and that meant he needed to know what drove him. But the connection that could stitch all these bits and pieces together flitted in space just ahead of his ability to grasp them. It was maddening.

He rose and would have turned away except a movement on the street opposite caught his eye. A man, a very familiar man, stepped cautiously into the sunlight. He looked both ways and then stared straight at Gamaliel. In fact, he stared at the house. Standing inside with the brighter light outdoors, Gamaliel could not have been seen. Nevertheless, the rabban shrank back a step. He did not, however, take his eyes off the man who now turned and shifted his attention down the street in the direction Loukas had taken. Gamaliel tried to concentrate. He felt sure he knew the man—one of the many familiar manifestations he'd run across over the past few days. The false priest? The man on the street on Shabbat eve? Both? Someone else? Maybe, with his lower face covered, the man who claimed to be in search of Ali bin Selah. Any and all of these possibilities could obtain. Which? He turned and went to his study. He needed to concentrate. Whether by instinct or Providence he would never know, but one or the other caused him to pivot back toward the window in time to see a second man move out from the wall and take a position behind the other. Now this man he did know.

He squinted his eyes against the sunlight streaming through the narrow slit and watched the two men walk away. Then, his mind made up, he grabbed his cloak from a peg by the door and yelled to Benyamin.

"Benyamin, I am going to meet with the prefect. If Loukas comes back, tell him where I am. If anyone else asks, tell them I am in the Souk searching for fabric for a new cloak. If I do not return in two hours you may assume that Pilate has had me put away."

"Yes, sir, and which of these stories will be the truth?"

"It doesn't matter, just be sure you tell the right one to the people I've identified."

Chapter XLIII

The Roman prefect had problems of his own, not the least of which was a wife, Procula, whom not a few of his acquaintances referred to as *dementis*, but never to his face. She wasn't crazy, but she did have premonitions that unfortunately or fortunately, depending on the outcome, often turned out to be true, or near enough. It had been at her insistence that he'd made this tiresome trip to Jerusalem. He confided to his friends back on the peninsula that of all the places he'd been posted, it was the most tiresome place anywhere in the Empire. This morning Procula had burst into his anteroom and informed him that he should listen to the voice of God. Her words exactly, *Listen to the voice of God.* Not the voice of the gods, which would be the way any normal person would have put it, but God, as if there were only one and he rated special attention. Pilate wondered if living in this benighted land with its constricting monotheism hadn't affected her mind and if he shouldn't petition the Emperor Tiberius for a transfer to a more salubrious posting. He'd earned it. He also knew that this Caesar had slipped out of the realm of rational thought and would as likely order his execution as his transfer. He sat with these thoughts, worrying them like a dog with a bone, when the legionnaire assigned to monitor his door announced the presence of the rabban of the Sanhedrin.

The voice of God?

"Show him in."

Gamaliel entered and greeted him with his usual courtesy, which Pilate felt bordered on the ironic, as if excessive politeness somehow satirized the relationship of Rome to its conquered nations and its citizens to their Caesar. In his more relaxed moments, which were admittedly few, he thought the rabban had it right.

"I will not tell you why, Rabban, but I have been expecting you. I can tell you that I have been thinking over what you reported to me earlier. I have made inquiries. I selected certain of my legionnaires who admitted to having acquired a taste for the stuff you described to me, and I have experimented. Aristotle taught us that the observation of phenomena while varying the circumstances around it can be extremely informative. It cost me six otherwise good men, but I have determined that *hul gil,* when taken in certain doses, will make a man useless for fighting. Furthermore, once they achieve a certain level of use it seems they require more of it and cannot willingly cease craving it. They will need the stuff and become quite unreliable unless they get it.

"Then you see the problem?"

"Indeed. What I do not see is the connection between it and the dead man or men, as you insist."

"That is the twist, to be sure. Like you, I have been considering the drug and the connection. Unlike you, however, I did not experiment with it, although my friend the physician did apply it to relieve the high priest of symptoms he said might have been fatal. I don't believe that, by the way. For any other man, they might, but the high priest is indestructible."

"Probably. And what did you conclude?"

"This is highly speculative, Prefect. I could be completely off the mark."

"I have it on reliable authority that you are not."

"Pardon?"

"Someone insisted I hear you out and, more than that I was to take you seriously. You do understand how difficult the last part is for me?"

"I suppose it must. I would apologize for your inconvenience but I doubt you would take it seriously."

"As seriously as it is offered."

"Yes, well then, there you are. Now, here is what I have so far. Something has changed in this material. Until this moment, it has been in the bag of every healer on earth. It sits in powders, poultices, vials, and blocks in hundreds, thousands of homes. To this point, no one has cared one way or the other about it. Some think it is a good palliative, others doubt it. Now, suddenly, it is the source of great attention. I have been reading, Prefect."

"Stop. We are talking about *hul gil* are we not?"

"Exactly. Something has changed. Someone, or several some-ones, has cultivated a strain of poppy that produces a sap that is more heavily endowed with the active ingredient."

"Or?"

"Sorry, what?"

"There is another possibility, you know."

"I see, and what would that be?"

"Improved processing."

"Oh, yes, that is a possibility."

"If the latter, we will never get on top of this except by banning its use on pain of death."

"And if the former?"

"We burn the fields and crucify the growers."

"If I am correct, that will not be possible."

"Not? Tell me why the Roman Empire with its legions cannot do exactly that?"

"Because it comes from a place beyond your reach. Your influence extends far to the east, I know, and you can even make people you have not yet subjugated bend to your will, but these flowers grow far away in the northern mountains beyond Parthia in Khorasan. The people there are gathered into warlike tribes and to date no one has successfully conquered them, not even the late great Macedonian, Alexander."

"I know the place. It is on the border of the world."

"That might be overstating, Prefect. I have no doubt here are countries beyond it which, if I'm not mistaken, supply the rare spices and fabrics you people covet. No, the problem is, and I admit I am not a strategist or familiar with the workings of armies, but it is more a matter of vulnerable supply lines and topography, I think."

"For a man who spends his days with his nose on sheets of holy writings, you seem to have acquired a working knowledge of logistics."

"I attribute it to some of my days in your company, Prefect. A man is a fool if he does not know his adversary."

"Well put. As my adversary, then, why should I take advice from you?"

"Alas, in this case you must."

"Because?"

"This new threat to the well being of your troops is like the wind. It blows where it will and knows no favor. That is to say it will blow on Roman and Hebrew alike. The problems it creates will affect us all."

"I take your point. Now what?"

"The souk must be cleansed, the border to that far away province sealed, and warnings issued to your people and mine."

"You shall be responsible for your people. I will attend to the souk and the Roman population. Anything else?"

"There is one more thing. The killer of several men is at the heart of this, I am sure. We must root him out."

"For what purpose?"

"As I said at the outset, what I am suggesting is highly speculative. I said I could be completely off the mark. To be absolutely certain, we must find this man and question him. I have a feeling, which I cannot justify in my own mind, that the problem is more complex than I have just described."

"More? In what way is it more complex?"

"I do not yet know. That is why we must find this man."

"Do you believe that I can do a better job at that than yourself?"

"Modesty forbids me to answer. What I do know is you have men, many men, who can be deployed wherever they are needed. They will do exactly what they are told. I have only myself, a few Temple guards who are otherwise occupied, and the physician."

"You are not suggesting I put my legionnaires under your command?"

"Oh no, never that. What I suggest is that you assign a tribune or someone with authority to be in charge and that he consult with me as to where and how these men are to be stationed."

"I will think on this. Call on me again in three hours."

Pilate waited until the door closed after Gamaliel and then he began pacing. Was Procula correct? It was beginning to seem so. Where would this end?

Chapter XLIV

Gamaliel left the prefect's apartment in the Antonia Fortress and made his way across the Temple Mount to his home. He had finished his prayerful soak in the *mikvah* when Benyamin announced the physician had returned. Gamaliel met him in his study.

"What have you been up to so early that warranted a trip to the water?"

"I have been to see the prefect again. We talked and planned. I acquainted him with the problem of the pain-killer and he informed me he had experimented with it and if his observations are accurate, it is worse than we thought. I feel like I have struck a bargain with *Ba'al-Zebuwb*. We are to be allies in our efforts to trap the killer."

"And did the two of you in my absence decide to bait the trap?"

"We didn't discuss bait or even the trap. I only asked him for men to set it."

"And he will cooperate?"

"I will know in two hours. That is when I must return and get his answer. It was an odd meeting, Loukas."

"When you and the official representative from Rome meet, it will always be an odd meeting, surely."

"Yes, but that is not what I meant. He said he was expecting me and not only that, but he intended to listen to whatever I proposed. Does that sound like our Prefect?"

"Not even close. Perhaps he has succumbed to a mental problem. Madness seems to run rampant in the Roman hierarchy. It seems like one Caesar after another is either assassinated, thinks he's divine, is demented, or all three. At least one of the two aspirants for Mad Tiberias' mantle is, they say, well on his way to becoming *non compos mentis*, and the other is a boy with not much to recommend him."

"If you say so. At any rate, we should be happy for any respect he might show us, irrespective of its source or his mental state."

"Is that what this is, respect? Or is it mere expediency? We determined that this new *hul gil* is potent enough to incapacitate his troops if administered in high doses. He recognizes the danger and experiments on his own and must act. He can use you more, I expect, than you him. What did he discover by the way?"

Gamaliel described the prefect's trials with some of his men and the result. Loukas shook his head in dismay. "He may have learned how to assess phenomena from the Greeks but he certainly missed the part about the ethics that is supposed to accompany them. You say he destroyed six of his own men to find out how the drug works?"

"So he said."

"Romans are a cruel people. Nothing new there, of course. The question is why will he help us find our killer? He can deal with his troops and people without our input. Why work with anybody—with you?"

"I convinced him that there was more here than meets the eye, and finding the killer and taking him alive would allow us to ask some important questions."

"I see. You do realize the unlikely pair you two make? Isaiah is correct, it seems—*The leopard will lie down with the goat.* I am impressed, Rabban. It must be that the Kingdom has arrived. Weren't we just discussing that lately? Next the mustard plants will—"

"Do not try my patience. All he did was agree to supply me with some men, or perhaps soon will. I hope so in any event. What that gesture will cost us in the end I can only imagine, but the Kingdom will not be ushered in by a pack of Roman dogs. We work with them because there are no other choices."

"You are correct. We are in league with the devil."

"It can't be helped."

"Can't? Surely you do not believe that. You can refuse. You could have stayed home and discussed this with me first. You could have—"

"I could have, but chose not to. Would you like to know why?"

"I don't know. Will I be better off for the knowing?"

"I'll take that as an affirmative. Very well, that drug is available anywhere and to anyone. It knows no borders, it has no loyalties. It is as insidious to you and me as it is to them. Think of our position. We are a Nation in despair. Who holds out hope to us? Many of us have decided that *Ha Shem* has abandoned His people. That being the case, who is more likely to succumb to this substance's mind-numbing properties, Rome or us? You know the answer. Listen, we all yearn for a savior, for Messiah to come and throw off the mantle of this oppressive race of people from across the Middle Sea. We ache for it. We cry out, 'Where is Moses now when we need him most?' Silence is our answer. We think to ourselves, what are the chances of it happening? Can you envision any person, any set of circumstances, that can make that happen?"

"Short of a miracle, no. You do pray daily for Messiah though, don't you?"

"I do. The Nation does. In *Esther* we read that whatever state we find ourselves in, we shall ultimately triumph."

"Do you believe that?"

"We live in hope, Loukas. Alas, at this moment in our history, Rome has its foot on our neck, and we can do nothing except pray."

"Pray and hope?"

"Yes, and while we cower in our prayer shawls, our young men throw themselves at the Roman killing machine and die by the hundreds, thousands. The prefect said we are a nation of women and children. Rome will not go away in our lifetime, Loukas."

"That is a pessimistic assessment coming from you."

"It is realism. If Rome falls it will be because of rot from within, from a succession of insane and cruel leaders and forces arising elsewhere, not from action on our part. We are a decimated people. We no longer have the sinew to resist. Our destiny must be simply to stay alive and pray until they are gone. Survival, Loukas. *Ha Shem* expects us to survive. We are his people, his chosen, and to commit suicide by trying to defeat Rome would be contrary to His will. So, we must wait and survive."

"So, for that we help them save themselves?"

"We do."

"I do not like this, Rabban."

"No more do I, but I promise you this, we will be here long after Rome has been gone and forgotten. We are His chosen. It is written. It is so."

Loukas paced to the window and stared out at the street. The two men were silent for a long time. Finally Loukas sighed. "Very well, Gamaliel. I do not like it, but I understand. What now?"

"Now we consider. Here is what I have been thinking. Tell me where I am wrong and quickly. I must be at the fortress in less than two hours now."

Gamaliel recounted what he'd observed from the window after Loukas had departed. He explained again the ease by which identities could be altered due to the stereotyping that characterized Jerusalem's population. He did not, however, repeat his suspicions about Ali bin Selah. Loukas did not need that piece just yet. He would find out soon enough on which side of the tent pole Ali slept.

"It is time to go to your Roman," Loukas said. "Have you a plan yet?"

"Not all of it. Too much depends on the level of support the prefect offers. If it is small and begrudging, I have no hopes for any plan. If he insists on running the whole maneuver, then I can't guarantee anything."

"But you do have something?"

"I have something. We shall see. I must be off."

"And me? What shall I do?"

"With Oren at your side, of course, I want you to act as if nothing at all was happening. We are being watched. It is like one approaches a hive of bees, Loukas, the less we stir them up, the better."

"Don't you think that when they realize you are conspiring with the prefect, they won't be in a state of high alert?"

"Probably. If the prefect goes along with us, I will have him disseminate a rumor that he has thrown me out of the fortress and possibly will soon arrest me. Then, I will suggest that he create the impression he is returning to Caesarea Maritima with his men. That should persuade them we are easy targets."

"You think they are plotting as well?"

"They, or he, is? Oh yes, no doubt. This is a complex game of move and counter move. I wish I had served in an army. It would make it easier to anticipate their next one."

"You as a soldier? Not in my wildest imaginings."

"Stranger things have happened. Who would have thought that David, the lyre-playing shepherd, would drop Goliath with a sling and a stone and then rule the land as king?"

"I stand corrected, 'Tribune.' Off you go to the den of iniquity—pardon, the Antonia Fortress, and its resident serpent."

Chapter XLV

Gamaliel spent nearly two hours with the prefect. He would later describe the meeting as remarkable for two reasons. First and foremost, the Roman's willingness to commit some of his troops to the pursuance of a killer, "an insignificant man" he'd said of him at the time, an estimate Gamaliel thought well off the mark but didn't say so. Then, what struck Gamaliel even more was his manner. In discourse and demeanor, Pilate, everyone knew, was sarcastic, arrogant, brutal, and invariably unpleasant—even to his friends, if he had any. Toward the Jews of the Palestine over whom he ruled, those characteristics compounded many fold. Yet this day, he'd been quiet and respectful. He'd listened and then agreed to put his men in play and, more or less, at the rabban's discretion.

"Are you feeling quite well, Prefect?"

"I am very well, Rabban. Why do you ask?"

"You are being nice to me. I just wondered…"

"Don't press your luck, old man, or you will see how nice the inside of my basement cells can be."

"Ah, you are back. I was worried there for a minute. Thank you for your troops, and I promise to deliver the man or men to you soon."

Gamaliel left the Antonia Fortress and prayed to *Elohim* that he could make good on his promise. As it now stood, he had at best only a guess as to which of two possible culprits he sought and how, if his guess was correct, he would trip up one or the other of them.

He stood at the top of the steps leading from the fortress down to the platform that formed the Temple Mount. He let his shoulders droop in discouragement and arranged his face into the best he could manage to appear defeated. His nemesis, who he felt certain would be watching somewhere nearby, needed to believe that the prefect had tossed him out on his ear. He proceeded down the steps and made his way homeward, looking neither right nor left. He did notice old Jacob in conversation with one of the priests and thought how wonderful it was that Loukas had restored the old man's sight.

But Gamaliel's thoughts swirled elsewhere. What if a man pretended to be something he was not, for example? Did he breach the Law? Would one be correct in accusing him of bearing false witness? What if the same man had saved his money to buy clothing beyond his station to make himself feel better, would that be a breach? If he did it to deceive or trick someone into revealing a secret, what then? Where to draw the line? In fact, couldn't his current posture of seeming defeat and despair constitute such a breach? Didn't he hope to deceive the watcher, whom he felt sure had him in sight? He wanted him to believe that he was depressed when in fact he was elated. It was a puzzle. He would put the concept before the senior rabbis the next time they met.

He knew ordinary people mocked him and his colleagues for the disputations they held. "Petty," they said, "splitting the hairs and bringing a dead man to court." But it had to be done. Perhaps a better example, curing a cripple on Shabbat, would be one they would understand. Doing so obviously broke the Law, Why? Because the next day and all the remaining days of the week the crippled man or woman would still be a cripple and still available for healing. He could think of no reason why the crippled person should not wait one day. A blind man, a leper, a demoniac, all would have the same condition on days when healing them would not force a breach of the Law; therefore they should wait and not be in violation of the Law. On the other hand, an intervention such as the one Loukas performed on the high priest, had it been on Shabbat, was a different matter entirely. One more day might not find him in the same condition. If an intervention had not been made, the man might have died. So, the question to be grappled with—where does one draw the line? Some instances were easy, others not so.

Now, take the case of a man who imitates a priest to deceive or…Wait, Jacob had been talking to one of the *kohen* a moment ago. Not just one of the priests, he had been talking to *him*. Gamaliel wheeled around and retraced his steps to the Temple. He had to speak to Jacob. He mentally kicked himself for allowing his mind to wander into the minute intricacies of Law when he had a killer on the loose and people in harm's way. One might put it down as an occupational hazard that fortunately or unfortunately characterized those like himself whose duty lay in defining the Law. As such it would be understandable, he supposed, but in this immediate instance it became dangerous and irresponsible. He would not dishonor the Temple by running, but he did step out briskly. Where had Jacob gotten to?

Jacob, as it happened lay unconscious, his head bleeding profusely, not twenty-five cubits from where Gamaliel now stood searching for him.

Yehudah, the Captain of the Guard rushed over to Gamaliel. "Rabban, quickly, Jacob ben Aschi has been injured."

"Is he hurt badly? How did it happen?"

"They say…I cannot believe it, but they say he was struck by one of the *kohanim*, but that cannot be possible."

"You remember your priest turned merchant in the street? Oh yes, it is very possible, Captain, very possible indeed. Take me to Jacob and send one of your men to my house to fetch the healer, Loukas."

Gamaliel pushed through the crowd around Jacob and knelt at his side.

"Jacob, can you hear me?"

The old man's eyelids fluttered, but did not open. "Is that you Rabban? I found him and would have brought him to you for a reprimand but he struck me. Why would he do such a thing?"

"You are lucky that is all he did to you, Jacob. He might have killed you."

"He would have," a voice from the crowd said, "but my friend and I saw him strike the old man and we rushed over. The man had a knife, sir. He would have done this man in if we hadn't—"

"Yes, yes, I see. Thank you and thank your friend. You saved this man's life. Can either of you tell me what he looked like?"

"He was a priest."

"Yes, so I gather, but his looks, his appearance? Tall, short, what?"

"Why would a priest do such a thing?"

"He wasn't a priest. He was an imposter and probably a murderer. Please, what did he look like?"

"Middle-sized, I guess. One doesn't notice those things when the first thing you see is what he is, do you?"

"No, you don't. It is the thing he relied on." Gamaliel stood and surveyed the crowd. "Can anyone tell me what he looked like?" People shuffled their feet and looked at everything and everywhere except at Gamaliel.

Loukas appeared and sat his bag down next to Jacob. "Everyone step back at least ten paces. I need air and light." He bent and spoke softly to Jacob. The old man shook his head. "Jacob," he said more loudly, "I do not think a crack on the head will have brought your blindness back, but I can't tell unless you open your eyes for me to see." Jacob opened one eye and then the other and smiled. "There you see, you see. Now lie still while I bandage that wound to your scalp."

"Will he live?" Gamaliel asked.

"What a question. Rabban, sometimes I think you were busy somewhere else when the Lord dealt common sense. Never ask a question like that with the patient within hearing. In this case, yes, he will live. All this blood is deceptive. Wounds to the scalp always bleed profusely. Now, Jacob. I want you to stay where you are until I can find some people to carry you to a couch. You should stay there until the tenth or eleventh hour and then have someone help you home."

"Before you do that, Jacob," Gamaliel said, "if you can, tell me what your assailant looked like?"

When Jacob told him, it was Gamaliel's turn to smile.

Chapter XLVI

The wind, no more than a breeze, shifted from east to north and brought with it a plume of smoke from the Altar of Sacrifice. It drifted across the mount and down. Loukas coughed.

"Do you think our man is watching us, Rabban, or has he slithered away and is hiding under a rock somewhere?"

"Slithered away, if I am any judge."

"And your meeting with the other snake, it went well?"

"The prefect? Amazingly well, our mercurial Pilate has given me men, ten to be precise."

"He has provided you a *minyan*?"

"Exactly, and authority to act in his name."

"Another ring for your finger?"

"Alas, no, not this time. I must say the ring he put on my finger the last time we had dealings had its advantages. Unfortunately, our roles are reversed this time. I am not doing his bidding, he is doing mine."

"And on the basis of no plan whatsoever, he has assigned you men and authority? How did you manage that?"

"I wish I knew. If I did, I would pack the whole Roman government along with the prefect himself onto the first ship back to that wretched peninsula of theirs."

"That is a grand thought, Gamaliel the Messiah, but since that won't happen, what do we do now?"

"Now we retire to my house, Benyamin will feed us, and then I will retreat into my study and have a long conversation with the Lord. I am missing something, Loukas, something small but exceedingly important."

"And you are hoping a meal and this conversation you intend to have with…Do you actually think He will reveal the thing to you?"

"I sincerely hope so. I pray so. Otherwise, I will have one very angry prefect on my hands tomorrow. Remember, we are not Roman citizens and, if he wished, he could consign us to prison, to pull oars in a galley, or to hang on that hideous cross his people seem so fond of. And if he so chooses, he could do it on a whim."

"Then let's eat quickly and put your mind to work. Once, when I happened to be in Egypt, I had an occasion to examine a body taken down from one of those crosses. I promise you, it is not an experience you want to have."

Gamaliel stopped so suddenly that Loukas, who followed him closely, nearly ran him down.

"Egypt, you said? Egypt, yes, that has to be it. You go ahead and inform Benyamin of our need for food and quiet. I will join you soon. I must be off."

"Off? To where must you be off? Shall I come with you?"

"No, you go and talk to Benyamin. Also, I left some sheets on the table inside the front door for you. They are in Greek. You read Greek passably well, you said."

"I read Greek like a native, not just passably well, Rabban."

"Of course you do. Read through them and when I return, tell me what you think."

Gamaliel strode away toward the steps by the Pinnacle and disappeared into the city.

Amun, an expatriate from Egypt, ran a small shop in the souk that specialized in metal ware. His reputation as a skilled craftsman provided a comfortable income, and he had become the unofficial leader of the expatriate Egyptian community. Gamaliel found him at his bench scoring a brass urn.

"Greetings in the Name, Rabban. What can I sell you today?"

"Amun, greetings to you as well. I need some information."

"That is free, but limited."

"Tell me what you know about an incense pot and a bowl. They would be marked with Hebrew letters and meant to be copies of those used by the high priest on *Yom Kippur*."

Amun thought for a moment and smiled. "I wondered how long it would be before someone from the Temple came asking about those two items. Am I in trouble? The man who bought them said they were for a synagogue in Greece. I asked him why he didn't buy them there and he said my reputation was such that he'd been commissioned to buy them from me."

"And you believed him?"

"No, but he paid handsomely, so I obliged."

"Who was this man?"

"His name was Alethos…somebody or other. Not his real name, I suspect, and he said he was *kohen*, a Levite living in Greece."

"Can you describe what he looked like?"

"Medium in height, beard, dressed in the fashion of the north, if you know what I mean. That, even as he told me he hailed from the Hellespont. He must have thought me an idiot."

"I see. It is odd, though, isn't it? When a person deals with a merchant not from his own country, he assumes the man must be slow."

"Or he doesn't care. He is not likely to be found out. I am Egyptian, not Judean. He will think, why would I care? I will make his vessels and forget him."

"Exactly. So, what do you hear on the streets, Amun? We have had a desecration in the Temple, as you have heard. We are told strange things by the higher ups associated with the palace. For example, the legatee from Egypt seems to have an opinion about our local murder. Why is that?"

"An interesting question, Rabban. You heard that? What else are you hearing?"

"That, my friend, is my problem. I am hearing nothing else. My friend Loukas has asked and no one can tell him anything. Who is missing? What rumors? Nothing."

"All I can tell you is that the yeast of trouble bubbles in the dough of some merchants who trade in the dark."

"The yeast…? Could you be less poetic and more to the point? Too many people have died in the past few days."

"Very well, but you did not hear it from me. I have a trade to ply and cannot afford enemies, especially among my neighbors."

"I will be discreet."

"And I will trust you. There are certain Egyptians who sell in the souk. They are in a conflict with those from the far northeast who also sell there."

"From Khorasan? Those people?"

"I believe so…yes from Khorasan. How did you guess?"

"Exactly that, I guessed. Many people sell in the souk, Amun. Fighting about what?"

"It is a territorial dispute about the marketing of a substance. It brings a high price—if there is no competition, even higher. The word is that this conflict has escalated to murder, and, even as we speak, dangerous men are on their way here from Alexandria and a similar number and kind from Khorasan also."

"Khorasan, of course. Assyria, Parthia, and beyond. Contingents of thugs and enforcers?"

"Now it is you who wax poetic."

"Hardly. Amun, I need you to do me a favor."

"Anything, Rabban."

"When this Alethos person returns—"

"Is that likely?"

Gamaliel felt the prickling on the back of his neck. "Oh, yes, he will be back, of that I am sure. When he comes in on some new pretense, I have some news I wish him to have. Something I let slip, you could say."

Chapter LVII

Gamaliel returned home in a little under an hour, looking thoughtful. He waved off Loukas' questions.

"We will talk after we eat."

Supper had been set out for them, and they ate in silence. Afterwards they settled on soft benches. Loukas looked enquiringly at Gamaliel.

"Now will you tell me now what drew you away so precipitously?"

"Yes. I would have sooner, but I needed time to consider what to tell you. I visited a merchant I sometime patronize, a seller of metal ware. He is Egyptian—from Alexandria and. like you, reads scripture in Greek. It is a practice I do not approve of, by the way. Holy words should be read in the proper order and in Hebrew."

"I know you believe that. Know this also, if Hebrew literacy were a requirement for one's continued membership, half of the Nation, especially those scattered across the empire, would disappear from the census overnight. But that is not the point, is it? Why did you want to see this Egyptian metal worker?"

"It came to me, up on the mount. You mentioned what you'd seen in Egypt, and I remembered that Caiaphas complained that the Egyptian legatee had objected to my investigation into the death of the man in the Holy of Holies."

"The Egyptian legatee, yes and so? I still don't understand what possible interest a foreigner would have in our local murder?"

"My thought, exactly. What business is it of theirs to meddle in our affairs? Anyway, when you mentioned Egypt, I thought of Amun. He is the unofficial leader of and keeps close watch on the local Egyptian community. It seemed a logical place to ask questions but I had not acted on that. I do not know why, but I hadn't, especially after I discovered the false vessels retrieved from the Temple. I hoped it would not be too late."

"Did you learn anything useful?"

"Some, yes. I learned that he made the replica vessels inserted with the body to confuse us for a man who called himself Alethos. He told me a dispute had broken out in the Souk over the sale of a substance. He did not admit to knowing what it was but I assume it must be *hul gil.* He told me there were forces arrayed across the empire and heading this way to settle the dispute, it seems. That can't be good. Beyond that, I am not sure. I need to think about it. What did you glean from the sheets I left for you?"

"Only what you'd already discovered. There has been a significant increase in the efficacy of *hul gil* reported here and there. Also, there seem to be two major sources of this newer variety."

"Egypt and the mountainous Khorasan."

"Yes. There has been an effort on the part of the people who raise the plants to restrict the efforts of the other."

"A war."

"That would be putting it a bit strongly. More like a serious competition between the suppliers. A plant is a plant."

"People are dying in the streets of our city. Temple guards have been suborned and probably killed. The Holy of Holies has been defiled because of this…what did you call it…serious competition? No, we are seeing the beginnings of what could be a veiled but very deadly conflict with significant money at stake."

"So, now what? Are we to insert ourselves into this conflict? If you want my opinion, I say no. I am a healer, not a fighter."

"No, we will not be combatants. We have my *minyan* for that."

"Then you intend to squelch the trade in it? How would you go about that?"

"I do not intend that either. Pilate, however, and the empire he represents, can try. The threat to his people and to the internal accord among its satrapies requires he do something. Caesar cannot have Parthia at war with Egypt, even at this level."

"It all seems strange to me. I have dealt with the substance for years. It is a component of many palliatives. Never has there been a problem. Now, because of the changes it looms large and could cause a problem for the Empire? Are you sure of this? That marketing of the opiate is the root of all the murders, strife, and deception?"

"I am as sure as I can be. There is only one way to find out."

"You mean to bring in this man who flits around the city as a priest, a merchant, a rabbi, and who knows what else."

"Not just him, Loukas: him and the man or men who follow him. If Amun is right, they each have a version of the story and we need to hear both. We must find a way to lure them into the same place at the same time and then throw a net over them."

"And how will you do that?"

"I will set a trap. I am hoping *Ha Shem* will give the killer a nudge in the right direction."

"Does the Lord nudge? A prophet might be nudged, or a nascent Messiah, but a killer?

A loud rapping at the door interrupted Gamaliel's response. Benyamin could be heard arguing with someone at the door. The rabban rose and joined his servant. Time passed. Loukas heard a murmured exchange but could not make out the content Gamaliel returned and found his place on the bench he'd just vacated.

"I had to instruct my *minyan*," Gamaliel said.

"And? Surely, the presence of ten legionnaires roaming about will only drive our man into deep cover."

"They will not be attired in their armor. I asked Pilate for the scruffiest men available and they are to be posted in the places I think most likely to lure the killer."

"Wouldn't the intelligent thing for him to do be to quit the city and wait?"

"If he were intelligent, he would have left days ago. He didn't. Therefore, he is not intelligent, or he has unfinished business. You and I stand in his way."

"We do?"

"If he thinks so, then yes, we do."

"He wishes to silence us."

"He does."

"He will attempt to assassinate us."

"I sincerely hope so."

Amun, the metal worker, puzzled over the rabban's request. He knew any attempt to plumb the old man's mind would lead him nowhere. He had tried once before and failed. If he said the imitation Greek Levite would return, he would. At the eleventh hour he began to cover his display wares and put his tools away. The hearth had been banked down earlier. He would have bolted the door but, as the rabban had predicted, the man who called himself Alethos did indeed push his way in.

"I am closing for the day, my friend. Can you return tomorrow?"

"What? Oh certainly, but I would like to place an order, if that is possible."

"Certainly. What is it you require?"

"A…candlestick. A branched candlestick…in bronze."

"Size?"

"Size, of course, that is important." Alethos described the item he wished the artisan to make for him in some detail. Amun had the impression he concocted the specifications as he spoke. "And, um…wasn't that the rabban of the Sanhedrin in here earlier?"

"It was. He is a regular customer, mostly for items for the Sanhedrin. He is quite an interesting man. Do you know him?"

"Know him? No, not at all; by reputation only."

"I can have your item in three days if that is satisfactory."

"Three days? That will do, yes. The rabban has been investigating a murder, I hear."

"He has. He mentioned something about it when he was here asking about the vessels he found in the Holy of Holies."

"Yes?"

"It didn't make much sense, not if you know the prefect. He said…I forget the details, but…"

"Yes?"

"Because of my position in the Egyptian community, he wanted to warn me. He said he believed the murderer of the man in the Temple was a…I can hardly believe it…"

"What?"

"Oh, yes. He said the prefect would be leaving the city for a time. Then he said he knew who the killer was and that he, that is the rabban, would report it to the prefect when he returned. So, the man's capture must wait, of course."

"He said that? He knows but has not told the authorities?"

"He said that."

Alethos thanked the metal artist and left. He would not return in three days to collect his candle stick. He stepped out of the glimmering light from the shops. So, there it was, his exit visa, as it were. All that remained was the elimination of the rabban. Of course if the rabban knew, the physician would, too. That meant Loukas must be eliminated as well. Too bad, that; great healers are rare. Afterwards, he need only wait a day, tidy up a few details, and go home to collect his reward.

Gamaliel, for his part, saw Loukas off to bed, lit his lamp with extra oil, this time for the last time, he hoped. He had Benyamin bring him a pot of boiled water, and he dropped some of the leaves he'd purchased from the herbalist. He would see if the seller had told the truth about them and he would be refreshed with his mind stimulated as promised. He certainly needed both if he hoped to force the solution to this increasingly complex mystery out of hiding. He would do it even if it took all night.

And, as it happened, it did.

Chapter XLVIII

The sun had begun its transit from east to west on what promised to be a crystal-clear morning. Gamaliel's front door faced north toward the Temple. From there he watched the sun rise above the walls of the mount to his right. He felt exhausted but at the same time exhilarated. A breeze lifted a handful of leaves and bits of straw and swirled them down the street and around corners. He thought it whispered to him, promised something, success surely, and an end to the investigation, a return to normalcy. He took a deep breath and called for Loukas to come and see the dawn.

"I have seen a dawn," Loukas muttered from somewhere inside. "I have no need to see another. Do you always rise with the sun? If I had known that I would not have stayed."

"Until this killer is in hand, I fear for your safety, and besides, I did not rise with the dawn. I never went to bed."

"I appreciate your concern, and I think you worry too much. Please understand, I stayed to ease your mind. This will be the last time. I don't like the hours you keep. Why were you up all night?"

"Because I had to. And now I know all."

"Really? Well I must say for a man who has not slept, you seem remarkably spry."

"I had Benyamin boil me some water and I made an infusion of some leaves I bought from one of the herbalists. He said it would refresh me and stimulate my mind."

"And did it?" Loukas picked up Gamaliel's cup and sniffed. "Tannin."

"What's tannin?"

"An extract from bark, among other things—like certain leaves—that is used to tan leather. Your refreshing drink reeks of it."

Gamaliel frowned and motioned for the physician to sit. "You don't think I have altered my insides? Tanned them?"

The two men sat at table to eat their morning meal.

"No, of course not. Tannin appears in small amounts in many things, most of them quite harmless. So, you have uncovered the killer. How did you manage that?" Gamaliel sat back and combed his beard with his fingers. His eyes narrowed. Except for the fact that his hand hid his mouth, he might have been smiling. "And did you think to notify the Roman authorities?"

"Notify? Oh, no, not just yet. First our man must be unmasked—he and his associates, you could say."

Loukas shook his head and rolled a crust of bread into crumbs. "It is only the first hour and already I am lost. You stayed up all night and have reached what you are convinced is the solution, am I correct?"

"Correct."

"And on the basis of your all night musings and under the influence of tannin, you are confident you can deploy the prefect's minions in a way that will capture the killer."

"I can."

"Are you going to let me in on this revelation or shall it be a surprise?"

"Which would you prefer? Pass me the remainder of that loaf while you consider which."

Loukas practically threw the wheaten bread at Gamaliel. "There are times, Rabban, when I sincerely wish I had never met you or better, that I saw you as the annoying old Pharisee everyone else does."

"Tut, Physician, you know that you love every moment of this. Who else of your acquaintance offers you so much adventure?"

"I give up. So, tell me. How did you divine how all this was done and who did it."

"Unlike you, I am happy for your acquaintance. You have taught me many things, geometry and Euclid, for instance."

"Geometry? You said you had no knowledge of either the subject or its innovator."

"I don't remember that, and you did and I do. Well, at least enough to use what I believe are the principles it employs to solve problems."

"You used…Please continue. I am fascinated at the Israelite who tackles geometry without having studied it."

"I said the principles. They are not so complex, are they? Look, if I understand the system correctly, there are certain things, facts you could say, that serve as axioms. These are the indisputable items. They stand. Against them, one arrays possibilities and if the possibilities are congruent with the facts, then you move forward one step toward the solution. Correct?"

"In a way, yes, I suppose so. Go on."

"Well, it seemed to me that the trick one needs to employ in the geometry of murder is to first sort out the axioms from the suppositions, the facts from the assumptions, so to say. Then one has only to put them in the correct order and the problem is solved. You may then assume the acuity of the angle or, in this case, the murderer and his motive."

"The geometry of murder?"

"Yes. Nice turn of phrase, don't you think?"

"If you insist. Continue with your lesson. What are the axioms?"

"What do we know for certain? Well, he was dead when placed in the Holy of Holies. We all agree with that."

"Except the high priest."

"Yes, except Caiaphas and the Temple party. But we will discount them for the moment. They will be brought into the solution later. We know the dead man was not Jewish, although there was an attempt to make it seem as though he was. From that we conclude?"

"Someone wished to lead us astray."

"Correct. But why, Loukas? Why such a massive deception? People go missing all the time. Why suborn two guards, pose as a *kohen*, and run such risks just to deceive people of one's real intent?"

"He wanted to send a message."

"Yes, but to whom?"

"Well, given the enormity of the project, the only answer I can think of is to us, to the Nation, to Israel, but I can't for the life of me think what the message could be."

"Then we must conclude the message was not for us."

"But—"

"Patience, you will see soon enough. Now, where was I?"

"The geometry of murder."

"Yes, let me ask you another question, Loukas. If you wanted to announce to an enemy that you had eliminated one of his people, someone important, say, how would you do it?"

"If I were a Roman, I would publically hang him from a cross. Otherwise I would send a neutral intermediary."

"Take the case that you wanted the enemy to know their man was murdered and in a very dramatic fashion, and you were not in a position to crucify him?"

"I give up. Tell me what you're driving at."

"In a minute. We need to establish a few more axioms."

"Gamaliel, you try my patience. If it weren't so early, I would be well into the wine by now. Just tell me what you decided."

"I stayed up all night working this out and you would deny me my moment, my geometry lesson?"

Loukas groaned. "All right, go on, but could you give me the short version?"

"There is no short version. To continue with another axiom, we know that there are two sources of this new *hul gil*, Egypt and Khorasan. We know that men from both places are on their way here to wage a small war over who sell it in the souk. We conclude that they represent syndicates, and we also conclude they do not wish to share the market. You remember that one of the shopkeepers said that the Hana store had a proprietor before the most recent one. From that we extrapolate that there has already been some murderous activity and perhaps this temple man was an act of revenge. So, to send the message, our killer perpetrates the most sensational murder in history. He assumes that we, that is, the Jews, will do nothing about it, believing that the circumstances were as the high priest wishes to us believe."

"But we didn't."

"No, we didn't, but that was sheer chance, a misadventure. I summoned you and you immediately suspected an alternative. Do you realize what our position would have been if you had been away or unavailable that morning?"

"You give me too much credit. You would have tumbled on to the ruse in good time."

"Possibly."

A loud knocking at the door brought Gamaliel up short. Benyamin announced that there was a man at the door who wished to speak to the rabban.

"Are you able to receive a visitor or shall I send him away?"

"I will see him." Gamaliel disappeared, and Loukas could hear him talking to someone. The door slammed shut, and the rabban returned.

"And that was…?"

"I needed to deploy my *minyan*."

"I thought you had done so already."

"Redeploy, then. This time in a way that will net us our killers. In an hour they will be set and ready to bring this to a close."

"And we? What shall we do?"

"In that same hour, we shall take a walk."

"A walk?"

"Exactly. Now where was I?"

Chapter XLIX

Benyamin, who had been standing in the corner seeing to the meal, seemed rattled.

"Excellency, please tell me you do not plan to walk about the streets. If there is a murderer out there, and if he is as clever as you say, he will also know you are onto him. He will come after you."

"Yes, Benyamin, that is the point of the walk, to draw him out. Now then, to return to our killer…yes, we were discussing where we might have been but for the perspicuity of our good physician."

Gamaliel had a faraway look in his eyes, as if he were experiencing something approaching the spiritual. Loukas just looked worried.

"The fact of the murder would have been abroad within moments of its discovery." Gamaliel continued. "Within an hour, everyone in the city would know about it. The faithful would wail and moan and wonder what *Ha Shem* would make of it. The *kohanim* and the pharisee would preach and scold, and the syndicate who'd lost their man would have received the message."

"But they would not report it?"

"In this case, no. They would not like the prefect nosing around the Street of the Herbalists and discovering what his troops, among others, were involved in and doubtless shutting them down."

"No, I suppose not. I need to pick up on Benyamin's worry. Why are we walking into certain danger?"

"Nothing in life is certain. Life, death, they are facets of the same ordinary thing, Loukas, but honor, and truth, and obedience, now they have value."

"And we will seek these things in our walk?" Loukas did not seem pleased at the prospect.

"Oh, I despair for you, Loukas. It is a problem to be solved, first. If you were the killer and you had on good authority that the rabban of the Sanhedrin knew who you were and why you killed, what would you do?"

"Find an opportunity to do you in as quickly as possible."

"And if you believed that no one else, with the obvious exception of his friend the physician—"

"Me!"

"No one else knew and further you had it on the same good authority, that the prefect had left the city for a few days or weeks, and that this rabban was waiting for Pilate's return before revealing who the killer was—"

"Rabban, he's going to kill us."

"He's going to try, certainly, perhaps even succeed. That's why we will take our walk. He will act as soon as he possibly can, and then the rest will be easy. You see, he thinks no one but the two of us care about the Temple man. With us out of the way, he will be free to set his men against the other syndicate and start the war over the drug. Simple."

"I have no wish to put myself in harm's way, Rabban. I have no wish to die in the service of the prefect, for that is what this comes down to. You are asking me to throw myself into the fire so that the prefect, the most hated man in the country, can round up a felon?"

"You will serve justice, not the prefect. It is an axiom that truth must overcome falsehood, righteousness overcome faithlessness."

"I wish I had never taught you geometry."

"I thought you said you hadn't. So there you are, my night's musings, as you so inelegantly put it."

"Not quite. We agreed the killer couldn't have inserted the body behind the Veil alone. Where is his accomplice, and shouldn't we worry about him?"

"His accomplice? I offer you two possibilities. One, he is the other man who follows the follower, or two, he is dead."

"Which?"

"My instinct says the latter. There is no reason for them to traipse around on each other's heels like that. My supposition is that the accomplice is, or was, a *hul gil* user who, because of his dependency, would do exactly what he was asked so long as he was supplied the drug. But people like that are unreliable and, therefore, he was either the man in the burned out shop who had been co-opted by the other side, or is dead somewhere else, his body with those guards in some remote place. We may never know."

"Why does the killer believe Pilate has left the city?"

"Because I told him so. Well, not me directly. I left him a message with Amun. You remember the Egyptian craftsman I visited. He produced the bowl and the pot and I was certain that if I visited him, so would the killer, if only to find out what I said."

"And you are certain he visited?"

"No, but I like the probabilities. See how I have mastered your Hellenic love of mathematics and logic?"

Loukas held his head and moaned. "Rabban, this is not like you. You are always so careful, you are conservative, and you are always sure. What has gotten into you?"

Gamaliel did not answer. Instead, he sat very still and stared at the far wall,

"Gamaliel, is there something?" Loukas studied his friend. His physician's habit he would say. Gamaliel sat quietly, like a volcano about to erupt, or the calm before a gale. Then, he stood and began to pace, at first aimlessly, then striding furiously back and forth. His voice dropped to a near whisper. His eyes flashed, which caused Benyamin to retreat into a corner.

"My friend," Gamaliel rasped, "you miss the whole point. This is not just some wonderfully concocted murder. It is not just about the possible consequences of some opiate invading the sensibilities of the Nation. Loukas, someone has defiled the Holy of Holies. He has done so for the basest of reasons and no one seems to care." His voice grew stronger, and by the end of his speech was nearly a shout.

"He has mocked *Ha Shem*. Don't you understand? The Holy of Holy has been desecrated, the Temple defiled! That cannot be allowed. Does anyone care about that? Does the high priest? No. It cannot, I repeat, it cannot be allowed. As long as I am alive, it will not go unpunished. You, Loukas and those like you, may drift comfortably along on the edges of near nonbelief and see only a foolish attack on an institution. In my darkest moments I believe half the nation is with you in that, but I will not abide it. The Lord expects more from us, and when he is attacked by some scheming, irreverent, blasphemous…infidel. He expects us to respond. Wringing our hands will not do. Pretending it is something it is not, will not do. This man must be brought to justice. Well, since Rome forbids us the exercise of capital punishment, I must turn this terrible person over to them to do it for us. Do you understand? I am the Rabban of the Sanhedrin, and I can do no less."

"And how do you reckon the risks entailed in the walk we are to take?"

"Risks? The risks are unimportant. If we are killed, is unimportant. The only important thing is that he be captured and brought to justice."

Gamaliel stopped his pacing and let out a wail of anguish. Loukas would say later he had never heard the man so upset.

"Rabban, calm yourself. This is not like you. Benyamin, some wine for the rabban." The servant scuttled off to find the strongest vintage in the cellar.

Gamaliel wheeled and, red faced and, his finger pointing at Loukas' face, barked, "This is the high priest's responsibility, not mine. He has no business sweeping this under one of those gaudy carpets he decorates his house with. He is our anointed high priest. He stands foremost in the line of Aaron, and it is his job, I say. But does he address it? No! He frets and fusses about a country rabbi and does nothing about the defilement of his Temple. It is an outrage! He is our shepherd, and yet he chases after mice in the feed bin while wolves ravage his sheep!"

Benyamin handed Gamaliel a cup. The rabban drank it in a single gulp. "It is time, Loukas. Time to walk, time to send our own message." Gamaliel headed for the door. "Are you coming? You do not have to. I am the man he wants."

Although his better judgment warned him not to, Loukas followed Gamaliel into the street.

Chapter L

It had been a long and dangerous day. Loukas sat in the late afternoon sun in his back court and contemplated his friend. While his nerves still jangled and his heart pounded from the morning's excitement, the rabban, sitting opposite him, appeared calm and quite pleased with himself.

"There are still some things I do not understand, Rabban. I listened at the fortress when Ali bin Selah and the other man were being questioned, but what with the Roman's shouting. Ali's screaming, and the other man's moaning, I did not learn much. I must say, as a healer, torture is contrary to everything I hold dear. I could take no more. In any event, I lost the thread."

"But we went through it this morning. You have been with me from the very beginning. Your difficulty arises from your friendship with Ali bin Selah and your innate reluctance to think ill of anybody, much less a friend."

"You may be right about Ali. I value friendship highly, and Ali was one." Loukas paused. "I confess that after I heard the part about our murderer believing you were waiting for Pilate's return before revealing the killer to him, my mind tended to drift. To tell the truth, not a lot of what you said this morning sank in."

"Yes, you said 'He is going to kill us.' I remember."

"Looking back on it, I suppose it went very well. I was able to control all of my sphincters, and I don't think I wept. I do admit to being very frightened."

"Yes, so was I, to be honest. I will happily fill in your gaps, if you produce some Cappadocian wine."

"You realize it may be the last you will ever taste now that Ali will no longer be traveling this way."

"A terrible price to pay for justice. In the future we must concentrate on delivering criminals to the authorities who do not require us to make such a heavy sacrifice."

Loukas produced the skin of wine, and they sipped in silence.

"As we thought, all this business is to be understood in the ruse of planting the dead man in the Temple. An Egyptian dealer in *hul gil* who traded under the name of Hana. After our Roman interrogators had created sufficient pain in Aswad Khashab, the poor man babbled that Hana was his brother. When he refused Ali's demand that he surrender the market in the more powerful *hul gil* to him, Ali murdered him. But, if the plan was to work, our dead man had to seem a recipient of *Ha Shem's* wrath and draw us away. At the same time a clear message sent to the dead man's allies. We might believe in Divine wrath, but they would know otherwise. As you noted, they would not report it."

"So, the Jerusalem authorities would assume that the dead man was a lunatic who believed he was supposed to communicate with *Ha Shem*. And the other side would say nothing but know what was afoot?"

"Exactly. It served the same purpose the incense smoke serves at *Yom Kippur*—to screen the high priest from the Presence lest he be struck down for accidently gazing on the Presence. In this case, the intent was to screen us from the truth."

"In this case, not with holy smoke."

"Not even remotely holy. Then, of course, to make it all work, I think they, that is Ali and whoever helped him, dragged the dead man up the ramp to the Altar of Sacrifice and tossed him on the coals left from the day's sacrifice. Remember, he was only burned to his knees."

"But you said nothing about Ali at the time, yet you suspected."

"There was nothing to say. He declared his intention to leave the city immediately, and the matter seemed moot. It was only when he reappeared at your door dressed as someone else that I had any real doubts. I assumed he must be connected somehow, but I did not know how. It was the business about the *hul gil* that changed suspicion to a near certainty."

"How so? Ali merely gave me a sample for Draco. I would expect no less from any visitor who happened to have a useful potion."

"Once I discovered the danger the new formulation of the substance posed and the fact that Ali had it, the wheels, you could say, began to turn. That coupled with the realization that it was probably he who, in one disguise or another, represented at least half of the people who'd been tracking for us the last several days. Remember, too, he said his brother Achmir had been murdered recently. When and where, I wondered. Finally, Jacob, with his newly functioning eyes, described his attacker, too well, it seems. Ali nearly killed him too, you know."

"I didn't know. I congratulate you, and as you are naturally more skeptical than I, it makes perfect sense. While I think of it, why did Ali even come back when he could have been away and clear after that first day?"

"I believe he had not completed his business in the city, there were the guards to be gotten rid of and he needed to return as someone else to do that. That would explain the fire at the store and the second death as well—tidying up."

"It seems like a lot of trouble. You'd have thought he would have had a neater plan to start with."

"You would. He overplayed his hand, it seems. Posing as a priest got him past the guards, but he did not have to kill them. Once they'd realized what they'd done, they'd have disappeared into Thrace or Edom, or some such distant place rather than face the wrath of the Sanhedrin and the Lord. And he killed his accomplice."

"He had to have had one?"

"How else carry a body into the Temples disguised as four or five omers of grain, except with a coconspirator? What I don't understand is how, or from whom, the killer discovered the intricacies of our rituals. How did he know about *Yom Kippur* or to tie a rope on the ankle, for example?"

Loukas' face reddened, and he fixed his gaze on the tiles. "That would be me, I'm afraid. I told you we exchanged information, not just medical. He told me he had an interest in learning about our culture. That's what he called it—our culture. So, over several cups of the wine he brought me, I told him what I knew."

"Not to worry, my friend. If not you, he would have learned it from someone else and perhaps in a less hygienic way."

"I am sorry to have ever brought that man into our circle, Rabban. I must be a better judge of character in the future."

Gamaliel poured the last of the wine into their cups and sighed.

"Do not distress yourself, Loukas. Men are deceived and betrayed by their friends all the time. Think of David, and his sons and his friends. My student, Saul, read from Kings when I asked him to parse the mystery. He quoted the part about Joab's deception. Joab, the king's faithful all, turned on him and rallied to Absalom."

"I suppose you are right, but I wish it weren't so. So the prefect has what he needs?"

"After some persuasion which involved a branding iron, Ali confessed to Pilate that he intended to do away with the Egyptian's trade in *hul gil*. As we heard, the Egyptian syndicate had got hold of plants from Khorasan and competed, too successfully, with his group."

"It seems so ridiculous that people should die for a pain killer. Any fool who tried it would immediately see the danger and avoid it afterwards."

"I am afraid you give people too much credit. In a despairing and hurting world, anything that offers a person a moment's release will be snapped up by the suffering like children after honey cakes. Pilate understands that. Remember, the legionnaires stationed here are not from Rome nor are they Romans. The Roman legions, the elite troops, remain on the Italian peninsula, honored and admired. The men who serve here and elsewhere on the dusty fringes of the Empire, are mercenaries. Their lot is only marginally better than ours. The drug would have the same appeal to them as it would to us. More importantly, were it to take hold, Pilate would have troops that could not function. That, in turn, would encourage rebels to more violence, which would be completely unacceptable."

"What will Pilate do now?"

"I expect when he is satisfied his people can't terrorize anymore information from Ali and what's-his-name—"

"Aswad Khashab."

"Yes, Aswad. When he is done with that pair, he will crucify them. Then he will notify his counterpart in Egypt who will deal with the poppy growers out there, and finally he will try to seal that northern border."

"Will he succeed?"

"With the crucifixions, certainly. The rest, probably not. There are some things, persons, events, or in this case a drug, which when they insinuate themselves into history, change its course, and their influence is rarely reversed. This opiate, this sap of the poppy plant, will curse this world to the end of time. It will be like your wild mustard, spreading and choking out everything in its path."

"That is not a very optimistic notion. There have been plagues, volcanoes, and disasters of every sort throughout history. Rome cannot last forever. The Great Alexander is but a dim memory, the pharaohs, gone and soon forgotten."

"Yes, but not your geometry and not our Lord. We must trust to the things that are absolute and true to bear us up against those that are deceptive and false. Evil will always be with us, Loukas, but so will *Ha Shem*."

"If you say so, Rabban. I admire your faith and long for some part of it. Perhaps someday I will find it, but, alas, not today. And, now what will you do?"

"What will I do? First, I will finish this very fine wine and then I shall return to my home. Benyamin will feed me my evening meal and scold me for taking so many risks—we could have been killed you know. I will sleep the night through without dreaming, and tomorrow I will resume my studies and tend to my students. All this I will do with a fervent prayer to *Ha Shem* that I will not see the high priest for at least a month, the prefect again ever, and murder, should visit this place once more, will not involve me in any way, shape, or form."

Notes

For those readers who have already experienced Gamaliel and his detective skills in *The Eighth Veil* some of these notes will be repetitious. For new readers, I hope they help clarify some of the complexities of life in Jerusalem during the first half of the First Century. They may be, as the little girl in the story once said, "It's more about penguins than I really wanted to know." If so, skip this part.

Primary Characters

Caiaphas, Yosef bar Kayafa; high priest of the Temple 18 CE to 36 CE. Although removed from office by Caligula, he saw his sons succeed him in the office later.

Gamaliel, Gamaliel the Elder, Gamaliel I: Served as the rabban (chief rabbi) of the Sanhedrin, the ruling body of Israel. While believing the Law of Moses to be wholly inspired, he is reported to have taken a broad-minded and compassionate stance in its interpretation. Gamaliel held that the Sabbath laws should be understood in a realistic rather than rigorous fashion. He also maintained, in distinction to his contemporaries, that the law should protect women during divorce and urged openness toward Gentiles. Acts 5:38–39 relates that he intervened on behalf of Saint Peter and other Jewish followers of Jesus.

Pontius Pilate, prefect (governor) of Judea appointed by Tiberius and recalled in 36 CE by the Emperor Caligula.

Procula, one of the names traditionally given for Pilate's wife. The other is Claudia; and occasionally she is called Claudia Procles or Claudia Procula. She appears briefly in Matthew's Gospel as having had a dream or premonition and warning Pilate not to persecute Jesus.

Yeshua ben Josef, Jesus of Nazareth.

The Cord around the Ankle

It is generally acknowledged among scholars who pay attention to this sort of thing that the practice of tying a cord around the high priest's ankle when he made his annual entry into the Holy of Holies on the Day of Atonement is a myth. The story surfaced several centuries after the destruction of the Temple in 70CE. The idea behind the alleged practice held that a cord would assure that the body of a person struck down by an angered or displeased God could be retrieved without running the risk to a second, prohibited person, who would have to enter to retrieve it. Scholars maintain there is no scriptural evidence to support the practice. And since the Torah contains such great detail about everything that was to happen on that day—dress, rituals before, preparations, rituals afterward, etc., it seems inconceivable that the practice would have been left out of the instructions. To my mind, that is not much of an argument, but then I do not make my living parsing Torah. We shall never know the source of the myth, but as with most folklore, there is usually a kernel of truth in them somewhere.

Yom Kippur

Yom Kippur, also known as Day of Atonement, is the holiest and most solemn day of the year for Jews. Its central themes are atonement and repentance. *Yom Kippur* completes the annual period known in Judaism as the High Holy Days or Yamim Nora'im (Days of Awe). *Yom Kippur* is the tenth day of the month of Tishrei. The evening and day of *Yom Kippur* are set aside for public and private petitions and confessions of guilt.

Once a year on *Yom Kippur*, the high priest would enter the Holy of Holies. First, he would prepare himself with ritual cleansing and then don a blue ephod (a narrow poncho-like vestment which extended to about his knees). Bells were affixed to its hem. He also wore a white linen tunic. In addition he carried a bowl of sacrificial blood, and incense would be burned to limit his ability to gaze on the Presence. While he was in the Most Holy Place, people waited outside. Some assume the bells were the means by which those in attendance could be sure the high priest still moved about. Others argue that the blue ephod with the bells was shed before entering. Whatever the case, when the high priest emerged intact, a shout of joy rose up from the people. The Lord had accepted the sacrifice and their sins were forgiven. The high priest would announce, "Your sins are forgiven" and utter the Name. The people would probably shout the *Shema: Shema, Israel, Adonoi elohenu, Adonoi Echad* or Hear, O Israel, the Lord our God is one Lord."

Measurements

Volume

An *omer* is an ancient Israelite unit of dry measure used in the era described here. It appears in the Bible as an ancient unit of volume for grains, and the Torah mentions as being equal to one tenth of an ephah.

The *ephah* was defined as being 72 *logs*, and the *log* was equal to the Sumerian *mina*.

Distance

Amah (*Amot*): the biblical cubit or 48.0–57.6 cm. Nearly two feet: Latin=*cubit*.

Ris (*stadium* pl. *stadia*): 128–153.6 meters, or 139–167 yards.

Mil (Milin): a mile 960–1152 m 1049–1258 yd. Time to walk a *mil* is 18 minutes. Roman tradition has it at one thousand paces (thus *mille* or mile).

Kohen or Kohanim

Hebrew: כֹהֵן, *kohen* pl. כֹהֲנִים, *kohanim*, is the Hebrew word for priest. Jewish *kohanim* are traditionally believed to be of direct patrilineal descent from Aaron, the brother of Moses. The status *kohen* was first conferred on Aaron and his sons. During the forty years in the wilderness and until the Temple was built in Jerusalem, priests performed their priestly duties in the portable tabernacle, a tent surrounded by a wall of fabric panels.

The noun *kohen* is used in the Torah to refer to priests, both Jewish and non-Jewish, such as the priests of Baal. During the existence of the Temple in Jerusalem, the *kohanim* performed the daily and holiday sacrifices. They were assigned to a cohort and there were (at least) thirty-eight such groups which took turns serving at the Temple. Obviously some time might pass between their calls to function as priests.

Speaking the Name

Orthodox Jewish custom prevents a person from saying the name of God. The pronunciation of the Hebrew, יהוה (the tetragrammaton, YHWH), which designates the Almighty, is sometimes pronounced Yaweh (I Am), Jehovah, or some other circumlocution. Even today, orthodox Jewish literature and web sites will print God only as G*d. Because our protagonist, Gamaliel, would have been at least as orthodox as modern-day practice, the term Lord, or the Lord, or *Elohim*, is used instead of God in order to make this distinction. Sometimes a greeting would be even more circumspect, and the person initiating it would merely say "Greetings in the Name, or just "The Name" (*Ha Shem*).

The Temple

Herod the Great began building the Temple in use at the time this story is set in 19 BCE. It replaced the temple built by Zerubbabel after the return from exile which, in turn, was erected on the ruins of that built by Solomon. That temple had been sacked and burned by Nebuchadnezzar years before. Most scholars assume it was an attempt by Herod, who was half Idumean, to appease the Jews, but certainly not a genuine desire to glorify God. Rather, he built a memorial to himself and to convince his counterparts in Rome, Alexandria, Athens, and elsewhere, that he could equal or surpass anything they might devise.

To avoid the workmen profaning the temple during its construction, Herod had priests trained as stonemasons and carpenters to serve as his *Bazal'el* or Temple workmen.

It is reported that the rabbis at the time (and subsequently) continually praised the Temple's splendor, but never mentioned that it was built by Herod.

Reading and Writing

Hebrew is written right to left. There are two things the reader should know:

1. There are no numbers in Hebrew (or Greek or Aramaic, for that matter) so a writer wishing to itemize would have to adopt Arabic numerals (with no zero), Roman numerals, or use the letters of the alphabet in order.

2. There are no vowels in the Hebrew alphabet (although there are consonantal vowels—but that is another matter.) Ancient texts assumed the reader knew the traditional pronunciation of the words as they appeared in context. For example:

TRN LFT TH NXT CRNR

TURN LEFT AT THE NEXT CORNER can be easily read. And it would be assumed that readers of Hebrew then could insert the correct vowel sounds in the words and sentences.

After the Exile, the ability to figure out the correct pronunciation seemed to have been lost, or the language became more complex. Either way, the practice emerged of making diacritical marks in various locations on the individual letters, which dictated the correct pronunciation.

These marks are called *neqqudot*.

To recycle papyrus, a sheet would be sanded and repolished. If the job were not done carefully, a bit of ink might be overlooked and when a new word was written, a mark might be introduced which could easily change the meaning of the word.

Hours of the Day

A day was divided into twenty four hours—twelve for daylight, twelve for night. Day began at sunup and ended at sunset. The hours were of indefinite lengths depending on the season, shortest in the winter, longer in the summer, but noon, when the sun stood at its zenith, was designated the sixth hour. As there could be no similar reference point at night, the phases of the moon being variable, the night hours had no time divisions except rough notations. Midnight might be described as the night's "sixth hour," but when it occurred would necessarily vary with the speaker and his or her sense of the passage of time.

Miscellaney

Ba'al-Zebuwb: Ba'al or Baal = Lord, is generic. All divine beings would be *Baals*. The addition of *zebuwb* or *zeebub* = flies. Thus *Ba'al Zebuwb* means Lord of the flies. In this case the reference is to Satan.

Bitumen, (pitch): a generic term referring to flammable brown or black mixtures of tarlike material, derived from petroleum. It is found in quantity near the Dead Sea and is used for a variety of purposes, not the least of which is cosmetic. If you have ever visited the Dead Sea, you will recall seeing people smeared with a black substance. If you were one of those people, you know that after washing off the application, your skin feels like silk for the rest of the day.

Gehinnom: a valley outside Jerusalem where garbage, trash, offal, and waste were dumped. When the rains came much of it would be washed eastward toward and finally into the Dead Sea.

Hul gil: opium or one of its derivatives. The history of opium is fascinating and scary. I will not attempt to capture it here. It is enough to know that poppy pods have been found in the Neolithic caves. Over time, the cultivation of the plant became more sophisticated and the ability to process the sap equally so. Thus, the sedating (and addictive) effects increased remarkably.

Mikvah (pl. mikva'ote): a ritual bath. Orthodox Jews cleanse themselves periodically by immersion in the bath. Some ascribe this practice as the forerunner of the baptismal practice instituted by John the Baptizer.

Minyan, (pl. minyanim) in Judaism refers to the quorum of ten Jewish adults required for certain religious meetings and worship.

Nomenclature, I heard from a few readers who expressed their disapproval of the practice of delineating the pre and post Christian eras with the notations, BCE and CE. Why the change from BC and AD? The latter annotations represented the notion that the Christian era began with the birth of Jesus (*anno domini*) and the years prior to that time were before Christ (BC). But we now know that Jesus had to have been born sometime before the Death of Herod the Great, and we know for a certainty that date to be no later than 4BCE (BC). Since the Jesus could not have been born before Christ, the notation has been changed. The use of BCE (before the Common Era) and CE (Common Era) are now pretty much standard practice. Not everyone is happy about that.

Shepherds: In the world of work at this time, a shepherd was considered to be one of the lowest occupations available to a man, just above beggar, which adds poignancy to the story of David, the shepherd who became King, and the tradition that a heavenly host first announced the nativity of Jesus to shepherds.

Souk: the area in cities devoted to street vendors and market stalls; a marketplace.

Wadi Kelt: is a large valley that roughly parallels the road from Jerusalem down to Jericho. At the time of this writing, the road to Jericho would have traversed all or part of this valley.

Finally, an apology to physicists, exponents of quantum mechanics, and admirers of Erwin Schrödinger. In chapter XIV, I stole his cat (and replaced it with fruit). Sorry about that.

To receive a free catalog of Poisoned Pen Press titles, please contact us in one of the following ways:

Phone: 1-800-421-3976
Facsimile: 1-480-949-1707
Email: info@poisonedpenpress.com
Website: www.poisonedpenpress.com

Poisoned Pen Press
6962 E. First Ave. Ste 103
Scottsdale, AZ 85251